Powder for Drying Wounds

Beraud Rock 2025

First published 2025 by Beraud Rock
Revised Nov, 2025 edition includes
editorial and stylistic refinements.

ISBN 9781-1-7643565-3-4

Author website:
https://www.peterbarrett-author.com/peterbarrett

Acknowledgments

Thanks to my partner Donna, a Graphic Designer and Book Design editor.
Cover images created by ChatGPT5 with the author's descriptive changes.

About the Author

Peter Barrett - Pen name: Beraud Rock, was born and grew up on Christmas Island in the Indian Ocean. He has spent a lifetime reading Evolutionary Science, Science Fiction, History, and comics as a child. He was not exposed to television until age eleven.

Peter has a fascination and passion for the natural world and our place in the Universe. Peter's world changed the day he examined tiny insects through his photographic lens and discovered their beauty and makeup. He is equally fascinated by the human animal, their degrees of humanity, the complexities of society and the future of the human race. Themes in his writing include Artificial Intelligence, sentience, problem-solving, disaster, and the evolutionary timeline and makeup of life on Earth.

He holds two University degrees, neither of which is related to his previous careers as a Cook, Photographic Technician, and Ophthalmic Technician. When not writing, he spends time with his partner, his chickens (Chooks, as Australians say), wildlife, and grows his own food.

1

Ichneumonidae - A family of parasitoid wasps, commonly known as *'Darwin Wasps.'*

"With respect to the theological view of the question; this is always painful to me.— I am bewildered.— I had no intention to write atheistically. But I own that I cannot see, as plainly as others do, & as I wish to do, evidence of design & beneficence on all sides of us. There seems to me too much misery in the world. I cannot persuade myself that a beneficent & omnipotent God would have designedly created the Ichneumonidæ with the express intention of their feeding within the living bodies of caterpillars, or that a cat should play with mice. Not believing this, I see no necessity in the belief that the eye was expressly designed. On the other hand I cannot anyhow be contented to view this wonderful universe & especially the nature of man, & to conclude that everything is the result of brute force. I am inclined to look at everything as resulting from designed laws, with the details, whether good or bad, left to the working out of what we may call chance. Not that this notion at all satisfies me. I feel most deeply that the whole subject is too profound for the human intellect. A dog might as well speculate on the mind of Newton.— Let each man hope & believe what he can.—Charles Darwin to Asa Gray, letter, 22 May, 1860.

Frank Fieldlight could still feel the slight tingling of the healed scar that dissected his face from the top right of his forehead to the bottom left of his chin. He stared down at the green pool at the massive crater's bottom; the result of the Allies' new 350-millimetre howitzer high-explosive shell. He continued to stare at the festering pool and the two dead Germans. His mind went into a trance, and he listened to his breathing through his nose, calming his brain as he thought about Donny, the sixteen-year-old who was now home with his Mother.

Donny's mother had written him a two-page letter with words of *thanks, love,* and *hope*, accompanied by a parcel containing a packed lemon cake, cigarettes, socks, underwear, and a razor-shaver. Donny sent him a picture of himself and his cattle dog, *Hector,* sitting beside him in a paddock, with one arm on his knee.

At the time, he felt nothing. A piece of whizzing terminal shrapnel he assumed had flown down at that angle, seeking to dissect his head on a diagonal, but had slightly miscalculated. What he couldn't work out was why the metal had glided like a razor across his skin, following the contours of his face and over his nose as the scar was unbroken. He would have supposed that the fine steel edge would have cut his nose off on the way. He often thought that perhaps the steel shard had been multi-toothed. It had spun one hundred and eighty degrees, and a longer tooth had taken over the path of the shorter tooth, like some machine that outlined human flesh for making skin clothes.

He remembered the blood streaming off his superficially severed face, and thought at the time, while carrying Donny Farrow, the sixteen-year-old, that he was certainly badly wounded. By that stage, he was about twenty metres from the German lines, an impossible distance. He had lost his rifle, and he could see the German frontline trench soldiers looking at him. There were several small fires on top of the trench line, and then he realised it was the machine guns smoking from the constant fire; the barrels were hot where the operators had poured water to cool them.

He hesitated, standing upright and staring at the guns, a delirious curiosity about the machines that had eliminated a generation, silenced his enemies and the five thousand legacies that would never be realised, never to go home. His mind wandered, a yearning mixed with memories parlayed across his subconsciousness.

Under swaying gum trees, and across from crashing course sand beach waves.

2

Beside the gurgling of bush-creeks and worn granite with cicada screeching above and the click of stripy marsh frogs and the whisper of the wind through Allocasurina trees before a storm on a barbecue afternoon...

Beside cold grave sites, where the living gather watching the descent of a terminal pine box, and white-ant fence lines, twirling hills-hoists that had lost their inner gear, that were spinning like carnival wheels, the clothing horizontal, the bars like sail booms.

The sound of Magpie wings and parrot's chatter and Budgie's whistle at dawn when the flock rose into the cool pre-dawn air, filled with the scent of Eucalypt and cockatoo, with the shriek of life's celebration.

He could smell lead, metal, blood and rosemary, a Grim Reaper's dinner menu entree. The sun shone brightly on the field, its light piercing through the rising haze that was abating but still swirling in white wisps in the sky. The shards of light struck the karkhi soldiers' kit and reflected brass and silver buckles and broken rifles and shattered bone among the grotesque shapes of now stopped spinning death. The many helmets seemed like thrown saucers at a mad hatter's tea party, lying upside down and flat like alien ships, some like empty nests on the ground.

The Germans held their fire, and his ears were ringing. He realised that the noise had stopped. The artillery was silent. Some Germans were shouting. He could hear the sound of leather boots on wood below the trench line. A large German sergeant with a spiked helmet bellowed at his troops, "Halte dein feuer!" and then watched them through the machine-gun emplacement gap, smiling, his yellow teeth advertising a glimmer of consideration and a thought of schnapps and sausage with him if the war hadn't intervened.

He turned, not quite understanding what the enemy was doing and why the enemy was smiling at him. He lifted Donny in a

3

fireman's lift. Red poured from his face and in congealed smatterings globbed onto the dirt below, and the soldiers' faces that he had to step on and over. The German Sergeant bellowed again, "Halte dein feuer!" He heard the phrase being repeated down the line behind him, thinking they were getting ready to let fly.

Donny was heavy for a sixteen-year-old. He had to step on his comrades, some of whom were crying out and moaning and gasping and writhing. That field of torsos stretched for four hundred metres back to the direction of the division lines and as far as his obscured red vision to the left could discern.—lumps of kharki in fetal poses, grotesque shapes where men had fallen arms akimbo and scattered rifles. Growing between the fields of rosemary were bramble bushes with small white flowers. Thick with bodies, red and brown white faces, wide eyes, the brambles and the faces became a plain lament; his path.

As he stumbled back, Donny, a crippling weight, the thin line of the Fifteenth's forward trench came into view. The body field had dispersed into a scattered, fallen mass, like a frozen cadaver spray that a giant had blown onto the ground in a jet, casting bodies thick at the aimed spot and scattering others to the edge. Donny was a grain sack, slipping with the contents of sifting entities, Donny's soul. He didn't care if they fired, but he noticed the poking periscope binoculars, which resembled insect eyes above the trench, and continued towards the lens. Two men came forward, the sappers who built the trench line and pulled him down the side of the trench wall. Donny cried out, slumped to the bottom, gasped, and then fell silent. He watched as the Doctor approached the bearers, waited, and looked up at the blue sky above before starting to shake.

§

Releasing himself from the recollective trance, he looked at the huge shell crater standing on the side of the shattered rock and rocky cordite face. His absolute daydream nightmare cast

4

away slightly as he saw his Corporal walking down the other side of the crater; he was needed again. He couldn't see any way but to be back on the front. The war hadn't really stopped since 1914. The brief three-month halt in the conflict echoed the failed armistice. The Germans had realised what would happen if the Allies had controlled Germany, so they said *"Nein"* and fought on.

He gazed at the dirt and pondered like a demented madman staring at a made up insect, grazing the soil with his boot, between glancing at the Corporal.

The Germans employed a new and straightforward tactic: defensive operations only. German trenches were superior to those of the Allies because they were deeper, often reinforced with concrete, and heavily fortified. The Krauts had made trench building, now in its eighth year, a new form of Germanic architecture, the *Sicherer Bunker.* They utilised their U-boats in the Atlantic with greater efficiency to stop Britain from cutting off their supply routes. The Germans waited for costly attacks and sheltered from the worst artillery barrages in relative comfort.

The tactics of killing had intensified through the years of 1921 and 1922, after the Spanish flu had its turn sorting bodies. He thought tactics hadn't gotten any more intelligent; only the firepower was greater. The French were literally spent and now fought with a depleted army and battalions that wouldn't attack, only watching the Germans from their lines. The Americans, New Zealanders, and Canadians realised their folly of charging steel walls of machine gun fire and pulled out.

The Corporal had crouched and was digging around on the ground with his bayonet. He looked up to the sky and then down again making sure he was below the crater wall and out of sight. His eyes were having trouble compensating the crater shade from harsh sunshine. He rubbed both eyes with his fists in correction and made sure he had the scuttling Corporal in sight. He continued to ruminate on what he had learned.

The US President lost a vote of no-confidence and was deposed. With a new President, the United States became isolationist. The Americans had been in Russia with little effect during the revolution and decided to change tack, leaving Europe to itself—a strategic decision. The British Prime Minister was furious. Reported comments he remembered, "Europe will be consumed by German Nationalism, Mr President," the Prime Minister was quoted as saying. "Then, Prime Minister, Europe will have to combat Nationalism, get on with it. The United States will no longer be pulled into European affairs militarily," the new President was quoted as saying. The Australian Prime Minister continued to be influenced by English opinion and pressure for larger numbers of troops.

The British had now lost over 1.6 million men and were on their knees; Australia had lost ninety-five thousand. The Scots, Welsh, and Irish refused to provide the Empire with more men, causing their frontline units to dwindle to small battalions and civil unrest to brew within the Empire. The slaughter continued over General's tea parties and lines on maps. Australia's finest were diminishing fast. Australia's Farmers were dying on French fields, and the Prime Minister was facing a simmering union movement riding the sheep's back.

All Australian units were recalled from the Middle East, where the Turks had driven them out, and placed in new divisions in the Western hell, now minus their horses. Britain was already facing a severe shortage of junior officers, protests at home, and a deep-seated weariness that felt like a festering cancer. Europe was almost bankrupt and on the brink of a continental collapse; starvation, cultural ruin and shocking casualties.

The Germans were now receiving reinforcements from Italy, the Middle East, Turkey, and Bulgaria, and the scales had tipped in favour of the Axis's defensive posture. He had heard the updated life expectancy for an Allied officer on the front was now two days. For his German equivalent, four months. He had refused promotion well before the new statistic, been disciplined, but was allowed to stay in hell. *I can't care about myself. The next step is to determine how to reach Flurry, which is still in German hands.*

"Sergeant, we found it, the dugout, they have gone, no booby traps" He nodded, he sort of knew. Corporal Harry Carter's chiselled twenty-year-old face and grey eyes reflected the blue sky and hid stories of horror and tainted secrets. Carter's kit and uniform were relics of a Western Front survivor's history. Helmet, trench knife, canteen and rifle stowed to a survivor's code, accessible, safe, silent, and all sound and deadly in their own inanimate object way. Useless weight had long been discarded; items of luxury were utilised or thrown away, while items of practicality were retained, repaired, reinvented, and crafted to withstand the brutal combat laws.

Carter, the former Priest, wore his helmet strapped, his belt secure, and no clothing was let loose, nothing to fall, make noise, trip or get him killed. His hollow artillery barrage eyes still shone, but the light was grey like a macabre picture showing the past origin of his blue eyes. Battle-scarred scribed hands, like some secret scroll, close-cropped hair, and movie-star looks that talked constantly to a sixth-sense intelligence and combat awareness of where to stand and not to stand.

"Corporal…" He paused, and looked down at the green crater pool for a clarifying moment like a rocket Scientist who had just realised how to ignite a propellant. "Down there in that green pool of demented hell water, I think it's a German *Gewehr 98* sniper rifle. I thought I saw a scope just above the waterline, and the gun seems too long for a standard rifle. Retrieve it for me, please"

"Sergeant," the Corporal said, smiling looking down at the swimming pool of hell and pretending that it did not concern him, turned and walked down the crater wall as if he was off to the beach. He smiled. Carter was a good man, and he loved him and enjoyed challenging him. He watched as the Corporal slowly checked the water's edge for a concealed bomb left by the enemy to avenge a crater pool. *He absorbs everything I teach him. Nothing exits from the other ear.*

The Corporal continued to slowly circle the pool, inspecting a piece of metal on the ground, digging around it with his bayonet, then picking it up near the green, decaying flesh detritus. He could see the two bodies in the pool; a German torso was bobbing in an upright stance, its face half visible. The other was face down in the mire in a bloated bottom-up pose. The swirling crater wind wafted the cadaver breeze around him, the rotting flesh a ripe miasmic horror. The bobbing German was gas-filled and buoyant, the torso somehow sealed and floating like a methane balloon, a child's pool toy.

The Corporal got down on his haunches and felt carefully with his bayonet, caressing the surface of the pool. The gas-filled German torso slowly whirled around with the swirling wind in the bowl and faced the Corporal, who looked up momentarily at it, then continued his stabbing of the water as if the dead man had interrupted his swim. He lifted the rifle with the scope out and let the terrible mess drip off the weapon, and rose and walked up to him.

"Sergeant, as requested," he nodded and looked at Carter like a happy Father. Carter then threw up on the ground, his stomach allowed to protest now that his task had been completed. 'Thank you, Carter. "Sergeant Carter rose, looked deadpan at him, and wiped a small piece of corn from the side of his mouth. He looked at the weapon, which seemed to be in working order, as he pulled the bolt and examined the breach.

"There was this also, sir, by the side of the pool" Carter held out a small cigarette tin and opened the lid, inside five cigarettes. "Bingo, keep them, Carter, you have deserved it." "Thank you, sir." "Hang on, wait." He saw some writing on the tin. "Sir?" "Give that here for a moment," he examined the writing etched on the tin."Ah, our owner's name, *Adolf, Adolf*

8

Hitler. He smiled grimly. "Well, Adolf, you won't be needing those," he handed back the tin to Carter, who grabbed a cigarette and lit it. "Sergeant?" He offered the open tin. "No, thanks, Corporal"

"When does the *Meat-Flayer* get here? "General Barn-Paler is scheduled to arrive at ten fifteen, Sergeant," Carter tried to conceal his smile and failed. "There's no unexploded ordnance in that pool, is that right, Carter?" "No, Sergeant" He reached down to the ground, picked up a pebble and threw it into the green pool. The plop sound in the water sent ringed ripples circling to the edges, turning the dead German around again with the current, and the body stared at them.

They watched as the corpse stayed in the staring pose as if it wanted desperately to make an announcement, like it had realised too late it was a great orator. Carter drew on Adolf Hitler's cigarette and blew the smoke out with his breath, which twirled with the swirling wind in the crater and then dissipated. They continued to look at the corpse, both in their own thoughts, as a distant motor sounded, then looked up to discern the sound and walked together towards the top of the hell-hole.

2

Grant Mudbank waited for Australia's official War Correspondent and felt the dead oak tree's rough bark as he sat and listened to the distant artillery cracking in the distance. The ruined house behind him was a casualty of the first years of fighting. The town, *Coq Fier,* translated to *Proud Rooster,* he noted with some interest. He turned to look at what was left of the house's roof and saw the windvane still intact, the rusted rooster looking towards the South. *It is still a proud rooster. I hope he has the goods. I am salivating at the prospect of that silk.*

§

The official Australian War Correspondent, Greg Fieldlight, left Tom, his *Batman,* with the despatches and sent his last group of photographs home for May 1923 to the Editor of the *Stringy-Bark Times.* The terror and nature of General Barn-Palers' and Riddles' death stuck in his mind and played in a coloured dream over and over. The high command was going berserk, two Generals killed on the frontline on the same day, and also, now the Germans knew, and were sending mock condolences across no man's land.

He had written the story and hoped it would see some press. Still, he knew that bad press was almost sure to be censored in its entirety, so he saved the story in his memoirs to protect its authenticity and kept it for the day when the Australian people would want to read about the evisceration of two Generals in one day.

A war that had started in Nineteen Fourteen and was in its disastrous, murderous and unrelenting ninth year. The Australian public was enthusiastic and willing to embark on an adventure for the Empire, Britain, when it began. This gave way to increased enthusiasm when the reporting of the disastrous Gallipoli campaign was somehow skewed to make it appear as if it had been a success. He badgered his Editor to send him to Gallipoli to see for himself and discovered a

10

tenuous foothold on a foreign shore littered with Australian corpses; the result of British war plans when implemented by a Politician and managed by inept Generals. Furious, he wrote about the debacle, which his Editor had said no to, and had to publish a feel-good story about a lieutenant's pet rat.

Tempered doubt followed after the true nature of the murder in a town called *Flurry* became known. Conscription was established two years later, after general enlistment failed to achieve its objectives. The electorate rebelled. Ports shut down because of strikes, and women demonstrated in city streets. Men objected to service, many preferring prison; the previous shame heaped upon those who shunned military service had turned to respect. The new Divisions were mobilised anyway. Nine Divisions was all Australia could wring out of its fighting men, and boys.

He walked to the ruined farmhouse, a bombed-out brick shell, the artillery had smashed whatever semblance of a box it had; long forgotten as a home where people sought shelter. His contact in the Intelligence department was Grant Mudbank, Seventh Division Intelligence Officer. "Grant" "Greg" The man stood, having been seated on a fallen oak tree trunk, covered in strange lichen and long dead from artillery. It seemed to him, the Intelligence man, that a Division clerk too knowledgeable for his position and way too cowardly or smart —he couldn't decide which —would want to risk his life to wear women's clothes.

"Lovely day, Greg, the sky is blue, the flowers are in bloom, and over yonder another attack looms, the dismounted Australian Eighth Division, I hear" Grant looked out towards the front as if searching for a secret box. "Indeed, very poetic, Grant, but what do you have for me?" Mudbank ignored the question and stared at him. "You know I would be taken out to the yard at HQ and summarily executed if they find out I am talking to a reporter?" He smiled, waiting for the response. "Frank Fieldlight."

Frank Fieldlight, his Brother. He thought about the name and played the guessing game Grant wanted him to. "Ah, yes, I know, the Sergeant that survived the *Flurry* attack" "Bingo, well done" "And? Come on, ten more points if you get the last bit" He looked out towards the landscape and tried to discern where green met death by the colour of the ground."Rescued the young lad Donny Farrow. "Well done, but now you have to give me the goods, not the other way around" He smiled and handed Grant the package: dirty photos, soap, a gramophone recording of *Wheezer on the Whizzbag*, his old camera, two pairs of woollen socks and the Grand Prize: Latest silk ladies' underwear.

"You got the clothes?" He nodded, still smiling. "Size six, you make a petite lady." Grant ignored him and put the package down carefully on the fallen tree log beside him like a child given rare, fragile sweets. Grant looked at him, detecting a change to the goods delivered. "The ladies are not French, sorry, not available, they are all actually German, no, hang on, Austrian, the only lovely photos available." "Thanks, I mean that as a friend, Frau's eh? Even better." Grant raised a photo of a plump Austrian nude smiling beside a pile of washing.

"Friends are we, Grant?" The Intelligence Officer smiled and looked back out towards the front. "So, let's hear it, Mudbank, before it rains and washes you away" "Ha!, trust you, Fieldlight" "Never had that one?" "Actually, no, I can't say I have, it's usually *mud-pile.*" He folded his arms in mock impatience.

"Ok, so your brother is missing. You asked to be informed if there was anything." "Missing?" "Missing" "How? Killed? What?" "No, absent without leave, the Captain clocked him at the front, where Barn-Paler apparently got shot by the sniper and survived, then he was gone" "What? Barnpaler survived?" "Yes, miracle by all accounts. Why, you didn't know?" "He looked very dead to me" His image of Barnpaler's lifeless form being thrown off the stretcher assailed him. "Frank was there as well?" "Yes, reconnaissance, old German line."

"So he's dead?" No, no, no, not dead, I take it you two don't talk much." He looked at Mudbank, not quite believing him, knowing Frank couldn't tell him anything even if they met more than once a year. "The artillery was intense. I was there, we were lucky to get out alive." "Yes, I know, with Riddle as well, was he really cut in half?" He hesitated in annoyance and blinked at Mudbank. "Grant, get on with it, I haven't got all day, and yes, he was cut in half by a shell splinter." He quickly suppressed and censored his mental image of Riddle being flayed apart.

"No, he wasn't killed. His Corporal tried to cover for him, but Thanatos is on to him, you remember the Greek?" "Your Intelligence whip?" "Yes, he brings in the sabatours, thieves, murderers and deserters" "Correct, our own *Greek god* serving the underworld" "And he will arrest him?" "I have it on good authority that wouldn't be in the public's interest and that he may disappear." "He would face Court-Martial anyway, and prison, it wouldn't look good for anyone, better he disappear"

"You are kidding?" "Thought you would need to know, Frank decided to stay on the line, seems a waste to get himself shot as ironically a coward deserter and being your brother." Fuck, Frank. Thanks Mudbank"

"Can you stop Thanatos?" "Me? ha!,no, er not officially. But you might be able to. The guy is no coward. People back home wouldn't like the idea of a hero like Frank being shot behind the line or disappearing." "Neither would I. He was on the line in the area when Barn-Paler and Riddle made their unfortunate visit, you say?" "Yes," "Ok, I get it, Mudbank, this is asking the right question, game is it not?" "Maybe" "So what is it, what do you know? Did Frank do something? Mudbank shifted and looked at the ground, then back out, squinting at the shining morning horizon.

"Shall I take back your parcel?" "Ha!, no, no, come on, next question, a hint. How did Barn-Paler get shot?" "Sniper" "Yes" "You are telling me he was the sniper?" "That's what

13

we suspect" "No, how?" "I can't say, but someone says they saw Frank exactly in that area, probably someone on the line, another sniper or a Balloon lookout, not the Corporal. "You are speaking in increasingly riddled circles, Mudbank"

"Frank, my god, from hero to zero. Why?" "Barn-Paler ordered the attack and killed five thousand men, there's that. In my book, he deserves a pass." "Yes, but that's war, I don't know, I" Mudbank watched as he trailed off in thought, perhaps ultimately realising the horror of that assault; the ultimate effect on his only brother. The fact that his brother may die descended on his consciousness, and an alarm sounded in his mind.

"Look, I have a solution, but first, there is something else." "What?" Mudbank swept his foot in a semi-circle on the ground, flattening the grass. "We think the Germans have cracked some genetic code. We have their potion, some sort of chemical or drug, the nature of which we are unsure; it's changing everything." "What? A weapon?" "No, not a weapon, The war Department is doing tests, it is changing people's behaviour, human behaviour." He gazed at Mudbank, questioning his sanity for a moment. "If this is a joke, Grant, this is the last time we meet." Mudbank raised his hand, fingers splayed.

"Wait, give me a moment here. As a consequence, it appears that a peace deal is on the table. "Peace deal! Now you are talking straight, Mudbank, when, how?" He was shocked, beautifully numb. "Tell me this is real" "It's real" Mudbank looked at him seriously and nodded. "Ha!"

He grabbed Mudbank and embraced him, then grabbed him by both shoulders and looked at him straight on. Mudbank continued. "Look, I'm dead if this gets out early, but you have the heads up" "What does all this have to do with a potion?" "Everything," he saw from Mudbank, a look that something fundamental had changed in the man, and gazed into his eyes as if the key lay there, like a rare fossil in his Iris or Cornea, set in celluloid stone.

14

Mudbank handed him a small, folded piece of paper. "If you want to help Frank, then get to the Seventh's Australian Field Hospital, near *Chanty.* There is a wounded man there, one of ours. If anyone can help you, it will be Tempelton. One of the Division's snipers. He will find Fieldlight, protect him. In the meantime, I will see what I can do to stop the order or at least amend it. I do this willingly to genuinely help as a friend, but also at the penalty of death, so I expect the underwear to keep flowing, understood?" "You bet, I will go berserk at Harrods, I'm due to go to London next month." He looked at Mudbank and realised he had misjudged the man. "Thank you, Grant," Mudbank nodded; a recognition their relationship had changed.

"Just give Templeton this. We think this is the last position we know of, but of course, we know where he is going, so it might help." 'Where is he going?" "*Flurry.*" "For what?" "One could speculate, I would say, to visit his dead mates, all five thousand of them" "Of course, *Flurry.* And the peace deal? What else do you know?" "It's going to happen soon; there has been a chat between the two top brasses. The thinking has changed, fundamentally." "And this magic potion?" "It's fundamental to the thinking" "How?" "You'll see" "I guess I will have to take back those photos, I just remembered." "Ok, OK"

"Well?" "I have taken it. Some of us were lab rats. It was tested; it turned out to be some sort of insect venom. It's, well, it's what man has been searching for, the magic elixir of life in a way." Grant smiled and looked at him like a cheeky child who was hiding something. "What Mudbank? Are you telling me you are immortal?" "Ha! No, not immortal." Mudbank smiled and looked him straight in the eye. "Different, like you start to understand stuff, fundamentally, in a clever way. A humane way, like you know you are part of the Earth, that sounds silly, I know, but" *Part of the Earth? Has Mudbank gone insane? I wonder.*

15

Mudbank gazed at his shoes, then crouched to pick some grass and throw the strands into the wind in earnest contemplation, and then looked at him. "You have memories about the Earth, dreams about other animals, plants, and the Universe. Look, I sound completely bonkers, but here, take some, then you will understand. You will know where you came from"

Rising, Mudbank rummaged in his tunic pocket and handed him a small glass, labelled with a red label containing a colourless liquid. "Mother of Earth, Mudbank, you never cease to amaze me. "Who made it?" "Unknown. All we know is that it comes from their side of the line" "What about its distribution? Aren't there rules about this stuff?" "What do you suggest?" He laughed softly to himself. "I don't know, I"

Mudbank gazed at him ruefully. "It's one hell of a story," he thought about Frank and realised he knew little of him, his brother. Mudbank's eyes glistened in the morning light, and he turned his head and gazed back out again across the field to where men were dying and looked like he had found a way to stop it all.

3

The purple-green river water reflected the brown and red haze that hung over the tin and wooden, stain-streaked factories that lined the watercourse. Spewing mercury, lead and carbon-monoxide fumes from funnels like a dead man's fingers cast upward seeking the real sky somewhere blue above. The choking pollution hung like a soiled baby's blanket; the humidity intermingled with the smell of old Sulphur and tanned hides, a metallic tang and ochre-orange slime cast a heavy pall over the oxygen-deprived air.

Sam Cowan watched his steps as he walked, making depressions in the mud path. With every step, a green fluid seeped from the compressed clay. He coughed and tried to ignore the terrible stench of dead animals and mercury in the air. His daily path to the insecticide factory, where new chemicals were planned in a small room by pseudo-scientists with scant regard for their effects or smell. The other workers he saw were filing through the massive steel factory entrance like ants getting ready to release a Queen.

The foreman had sat with him in the cats-piss lobby on the tattered grey sofa to interview him for the position. He had drifted off as the thin, skeletal, wrinkled and worn-out man chattered like a vending machine at a Carnival. He advertised the wealth, future and grandeur of the company like a used scissors salesman; the firm's path to dominance was explained by those who killed insects along the miserable river.

While he nodded physically and drifted mentally, he wondered what the man was like and what had made him like the nub of a withered pencil. He examined the grey sofa and saw suspicious stains down the side, as well as a yellow, congealed stain. He wondered if the separate tears in the couch represented a meeting, action, or furious altercation.

"Mr Cowan, are you with me?" "Yes, yes, apologies, the future of the company sounds bonzer" The man smiled and started on another tangent of pointless diatribe. He knew he had a terrible job; no one could find workers along the river, many had gone to the country and were working the land that the Government had released for lease and productivity.

The light above annoyed him with the green cast and puzzled, strange shapes on the man's face, making him look like some hell-bourne gate-keeper. The sounds on the factory floor outside resembled a shaking wet dog, then a hissing cat. Loud thumps then started, and the clattering of hollow tins. Several men talked outside, and an acrid smell permeated the small room.

He clocked on at the metal box and placed his card in the metal tray. Several men nodded to him as he passed them, the night shift over, looks of "Good luck" and "It's hell in there" The conveyor belt vibrated the insecticide cans, which fell like dead flies onto the mats below, where several men and women collected the tins and packed them into the wooden crates. There was a man on a ridiculously high ladder replacing a roof light bulb above the factory floor, and he could hear the foreman in the rear telling someone off. The hiss of the carbon-dioxide pressuriser permeated the air at precise ten-second intervals like a constant, annoying friend.

He was awaiting approval for the plot of land for which he had submitted his application. It had already been three months, and he wondered and wondered. He dreamed of a clerk finding his application, quickly perusing the contents of the following folder on the pile, and stamping it in red, which meant it was *approved*. The city and factories made millions, but no one else did, and the place resembled a mechanical tyrant. *I have no choice.* Reaching his work station, the labelling section, he took his cap off and looked at the machine. The previous worker had left it in the correct standby mode and cleaned the operator sections. *Who was that guy that night? Hatter or something like that? He always does his job correctly.* Sometimes workers would leave it running or leave rubbish around.

He looked up to see how the man on the ladder was progressing. *How long does it take to change a light bulb?* He noticed a small bird on one of the steel rafters high above the factory floor, watching him and the ladder man. *He's making every second count. He's been relieved of his floor duty; the poor guy works on the compressor.* He glanced over to the compressor operator. The man was eyeing the ladder man with a scowl, waiting for him to finish, knowing he was stalling. "How long does it take to change a light bulb, Pickard? The compressor awaits." The foreman had seen the display of stalling for time and shouted at the ladder man, who remained still on the ladder. He held his breath, but the man was aware of his footing. The foreman laughed, and the compressor stand-in smiled, hoping to scare him. The ladder man descended, smiled at him and took his place back at the infernal machine.

The compressor looked as if it had been invented on some medieval battlefield. It had three victims that he knew of in his short time there. The machine was intimidating because it was under pressure and primed to spray the insecticide can. The operator had to prime each can on a conveyor belt; the drudgery of the job was continuous and unrelenting. The first poor man had pierced a can, and then it exploded into his face, the burning chemical blinded him, and he was carried away in an ambulance that took one hour to arrive. Afterwards, two men came, some Government inspectors.

He saw the Foreman give them a paper bag, then they left, and the compressor stayed. The next was a woman who pierced her hand with the compressor needle that drove the air into the cans. With a stricken scream, she fled the machine. The Foreman ran to her aid but seemed oblivious of what to do, seemingly more concerned with the conveyor belt. The woman's hand wept spotted red everywhere, and she knelt on the ground sobbing. Pickard, the light bulb man, came to her aid, grabbed the first aid kit he had brought to the factory

19

himself, and bandaged the wound after pouring some fluid on her hand. It was then he realised Pickard was different. He stayed with the young woman and comforted her. He helped repack the aid kit. Pickard gave him a thank-you look, and he placed it on his workstation table.

He helped Pickard carry the woman to the waiting ambulance, accompanied by the driver and the nurse. They looked at one another as if to say, *"What are we doing here?"* Pickard was older than him and looked strong, capable, and intelligent. The next unfortunate got hit with a high-pressure compressor pipe, which hissed off its mount and struck him in the face. The man went down hard on the floor, apparently, as the night-shift team had told him. Barney Hatter apparently checked the man to see if he was dead, checking his breathing. The man's heart had stopped, Barney had said. Barney administered a strange procedure he was told, pumping the man's heart with his hands and breathing air into his mouth.

The Foreman, he was told, was aghast and roared at Barney just as the man spluttered and sat up. The entire factory floor team watched, and the Foreman stood still in a rage, thinking Barney was mad. There was apparently a stillness afterwards as Barney walked back to his station, after the man was taken away as if they had seen a Roman god walk across the floor. The foreman had it in for Barney after that, but was visited by two men, doctors who told him it was a new technique for starting someone's heart invented in 1903. The foreman accepted the explanation, and Barney was reprieved.

Nothing had happened to Pickard, and he was pleased. He seemed careful with the beast, his intelligence shining through. Pickard changed the hose clamps on the Compressor lines and oiled the beast. His turn on the infernal machine was looming, however. The rotation was in place, and every worker had to sit on the thing for two months at a time. He hoped every day that the clerk would stamp his file, but months passed, and the time came as he stood in front of the beast. The foreman laughed and walked away, giving him a brief, rushed lecture on how to operate the machine.

20

Pickard approached him and watched while the foreman disappeared into the back of the factory. The other workers had stopped the production line, but kept the noise up so as not to arouse suspicion."Listen, Cowan, the trick is to calibrate the needle, which means correcting the amount of gas it uses; the idiot doesn't even know what that means. I looked it up at the suppliers one afternoon." "Neither do I, to be honest," he said, looking at Pickard, smiling. "Don't worry, I'll show you," they both said, looking around to make sure the foreman was not coming back. "Teddy is creating a diversion, and he'll be a while"

Pickard explained the machine's workings and how to calibrate it. He watched as Pickard talked, like a concerned father to a nervous son. "Thanks, Pickard" "Call me Johnathon, and it's actually Pike-Pickard for your information" "Thank you, Johnathon. You have saved my bacon." "No problem. Please let me know if you need any further information." Teddy Barnett walked back around the corner, smiling.

The foreman walked a few paces back. "Don't come back, Barnett, you're fired!"Great!" Barnett said, turning to face the foreman. The Foreman stopped. He noticed some marks on his cheek and realised Barnett had ruffed him up. The foreman looked scared, and Barnett looked at him menacingly for a second or so and then smiled at him as he walked out the factory entrance. Jonathon stole him a glance of compressed laughter, and he sat down and started the calibrated compressor.

For the next three months, he dreamed of arming compressed cans of insecticide during the night, which drove him crazy as he awoke to start work at the factory, where he would pierce the cans all day. The next day, he watched as the injured woman returned to the factory and walked over to Pike-Pickard and hugged him, crying. She said something else while holding one of his arms, then came over to him. Pickard hesitated, then sat down and started labelling. *Mary Somers, I*

21

think that's her name. "Hi Sam, thanks for what you did to help.

"That's ok Mary, how are you now?" "Ok, I can't work yet, though, it went straight through my palm." "Ouch." She went down to her station, talked to the other women, and then left. The foreman said nothing, watching, arms folded in the dark corner. The next day, he jumped up from the compressor in fright as an insect bit him on the back of his leg. An intense pain then red and sore, he inspected the site in a mirror, then forgot about it.

4

Johnathan Pike-Pickard watched the old lady climb the tram stairs. At the same time, the driver waited, and the other passengers remained patient, adopting the public transport demeanour that passengers typically exhibit: a deadpan look and a racing mind. "Thank you, driver," the woman said. She walked down the aisle, and he stood for her. She smiled and took the seat. He watched the street, a man sweeping, a truck loading and a baker in an apron pointing to something, something he couldn't see as the tram passed the area and turned on its way to the western suburbs.

He unfolded the letter and saw that his application had been successful, admitting him into officer training. A school had been established in the town, and the days of makeshift camps and drill training were over; officers now learnt first how to shoot straight, drill marching became a distant last. The drain on men being killed in the Great War had necessitated the need for specialised instruction on staying alive. He knew he would be taught skills that he could use in the trenches, including fieldcraft such as camouflage, weapon repair, and grenade throwing.

Tactics of trench warfare had been honed, and they would be taught which weapons worked the best, how to take proper cover from artillery, and how to flank a machine-gun position. Reconnaissance was a significant part of training, and map work and sniping became an art form that had its own school. Tanks had reappeared on the front, and the Australian mechanised corps had been formed with new machines, although it was all hush-hush about what they were.

He stood like a statue on his balcony, reading the letter. His deceased parents' home was still his home; the weathered floorboards and hardwood frame were his Father's legacy, a carpenter by trade. Worn out, his Father passed away, and his Mum died of cancer shortly after, and he was sad but relieved he was over twenty-one and an adult; they couldn't tell him what to do. His Dad's Solicitor had the will, and his Fathers dead ear. *Why do I want to join up? Tell me again, Jonathan, seeing my life expectancy on the front is three days.*

He grabbed the screen door and rattled it open, and went inside because his nosy neighbour, Mrs Alle, was pottering around, a covert gardener pretending to hose something. He sat on the weathered sofa and placed the letter down on the polished hardwood table his Father had made. His reflection stared at him from the wooden tabletop; a dark, menacing figure within the grain of the dark wood. *So, what do you say, Johnathon? What does my dark side say? Expect hell, that's what I say.* He thought about the war and how it had to stop, and what he could do about it, and that was his reason, to do something, try and win or more fanciful aims like making it to General and making it stop.

I honestly don't know why I am going, that's the truth. If I don't go, I will be a coward; Mrs Allen will see to that. Is that why I am going? No. Let's see, because I am bored, maybe. Because I am alone but not lonely? Maybe. King and Country? Definitely not; they made a hash of Gallipoli. They seem not to acknowledge the losses.

There was a soft knock on the screen door. He hesitated and prepared for Mrs Allen, but he saw it wasn't her through the glass, a man, bigger. Sam stood holding some eggs. "Sam! How are you?" "I thought this might be the best time. I had to go through town for Mum, so I took these with me this morning." "Of course, come in, mate. Wow, Sam, these are great."

He looked at the brown eggs arrayed in the cardboard container. "It's a new invention, the egg carton, it has the lid and locks down with the holders there" "So I see, it does a great job, so fridge, I assume?" "Yes, will keep longer" "So we said trade right?" "Yep, but it's no issue, if you can't make it, then it's fine" "No, no, no, my friend, a trade is a trade. Come and see." "What, you have made it?" He smiled, creating suspense for his work colleague, and walked to the back door, holding it open.

They stood looking at the crafted wooden box. Sam smiled, bent down, opened the lid, and caressed the wood finish, then touched the wire lid. "Wow, this is too much, Johnathon. I have to pay you." "No way, a trade is a trade. I enjoyed making it for you"

"So I made it as a dual purpose box" "If you have to carry them, which is what you asked for, the wire lid gives them good ventilation, but you can tip it to one side and it becomes a laying box, here I'll show you" He opened the lid and tilted the box, Sam was thrilled and his face was beaming. "Then place the partition in and you have two laying boxes, but as you say they only usually use one box anyway" "It's magic, thanks, I don't know what to say." "So, I have the truck, Dad's truck, when you are ready we can drive to your place, carry it for you" "Well, I.." "That's settled then"

"When's show day?" "Saturday week, "I'll pick you up, tell me the time" Sam nodded unwillingly and was too thrilled to argue. He felt relieved and elated that he had made the box; it had made Sam's day. Sam bent down and inspected the box again as if imagining his chooks inside. He glanced over at his Fathers tools in the shed and thought that his Dad was almost certainly there somewhere, smiling at him and pleased with his craftsmanship. "So how many are you entering?" "Two, Potts and Trumpet." "Ha! So you do name them?" "Er, yes, I can't help it, they are all individual characters" "Ha!, ok, Potts and Trumpet it is, Saturday week"

As darkness encroached, he walked back to his flat through the wilted grass and lifeless riverbank. There were no insects, no birds and no fish that he could see. The miasmic wind blew from the smelter to the East, and he covered his mouth trying to stop the foul air from entering his lungs. Leaden grey clouds milled in an Easterly path as if in agreement with the destruction below. On the other side, past the rusting walkway across the river, a mass of rubbish and machinery from the factories was piled. *How many people gave their lives for those monsters?* He passed a huge discarded water tank and a lifeless tractor, a tyre hanging off to one side of the rims. A green glass beaker sat on the grass awaiting solution, ironically, he thought from the locally poisoned sky. A pair of white socks with red stripes hung on a steel bar that jutted from a spiral apparatus of some unknown purpose; a giant corkscrew.

The flat grass area stretched around a large pond. He watched the water mill in the breeze, a relatively untouched source, set away from the miasmic river flow. Beyond the pond and the grass plain was the freeway, and smoking trucks trundled along like ants. He could see the walkway over the traffic in the distance, his beeline for home. A distinct clicking sound emitted from the pool of water, and he stopped to listen. The sound repeated every three seconds, a *toc toc* sound. He crouched and tried to locate the source, gazing into the pool of untouched water. A single rush stalk jutted from the pool in the middle, and a factory wooden pallet was floating at the other side. The toc toc sound continued, but the wind shifted the sound. He rose and went to the other side of the pool, where the pallet shifted like a ship without a mooring at the mercy of the wind.

He crouched again, and he saw the small frog, a tiny creature, reddish and brown with yellow dots on its back, perched on the lower part of the pallet. Its glistening skin shone on the cloudy day, and he watched as the frog halted its tune and dove into the water, swimming with its hind legs in a propelling V-shape down into the depths. He smiled and shook his head. *That's the most beautiful thing I have ever seen: a frog swimming. I have never seen a frog, actually, have I? Does it survive here? In this terrible place?*

He sat for a while on the grass in the place that just passed as clean, hoping to see the small creature again, but he didn't reappear. He looked at the leaden sky, seeing shapes in the clouds, a man's face grimacing, a kite with a tail and a glass of beer. He pictured the frog swimming again, its legs jutting from its body in expert strides. He felt tired; the factory line never let up, and he had only a half-hour break in his ten-hour shift. He lay back and rested in the acceptable grass.

After a time, he heard the frog again, the *"toc,"* emanating from under some grass at the edge of the pond. He didn't try to disturb the creature; he listened and smiled and felt something shift in him, a small aligning of thought about the natural world that he had never even considered; that it was there and always present, and he and all the creatures on Earth were the same and not that different. He realised that there were probably many creatures he couldn't see around the pond, maybe ants and mites and fleas and slugs, snails and water dragonflies. He looked out at the single reed in the middle of the pond, where a small bird, a tiny red and black avian wonder, grasped the reed stem and looked at him. Immaculate feathers, a tiny three-gram species that seemed ideally suited to stem-perching on stalks of grass. He rose to get a better look, but the bird flew off into the air, away across the dark field.

He fell asleep, and in his dream, he drifted through tall grass as if he had no legs.

The wiry strands grazed his torso, and then he could feel the footfall of his feet on the ground; a raspy swish and crack of dry detritus. The grass stalks had small white seeds that stuck to his skin, and small ants alighted from the strands and scuttled over his arms, before making their way back over the tubular phylem subways, much like commuting workers. The sky was a deep blue, with wispy green clouds drifting through it. He gazed skywards, marvelling at the torrents of cotton-wool and scourer-textured shapes that moved at pace through the ancient stratosphere.

As the grass became reeds and the footfall echoed in the slush, he looked around and knew several thousand creatures were below in the mud and the shallow water. Smiling, the memories within the dream lingered in consciousness. A sea

27

creature with fins, a hard-shelled anthropod, and a flying black carapaced aquatic beetle. Chemicals within, synthesis of sorts, instinct.

Ahead, a creature stood waiting. A female insect, but like him, a biped of sorts as well. How is that possible? The water-grass subsided to a fine pebble shore. Glancing at his feet, they seemed not to be troubled by the harsh angles of stone. The female had beautiful wings that shone with a reflected green and an ochre hue of red in the sunlight that was now above in the noon tempest. Then the creature was a woman, and he squinted, made sure, and berated himself for the silly error. She smiled as he approached, and a wave of contentment swept over him like nothing he had experienced: the attractive woman, the warm sunshine and the memories that he had been an integral part of the Earth. He stood before the Queen. She still smiled and embraced him with her beautiful, delicate, cellulite wings; the soft rasp he could hear as they grazed him.

Awakening slowly, he fought the dream's imminent closing curtain, not wanting to enter another world and leave the Queen's wings that comforted him. The sound and feel of a dark, grassy landscape. He spluttered upwards, shocked that he had passed out. The moon had risen, and the pond reflected the shine in a slight wind-generated pattern of ripples. The *toc toc* of the tiny frog was audible again in the darkness.

He crossed the freeway, the black ants with beaming eyes lined up and spewing pollution in six lanes. The overpass shook with a rattling vibration of the walkway deck. Beyond the freeway, he crossed the railway tracks and the slums of the Western district, a squalid place, where rubbish adorned the alleyways, discarded by rejected squatters and evicted tenants. The stained terrace houses crumbled and sat like ruined hives of a past society of intelligent insects. Single street lamps barely illuminated anything; darkness was the flavour. The Industrial river wind was blowing across the street, and bits of paper floated around, swirling upward in eddies and rising to fly onto the rooftops to replace the daytime birds that were usually nowhere to be seen.

An older man was crossing the street with a walker ahead of him when a young teenager threw an empty can at him, striking him on the head and causing laughter from the four boys. He stared at the boys, and one of them glared at him. "Hey, nong head, come here," he said. He ignored them and started across the street, saying nothing. "Hey, nong nuts, I've got a gun, stop" He calculated the likelihood of the lad having a gun and kept walking. "Hey, stop or I'll shoot" The lad was behind him as he continued to walk, catching up with the old man. "Hey, stop or I'll shoot, I'll count to ten. Ten, nine, eight," He continued. His mate said something to the effect of "Put it away, he's an idiot," and he caught up with the old man.

"Are you ok, mister?" "Oh yes, it'll take more than that," the man said, looking at him, with a smile. He noticed the man had a pin from the last war on his suit, a wattle leaf and flower that illuminated in the dim streetlight. The man stopped and caught his breath. Ahead was a woman in a nightgown and pink slippers putting something in a bin. He heard one of the boys call out "Bang Bang!" Laughter ensued." "Can I do anything for you, sir?' The older man looked at him, still smiling. "Actually, you could get my keys from my pocket, I'm having a wobbly here" "Sure." He reached into the man's pocket, a clutch of keys on a string keyring. "My house is that red shit-hole over there," He pointed, taking one hand off the walker, nearly falling.

He steadied the man and unlocked the door. The nightgown stared at him suspiciously as she went back inside. "Thanks, my fine fellow, I thank you, may all your desired future fucks be granted." He smiled and tried not to laugh. "Major Thomas Farrington, Seventh Division" The man shook his hand. "Sam Cowan, destitute factory worker" "Hah! You'll be right at home then, come on, have a port, it's the least I can do"

The Major brought him the port, a large crystal glass filled to the brim. "There you are, bottoms up, now I have to ask, what's a lad like you doing in this shit-pile of a place?" The

29

Major sat down in a brown, worn sofa chair. He sat across from him and sipped the port. "Waiting for my land grant." "Ahh, the mystical land that never is released"

"Say what?" "No, won't happen, Sam, they haven't even given the Veterans their land yet, I suspect they won't either, money-grabbing cretins. I have been waiting for five years now, and I'll probably die here, which of course suits them nicely" "But people have been leaving, they were approved" "No, no, not approved, applied, there is a whole lot of gap between those two Government-generated terms. Can you tell me one person who has got their land? Tell me and I'll change my tune." "Well, actually no, I just assumed they had moved to go to their plots," he said at his port, smelling the fumes of the fortified wine.

"Never assume, Sam, it will bring all sorts of dire trouble tumbling down on you like a wall of tainted shit covered bricks" The major sipped his port and stared at him above his black-rimmed glasses. "Besides, I hear that the Great War armistice, just like the last one in Nineteen eighteen, has been short-lived. It won't be long now, and we shall once again be at war" Sam almost choked on his port. "And that's why Sam, the land has not been given out. They need it to use it for war production."

"You can't be serious?" "Oh, yes, they seem not to understand what the German philosophy is" "Which is what?" Sam held his port in grim disappointment. "Well, an uneven-sided armistice would be a disaster. Just because you are first to suggest an armistice doesn't mean you are ready for unconditional surrender. Armistice literally means *Stop Arms*. So on it will go and your land will probably be used as a site for an arms factory or something similar."

§

He made sure the Major was ok and left. He lifted a heavy box for him and packed his groceries and walked down the street in the filthy gloom. The fortified wine had gone to his head, not having eaten anything. Still a minute's walk from home, he crossed the park bridge where the dead river flowed under on its way to the Industrial hell. The monument to the last war stood in the gloom; a soldier with a bayonet pointed to the ground, his head bowed, below the names of the dead etched in stone from a town that was once a thriving port city. The surviving old trees of the park seemed not to care, living monuments themselves and witnesses to crime, passion, happy picnics, and the soldiers who once passed by on their way to war, now inscribed upon brass plaques.

Several of the great gums rose to thirty metres, and the canopies swayed in the evening sulphur breeze. Beside them were the casualties, the leafless stands of poisoned companions that had succumbed to the toxic river wash.

The park was illuminated by the rising moon, a waxing crescent smile, casting enough light for him to make out microbats flitting through the gum flowers. He knew what the micro-bats were as they visited him at night in his small apartment, the light outside attracting the mosquitoes. The bats fluttered in like a vampire movie, one becoming trapped once when he had closed the window and hovering before him, *Nosferatu* wanting to go outside. He had checked himself the day after discovering them, looking for vampire marks, but he was not a vampire, and the bats were harmless, curious and mammals like him. He found out when he listened to a radio show about wildlife.

His door creaked, and he entered his one-room apartment. The expensive shit-hole took a third of his pay every month. His cool box sat near the wall on a wooden stand, with its ice block delivered every morning by a bearded man using a horse and cart. His Mum had given him a radio, and it sat near his sunken bed on his wobbly bedside table, upon the rattly lamp. The gas stove was the only other piece of furniture, consisting of a cast-iron oven and a gas cooktop connected to the main gas line, the only utility.

The shared bathroom block stood in the middle of the surrounding dwellings, concrete and tile surfaces marred by mould and mildew. *Geez, I forgot. Tomorrow is Saturday, thank god.* He sat with palpable relief on the side of his bed, eating a bit of cheese, as he realised he had two days off from the compressor. *During the day, anyway.*

He lay waiting for the tiny bats, their distinctive fluttering of membrane wings visible in the darkness. The dream factory was different, of course, more malevolent than the real place; the foreman was bigger and more threatening. The compressor made less sense than the absolute beast, with extra buttons that did nothing he could discern in the dream world and existed only as a byproduct of his brain's chemicals. The compressor did, however, fail more, and he was constantly looking for lost cans, realising with a shocked moment that he had come to work naked; the other workers were staring at him in horror.

5

He awoke to the fluttering sound, relieved he was free of the dream factory. The warm night brought the smell of garbage from the street and someone's piss in the alley. He saw the shadows of the tiny bats as they passed the street light filtering above his bed, catching the mosquitoes. He smiled and stayed still; the display was always a delight for him. He wondered if they sat next to him when he was asleep and examined the human, curious as they seemed to be.

As the sky grew light, he awoke as always, feeling the texture of the sheet on his aching ankles, his ten-kilometre walk on Sunday. He thought about the day's schedule, relieved he hadn't gone to work by mistake. A fly buzzed on the ceiling, unable to distinguish the plaster from the sky. Outside, the cartman left the ice blocks, the sound of scraping and hessian.

He walked down to Charmer Street and caught the tram to his Mum's place, a ten-minute ride through the contrasting central business district of empty shop fronts and imposing buildings of stone architecture history, housing banks and Industrial giants. The butcher was busy already, the gift shop he could see had a stand of hats outside and the grocer was taking a delivery off a truck.

The pub remained eternal, feeding the workers. Several people sat on the wooden tram seats, reading papers. Some stared into space, wishing they had a paper; some were horrified, while others smiled at the thought of having to address the harmless madman who stood and directed new passengers to their seats, dressed in a purple gown and holding a small tabletop lamp.

§

"Sammy, my love," she hugged him in the landing. "What sort of shirt is that?" She looked at his only non-work shirt with disdain. "It's my best one" "Mmm, come on, want some breakfast? "Yep," "Bacon and eggs?' "Yes, please," he said, and sat and looked at his Dead Father on the mantle piece staring at him. *Never found.* His Mum rifled through the fridge, a new, expensive invention and legacy of her Husband's pension payout. "What's that refrigerator like?"

"Oh, Sammy, it's wonderful, no more carrying ice, it runs on electricity, you know?" "Wow, so you can keep food for longer?" "Oh, yes, it's the best invention since sliced bread" "Are they the chook's eggs?" "Yes, they are in the back, they love you, those chooks. You cared for those hens for years." "Yeah, I love them too, I'll have a chat with them shortly" His Mum smiled at him, then started to laugh, placing the streaky bacon in the pan.

"How's work?" "Awful" "Mmm, I can't say I blame your disdain, that terrible factory area. Any news on the land?" "No, a man told me it's never going to happen. I helped a veteran last night. Some kids were harassing him." "Oh, really? What division was he from?" "Seventh" "Not your Dad's then" "No, not Dad's the Fifteenth" *Shit, what are you doing?* He wished he hadn't said Fifteenth, but it was too late. His Mum said nothing and stroked the bacon, staring at the pan. "Sorry, Mum"

"Don't you be sorry, Sam, it's the Government that should be sorry and that General, what was his name? "General Barnpaler" "Yes, that's the murderer, still with the high command, would you believe?" "Wasn't there an inquiry?" "Yes, a Government inquiry about themselves, their favourite type, we wouldn't have ever known the truth if that Journalist, um, *Packard*, no, *Fieldlight* from the *Stringy Bark Times* hadn't been there at the time." He hesitated, not wanting to upset her further. "That man lost five thousand men in one day, Sam, *one* day" She started to cry, and began to shake, a single finger raised to the ceiling, the other hand grabbing the benchtop as if she was in a high wind storm. He rose and put his arm around her, both of them looking out the kitchen window at the out-house, the tilted timber thunderbox as if his

Father was in there. He swallowed and held his welling tears for his Father, but also for the other four thousand nine hundred and ninety-nine, not being able to comprehend such a loss.

"Sorry, don't mind me, what about the land?" His Mum composed herself, gazing at him with red eyes. "The man said he's been waiting, and he is a veteran, they got first grab" "Oh, no, really?, I thought people had approved?" "No, I told you that, hastily probably, apparently the Government is saving plots for war production." "Can you find out the truth?" "That's where I'm going next, the land services office" "You're a nice man, Sam, for helping that veteran; your Father would be pleased" *I'm glad the lad didn't have a gun. Mind you, maybe the Major did.* He could smell the bacon and the sizzling eggs, and the aroma made his mouth water. His hunger set in him, and he realised he hadn't eaten much for days. They sat and ate while his Mum fussed and his Dad looked on. He cleaned his empty plate with a piece of bread so it looked unused, his Mum watching him with a smile.

The hens came running towards him and milled around him, his childhood friends. He sat with them and strung some corn up for them on a string, and they savaged the corn like crazed entertainers on a stage savaging a microphone. His Mum sat on the wooden stool outside the enclosure and peeled some potatoes, smiling. He picked each girl up, checked their feet for Bumble-foot, and massaged their lappels, which they hated but sort of loved.

The day with his Mum went from sunny morning to cloudy afternoon, then panting humidity as the afternoon got hotter as the day got shorter. Chicken routine followed the weather; hunger to curiosity to dirt bath introspection.

"See you then." He stepped out onto the landing. "Any potential grandchildren on the way?" "Ahh, I have to find a partner first. I'll let you know," he said deadpan. *That's if the insecticide or the Compressor doesn't kill me first.* She smiled and quashed a twenty-dollar bill into his hand. "Mum, it's ok, you need it" "No, I don't, there's only one of me, I consume like a flea" He smiled and hugged her. "Oh, a frog is living in the pond East of the factories" "Oh?" His Mum looked at him as if he were mad. *What did you say that for?* "Anyway, I'll be off, love you Mum" "Bye, sweetie" She grabbed his arm as if he was leaving for good.

§

Johnathon picked him up as promised on the second Saturday for the poultry show. They entered *Trumpet* and *Potts*, the president eyed them as they stared at him though the carry box and stamped their entry. The cacophony of crows split the din in the large shed, some hens sat and waited as though they already knew the outcome. They watched as the attendant placed Trumpet in the display cage, his hen watching and seemingly wondering if that was that.

They waited in the bar tent as the judging commenced as a storm broke in the afternoon and dumped a hail of ice on the ground to ladies concerned voices and men's stares. The storm cleared and the cool aftermath signalled the competition winners. Potts's cage had a third place ribbon and Trumpet's a second and he smiled as Jothnathon laughed out loud as they approached the cages.

At home his Mum pinned the ribbons on the new fridge and he and Johnathon had a final beer; Pott's and Trumpet returned heroine chooks. They laughed and celebrated and ate and his Father watched on the mantlepiece. As the Grandfather clock struck six Johnathon rose. "Thanks Mrs Cowan, for the delicious food, delicious." "My pleasure Johnathon, thanks for helping Sam." The three of them hesitated and looked at the ribbons for a moment, then smiled at the day. "See you mate, well done, now you can boast show chooks" "I plan to." The roar of the truck signalled Johnathon's departure and he sat for a while longer and listened to the chicken-chat outside.

6

General Barn-Paler sat down and read the action report from the last battle he commanded, just South of a small town called *Flurry*. *Damn good fight, that one. If the Ninth Division hadn't messed up on the right flank, we would have taken that area.* The intelligence report described the time of action and details about the division, the Fifteenth, his lost baby. *Hang on, there's an attachment here; this is additional information from the Intelligence Directorate. Fucking Journalist? Oh yes, who else, Fieldlight. Stringy bark face Fieldlight. Who let that idiot into the division?*

'Barn-Paler ordered the attack on several high ground machine-gun positions with a commanding field of fire despite clear evidence that the opposing forces operated them. Second Unit Guards Division, the army's most capable unit, with seasoned veterans who had survived the last great wars' stalemate battles. The known machine gun emplacements, confirmed by intelligence reports a week earlier, were designed to complement each other's field of fire, effectively creating a large killing ground.'

This report has been censored in full.

Let's move on, shall we, Bark-Face.

The General perused the after-action report about the casualties and the wounded. *5553 casualties, in the day, 5516 dead, 20 missing, 17 wounded, of which most appeared to survive due to being hit near their trenches on the battlefield in the early minutes of the fight and being retrieved by their comrades. One soldier, Sergeant Frank Fieldlight, was uninjured and cleared of cowardice after it was confirmed by the enemy, no less, that he had carried a wounded man back to the lines, a distance of four hundred metres. The enemy had chosen we are assuming not to fire upon him, seeing that he was unarmed, knowing the battle had been won, and witnessing his courage.*

The confirmation came the next day, after Major Winter-Tattle and Colonel Joseph Pitecaraer from the opposing divisions met in no man's land to organise the burying of the dead. This monumental task took the next three days to complete. Colonel Harris was not present due to being a casualty late on the day - see action report on Colonel Harris, 5th Feb - Apparent disregard for own safety and walk out into no-man's land.

He thought about Harris, whom they had talked to the previous day; Harris was not happy with the frontal assault. *Harris, Harris, where is that report? Ah, here.*

5th February, 1921. Colonel Harris becomes the division's final casualty.

Five men from the special signals unit observed the Colonel walking down trench 3A at ten minutes past six. Shortly afterwards, the Colonel was seen talking to Captain Fuller, the Intelligence Officer in charge of the failed attack. The two men seemed distraught, Captain Fuller in a state not befitting an officer. Colonel Harris then mounted the parapet shortly after and was immediately shot by an enemy sniper, the Colonel in an upright walking position at the time. Captain Fuller took his own life on his return to his home in Cahnt City shortly after the conflict.

The Eighth Division was unaware that the attack had started and was late in organising a proper flank diversion. It has now been established that Captain Fuller, the Intelligence Officer of the Fifteenth Division, neglected to inform his Eighth Division counterpart before the assault went ahead.

SECRET AND CONFIDENTIAL
Colonel Harris's Psychological assessment sheds no light on his behaviour, but it is assumed he decided to take his own life after the disastrous failure of the division's attack.

Division disbanded - HQ staff and auxiliary units, including Artillery, amalgamated into the Seventh Division: 20th March, 1921.

"Poppycock! Blunderbuss nonsense! It was a good day, Stouch, Harris, a weak individual, I always thought he was a straw-man." He looked at himself in the mirror across from the oak desk and smiled. *I do like that slimming mirror; it casts me in the correct light. You old devil, you. With luck, this next brewing conflict will arrive soon, and I can retake command.* He twirled the end of his moustache and sat back to continue his reading of Edgar Tennents' new novel: *The Heroic Dawn of the Modern Soldier.*

7

Three weeks after his victorious hens came home he walked to the Lands Office. Expecting to see a Victorian architectural masterpiece, he instead looked at the tin shed in the overgrown grass area behind the cart repair stables. He walked through the entrance, and a man was at a single desk typing; piles of files were strewn around on other desks beside him. A secretary was carrying a pile of folders to a cabinet and looked at him as he came into the makeshift reception, a single office chair." Won't be long," She smiled, and he took the seat. The typing man looked up at him momentarily as if he were his maker come to take him away.

The tapping was incessant, and the man typed fast. The secretary moved files and brought others. A truck arrived, and a man with a trolley carried in ten more boxes of files. He smiled at the typist as he left, and the typist frowned. *Why is there no one else here?* He caught the secretary's eye, and she stopped looking at him. "Sorry, I am at the right place, the Lands Office?" "Yes, Sir. Can I ask your inquiry?" The woman approached him. "Well, I made an application for a land grant three months ago. I was wondering when the application would be approved"

The typist looked up at him as though he were mad. "Oh, I'm sorry, Sir, the land grants have been rescinded. We sent out letters several weeks ago. "What? Rescinded?" "Yes, the Government has decided to batten down the hatches as the war is becoming a drain on resources. The land may need to be sold or used for revenue purposes. "Oh, his heart sank as he digested the news. "And they are apparently introducing conscription" The typist had stopped typing and stared at him, implying his age. "I'm so sorry, Sir, didn't you receive the letter?" "No, I'm afraid not" A horse from the nearby stables whinnied, as if on cue and the typist began typing again. "Can I ask what plot you applied for? I will just check to make sure. Are you a returned veteran?"

"No, I'm not, and it was farmland in the western interior." "Ok, let me see" The secretary walked to a blue cabinet and opened a drawer, rifling through some manila folders. "And your name?" "Sam Ronald Cowan," "Sam Ronald Cowan, let's see" "Here, forty acres, Western Hills" "Yes, that's right" "Ok, it says here, ah, land had been frozen for possible Government use. Wait, it says here that it's allocated to war production; it's a green file." "What does that mean?" "It means the land *may* be reserved for a serving soldier, but indicates that it is more than likely it will be reserved in case it needs to be used by the Government." "I see"

He suddenly felt useless, and images of the Compressor came into his mind, mocking him. The typist stopped typing again, and the secretary and the man stared at him before exchanging glances as if to communicate. The typist nodded at the Secretary, who seemed to be asking him something non-verbally. "They haven't told us not to," the typist mouthed to her quietly.

"Mr Cowan, we shouldn't really tell you this, but we see a lot of Military governance files that are bandied around from the high command to the different Government departments." "Ok," he looked at her inquiringly. "The conscription bill has already passed parliament in a secret session," she said, turning and looking around to ensure no one had entered the office, and also glanced at the typist, who nodded. "All males aged sixteen to fifty will be called up for military service"

"Sixteen? to Fifty?" "I'm afraid so, they seem to want to continue this madness," the secretary said grimly. "They are a bunch of murderers," the typist whispered, looking behind him, then staring at him wide-eyed. "Can I ask how old you are, Mr Cowan?" "Nineteen," he replied. The typist looked down at his typewriter. "When is this going to happen?" "We hear it starts sending letters tomorrow, that's what these boxes are, I think," she pointed to the boxes the truck driver had placed on the floor. He stared at the boxes and back at the typist, who had the look of a schoolgirl who had done something terrible. The typist looked at him as if he had smallpox.

§

Over the coming week, Sam knew it was only a matter of time before he was called up. The signs were evident as he saw sixteen-year-olds in uniform on the street, some looking like potato sacks, the kit too big for their frames. He had received no letter and hoped they had missed him somehow, allowing him to be overlooked. Then he thought that wouldn't be any good either, because people would ask him why he wasn't going to the front. He hated the factory, but the war had nothing to do with him. *Is it anything to do with me? Where's Belgium?* He watched as the sixteen-year-olds gathered around the street corner, looking at the girls, who smiled and walked faster in response. He also saw older men in uniform, some of whom had grey hair, and that didn't seem right either.

8

"Sixteen?" "I'm afraid so, Sir" His Battalion Commander, Harold Finch, the Colonel, looked at him sitting in the leather chair within the officers' lounge, his report papers beside him on the oak desk. Six months after finishing training and being surprised at getting a payout at the factory, here he was in France.

He could hear artillery fire in the distance, and he steeled himself, wishing he were in a trench instead of not trusting a roof. "Sit down for Pete's sake, Johnathon." "Sir." "And you can call me Harold in here, that's an order." "Harold," Jonathon sat next to Harold in the red leather armchair, and the waiter came immediately. "Would you like something, Sir?" "He'll have what I'm having." "Sir." The waiter bowed and walked away briskly. "I don't drink." "You do now," the Colonel said sternly.

"Listen, Pike-Pickard, you are my best Company Commander, and you have only been in the Seventh Division for a month. What does that tell you?" "That I may be out on my bottom tomorrow." "Ha! Nice try. No, if we have a chance of winning any battles at all here, it will be won at the Company level, with officers like you. Furthermore, your junior officers have permission to make their own decisions in the heat of battle. Do you understand?" "Yes, Harold," he said. "If you think something's off about the plan, change it or scrap it, you have my full support." The waiter returned with a whisky, which he ignored. "I expect that to be consumed by the time our conversation is over, that's an order." "Harold."

"How did they get that bill passed?" "War footing emergency, I hear" "Yes, I hear too, but who pushed it through? Barn-Paler will be pleased." "No doubt," The Colonel looked at him over his glasses. "Say it, we are friends in here, not Captain and Colonel"

"He sees men as an unreaped cornfield." "That he does, but keep that to yourself. What happened to Fieldlight?" "He has been transferred to us, the Seventh. He also refused promotion and a return home." "Look after him, Johnathon, give him something behind the line" "Already have?" "Which is?" "Intelligence unit, inspects cleared areas." "Good, keep it that way." "I plan to. Still, a word in the Major-General's ear may make that stick, and may I add, the disciplinary action to evaporate after his promotion refusal." "Who authorised that?" "The Corps command, General Sommors." "Sommors, why did I even bother to ask? He's a wet fish"

"Done. General Arlingfaller, an old high school friend, is now in command of the third Australian Army. Now listen, Major Hobbs is your superior by rank, but I want you both to command the company, you hear?" "Harold." "You both bring good skills, you are smarter than Hobbs, but he is far more clever, you get my drift? He will be with the Division in three days, transferred from the disbanded Fifteenth. You two get on, don't you? Don't lie." "Yes, he's an exceptional leader and friend, worked with me at the same factory just before our foreman fell into a vat of insecticide"

"Good grief." The Colonel sipped his whiskey. Seriously, Jonathon, this is going to be very rough. The Germans have regrouped, and they were formidable when they were at their weakest, if you catch my drift." "That's what I'm led to believe." "What?" The Colonel detected his strain. "I don't want to send sixteen-year-olds to their deaths" "Neither do I, nor fifty-year-olds." He drank some of the disgusting liquid and immediately coughed. "See? That's why I need you as my 5th Company Commander."

"Here, for pity's sake, pour it in there," He pointed to his crystal glass. He coughed at the fumes of the brew. "Hilarious, Pike-Pickard, you really are. I was going to offer you a cigar, but I suspect a similar reaction would ensue." "You would be right, but thanks for the thought. When do we leave?" "Two weeks, and that is between you and me" "Where?" "Next to the Australian Eighth Division at Ypres, experienced." "My god, Ypres again?" "I am afraid so, the Germans are holding the high ground" "The place is already the biggest morgue in Europe. Who else is with us in that area?" "Full briefing on Thursday at the command tent, but you will have what's left of the Irish Sixteenth on the left flank and the Ninth Scottish on the right." "What's left?" "Two Companies, between them" "Great"

"Marvellous, but where are the English?" "*Messines*, in their own hell, now listen carefully" The Colonel leaned towards him. "I have placed all the sixteen-year-olds in the artillery units and many with the sappers behind the lines, not with the miners, in carpentry shops and the like, you know, the old men of the division, criples and past badly wounded. Keep them away from joining any assault's, you hear?" "Harold" "I will take any heat that comes my way"

"Also, and this again, is not from me; I know nothing. A new tank has been manufactured. I expect that this new vehicle will be available to you in approximately one month. The new *First Australian Mechanised Division* is going to join you, "Tank?" "Yes, an iron beast, I saw it at the technology park, all hush, hush" "What's its name?" "The Tank?" "Yes" "The *Hughes Destroyer,* after the Prime Minister"

9

He smiled. Looking through the periscope binoculars across the barbed-wire emplacement across no-man's land, for a moment, he pretended he was by the seaside looking through the beach binoculars you had to pay for with a ten-cent piece. He saw the bloated German body, and the seaside excursion evaporated. After his meeting with Finch he had made his way back through the line hitching a ride on the supply section truck feeling safer at the front than in a house.

An artillery shell coursed in, and he fell flat. The round hit the communications trench at an angle behind and exploded, throwing a mighty amount of soil and sandbagged material into the air. He heard someone call. *Trenchmen! Bearer!*. "Are you injured, Johnathon?" "No, no harm done, Tom" Major Hobbs rose from the ground beside him. Tom wiped the dirt from his shoulder. "So, yes, it's pretty funny, Finch loves to banter and play us off with each other. He told everyone they were his best Company commander." What else did he tell you?" "That I was smarter than you and you were cleverer than me" "Ha! That old rogue." Two stretcher bearers ran past, saluting as they ran with the canvas bed.

They continued to look through the periscope binoculars, taking turns and watching the far German forward trench. A Sergeant and four enlisted men sat drinking tea on soap crates, while several others cleaned their weapons and slept. The forward trench was lightly manned in case of a heavy artillery bombardment. "Don't fret, Sergeant, we won't be long," he said, smiling at the man who smiled back. "Sir"

He knew officers were a magnet for heavy fire, and if a German sniper got a whiff of a Captain and a Major, it would be a trophy for the cabinet or an artillery barrage. He and Tom had discarded their caps and donned helmets; he had left his binoculars behind, and they wore no officer badges. "Can you see it?" "Yep, you're right, there is a section there, a blind spot."

"The rise blocks their view for about ten metres" "Mmm, maybe" "Sergeant, have you noticed that blind-spot?" The Sergeant rose and knelt beside them. The man had a bandaged right arm and a nasty scar on his neck."Yes, Sir." "And?" "Seems odd, Sir, the Jerries are normally very good at trench preparation, particularly their fields of fire, especially on the forward line." "So you say odd, spit it out, define odd." "The fact they haven't fixed it if they are prepared to defend it. I would say it's lightly operated and they plan to pull back to a better defensive position. The Germans are extremely crafty, as you are no doubt aware." "Who is your sniper?" "Tempelton Sir" "Next time he comes in, ask him what he thinks" Will do, Sir."

Frontal wave assaults were now a rare occurrence, but only Barn-Paler, now in command of the Seventh, Eighth, and soon Ninth Australian division, still considered it a noble form of attack. He and Tom planned the night raid, a section of men exploited the German forward communication trench, taking three prisoners and gathering intelligence, then exited before the inevitable artillery barrage descended and blew the trench-line to smithereens. The section of no-man's land now stretched for about half a kilometre rather than two hundred metres.

"So, Jonathan, here," Tom said, pointing to the document —a big German action plan. The scroll, unravelled on the dugout table, was the plan for a major offensive; several lines dissected the contours, the German divisions clearly marked. They both shook their heads and smiled. "Clever Fritz, nice try, Hans," Tom said, sitting down and rolling a cigarette. "They know Barn-Paler's tactics; this is so predictable. They know he will attack to pre-empt their fake plan, then make mincemeat out of us." "Yes, that's why they pulled back, so they can get a better field of fire, not to prepare for an attack"

"No casualties from the night raid, we got three conscripted lost German University students, what does that say?" "Do they trust those guys with a major offensive plan?" "It was at

47

the bottom of the trench," he said as Tom handed him the rolled tobacco. "You know I don't smoke" "Sorry, I forgot, everyone smokes" "Well, they shouldn't, I don't trust it" "Why?" Tom smiled. "Well, you wouldn't want to breathe in mustard gas, would you?" "What's that got to do with anything?" "Lungs are for air, not smoke." Tom looked at him as though he was mad. "That won't matter, our life expectancy is three days at the moment"

"It was in a satchel, though" "Yes, and some clumsy runner happened to leave it behind in the empty forward German line, no, I think not, planted, and they knew about the blind-spot" "What do you want to do?" "Burn it, if Barn-Paler gets wind of this, we are doomed" He looked around to be sure no one was hovering in the dugout entrance, and gave Tom a look of: *Keep your voice down.* "You know the division has given him a nickname?" "Oh?" "Yes, *Meat-Flayer,*" Tom said. "Can't argue with that one," he added, looking at him grimly laughing. "Yes, but there is always the single element of doubt, that it may be real" "Well, let's analyse it before we dismiss it, and then get it to Finch"

Another artillery freight train coursed overhead right on time, Fritz's dinner-time gift. The shell crumpled in the near distance, and the dugout vibrated, and sand fell from the ceiling, and the overhead light started to swing slowly, casting shadows on the German map through the cigarette smoke haze. He and Tom gazed at the map for a moment, then Tom shifted forward and began to examine the plan closely.

§

Frank read the reports for the upcoming raids. They were always approved by Finch, who sought small victories over slaughter. *Pike-Pickard, Captain. Infiltration of German communications line, one section, two officers. Blind-spot located ten metres from the main line trench. Ok, could work. Blind-spot eh? What is the time of the raid? Midnight.* A fake plan and a gamble on lives, something he was loath to do, but if he could get Barn-Paler close enough to the front-line, there might be a chance. *As soon as he hears that the Germans plan an assault, he will want to attack, no doubt. That is the tenet of his strategy, defence with costly futile attack.*

Barn-Paler is also a man who might take a risk to satisfy a frontline recce; his thirst for attack is unrivalled. He will want to see the field where he will send the boys over. It's like he has some sort of salivating desire to see where men will die. He was at Flurry the day before and apparently at Messines when he was seconded to the English for the attack on the city.

What is his motivation? Old school cavalry charge fortitude? No doubt. Send the Cavalry through, older man, then there will be a rout! What did he say before the attack? It was passed down the line. 'Strength and Vigour', something like that, no hang on, 'Fortitude and Rigour,' that's it. Well, let's see if I can inject some Fortitude and Rigour into this situation.

§

"Place it, bottom of the trench, and get the hell out. The raid starts at midnight, so you have to be out fifteen minutes before, unless you want your balls shot off by the raiding party. Sergeant Miller owes me one and has agreed to hold the line for you. It's a long shot, they will probably find it before the raid, but you never know"

Carter tried to work out what Frank may be up to, filtering out in great danger before the raid with his Sergeant's meticulously prepared map in the captured German runner's satchel. He however was busy with his own designs, he had received a message from the enemy, a request for a meeting. *They have a plan to end the war, I can't say no to that one. What I can't figure out is why they haven't gone through the official channels. Could these guys be from the Olduvai?*

§

In the darkness near the German forward trench he heard the German sentries bantering and laughing in the next line back and realised the forward line was virtually abandoned. He threw the satchel over and partly covered it with some soil, then crouched back through no-man's land while the Sergeant grabbed him and patted him after he slid down the parapet.

10

Barney Hatter walked down into the port stone district, the roughest part of the city and opened the door to the *Sailor's Arms Hotel*. Outside, a man faced the tiled wall, standing with arms splayed, palms on the ceramic, blind drunk and unable to move other than shuffle his feet sideways, his hands following one tile by one tile to stop him falling. Inside the dock's patrons eyed him, and he passed the entry test and sat down at the oak-polished bar with the brass footrest and the mirrored spirits section that reflected a factory worker, his gaze among bottles of lost dreams, and smiling gentlemen on whisky. Cigarette smoke permeated everything, and a low-lying tobacco troposphere had settled just under the bar ceiling and was slowly being sucked out through the open window high in the far bar room wall.

The barman tilted his head to say, *What'll you have?* "Schooner, thanks," the man poured, and he looked around to see the other patrons. Several dock workers sat at a table in the middle of the room. An old codger was stone drunk in his designated space, the brass nameplate that denoted his spot at the bar since time immemorial. All were men who had clocked off and sat and smoked and yarned and blustered. He didn't detect any angry drunks or simmering louts. A recruiting poster reflected in the bar mirror depicted a man questioning a young lad's commitment to his country, urging him to sign up. In contrast, a chiselled-faced man and an attractive woman watched in the painted background.

No need for that now. He unfolded the conscription notice to see if he had read it correctly, and by some miracle, he was exempted. He made sure no one was looking. The last thing he needed was a display of *"Good on ya, son."* The barman set down his beer and gave him the exact amount. The man nodded in satisfaction, and he almost got a smile.

...required in service for Australia and the Empire, to counter the significant threat of German...
Two fucking weeks, yes, fucking, that's ironic, then I will probably be dead. I haven't even had sex yet.

He sipped his beer. He had thought about how it would be great to get out of the factory, but then remembered the man, the soldier he had seen on the tram, half a face, a monster. He held the woman, whom he assumed was his Mother, as they got off at the Hospital like a child, and they crouched off the tram, him stumbling down the steps and falling. He quickly helped the man, who nodded and held his arm to express gratitude, unable to speak, while the woman thanked him.

They then crossed the road and disappeared through the main entrance. The tram driver waited for him, knowing with street savvy what had occurred, and he got back on, shaken, not understanding how such a wound did not kill the man instantly. It was then that he realised it was not going to be beer and skittles, and he grew frightened sitting there at the lonely bar, wishing he were a dock worker who was now exempt from service.

He had thought about visiting a prostitute, but was repulsed by the story of Mick Blanchard, who said she just lay there and looked at the ceiling like a beached whale, her head turned to the side so she didn't have to look at him. *"It was the most unsatisfying disappointment of my doodle,"* Mick said deadpan. They all laughed. He remembered the first girl who liked him, and they had kissed; the feeling as a teenager was incredible—her smell, her hair, her skin, and the sensation of her hands touching him. He thought of the emotional satisfaction gulf between that and Mick's experience and decided. No way, I'll wait.

"Sam!" Sam could see Barney at the bar, his arm raised. He walked over, the men stared at him momentarily and knew he was underage but let it go. "There's a guy out there hanging on to the wall" He sat, and Barney signalled the bartender for another two. "Yeah, he's on his last hurrah, I reckon" Two

Scooners appeared, and the barman let Sam go as well. Barney raised his glass. "Cheers" "So, you got your notice?" Barney looked at him inquiringly. He nodded. "Crap. What Division?"

"Ah, let's see. He opened his letter, Barney held up a hand to say Hide it. He obliged and read it below the barline. "Ah, Seventh Division," he whispered. "Bingo!, me too, well I think it's all Seventh Division to replace the Fifteenth, the Division that got wiped out" "Wiped out on paper, I mean" *I better not tell him that.* "The ship leaves in two weeks." "Yep, I saw" "What about your beloved chooks?" Barney asked, smiling. "Mums got their backs" "Ha!" "Don't laugh, chooks are descended from Dinosaurs, did you know?" "Is that a fact?" "It's a fact, my fine Compressor fellow"

"Ha, yes, it was my turn next on the beast. I am not sure what is worse, getting blown up or impaled by the compressor." They both laughed. "If we stay here, we'll end up like that guy outside" "Yes, or poisoned by the insecticide, there are pluses to leaving for war." "So you know?" "What?" "The factory is closed." "What?" "Yep, the foreman disappeared, closed up shop" "I don't know whether to cry or laugh." "Now listen, here" "What's this?" "They paid us all out, Mary even got money for her operation" "You are kidding? How much?"

"Forty pounds! No wonder you are shouting." "Very funny. Here it is." Sam. Barney carefully gave Sam the notes under the bar, glancing at the patrons. "The terror of the compressor paid off in the end. "So, who paid us?" "I don't know, I think it was the owner of the factory." Sam pocketed his cash carefully and stealthily. "Geez, that's a switch, someone who cares."

"Look, sorry about the land, that's a raw deal" "Yeah, but at least now I have applied to purchase it as a soldier, when I enlist, it's a different story." "How so?" "Enlisted men can get a plot. But I met a guy, a veteran that didn't, so Geez, I'm not sure"

The old codger fell off the bar and crumpled to the ground. All the patrons stared and the barman helped him up. He watched while addressing Sam. "Oh, did you hear, Pike-Pickard, remember?" "Yeah, "He applied for Officer school, and he's gone over." "Fuck, he's keen" "So, remember the foreman at the Factory?" "Yeah, I didn't like the guy, but hell, that's not the way I wanted him to go" "Yes, killed in a vat, lovely." "He was drunk, wasn't he?" "That's the story," Barney looked at him mysteriously. "What, there's another version?" Barney leaned in to him and held his ear. "There was talk about Barnett" "No!" "Yes, he wasn't pleased, you know, he roughed him up because Pike-Pickard wanted to show you the Compressor that time, but there is something else" "What?" Remember Mary?" "Yes," "They were an item." "Oh, I see." Barney nodded knowingly. "And, Barnett is also with the Seventh, by the way, we might be able to quiz him." He laughed, and Barney nodded. "Anyway, the factory closed its doors shortly after. Pike-Pickard had gone by then, so I couldn't say goodbye to the old goat."

As he walked home, having said goodbye to Barney, he thought about the Foreman's demise. I can't even remember his name. Did I ever know his name? Did he tell me? It was just Foreman. Mr Foreman Foreman. I wonder who the factory owner was.

He walked back down to the pond. He was surprised that the place was always deserted; there were parts of the city that people just didn't go to, didn't know about. He shone his small flashlight on the little frog that sat on the pallet. It seemed unconcerned and sat still, looking at him. He sat down, switched the light off, and listened to the sound, a *tic tic* call from the crickets.

After a time, another *toc toc* emanated from the grass and replied to the small frog. He smiled and sat back, watching the stars that shone as a clean, stark contrast to the poison below, which washed in the river; he could hear it in the stillness of the night. He realised he didn't know anything about Europe, except that Australia was part of the Empire. He hoped that he would return home, and his chooks would come running when they saw him, and his bats would flutter around him at night and eat mosquitoes.

11

Wilhelm Scumarterchwartzer potted in his laboratory, with the glass beakers hiding part of his form and distorting his figure as he watched the liquid bubble. The paste heated and ran from a clay consistency to a red-brown liquid, then fell into the boil from a small glass tube heated by a long gas burner. It emitted a green fume that wafted upwards into his extraction fan. The elixir was simply a work of creating a drinkable, nice-tasting substance. He had been stung by a wasp and thought nothing of it apart from the initial searing pain and hopping like a madman around the laboratory bench, then crouching like a distraught child in a fetal position as the pain coursed through his ankle, then feeling the acid make its way up his leg though his bloodstream.

Then, his mind cleared and he could feel the wasp venom moving through his circulatory system. Parts fitted into the whole of every picture after, and in a short few minutes understood the puzzling things in his life past and present in their contexts like sand guided through a timer; the direction found and the mystery solved.

Why was he raised as he was, by a caring family and not a cruel one?, why he didn't smoke and why he was good at mathematics and chemistry and bad at geometry. *Why was his son on the Western Front fighting for Germany, and why do humans continue to be savage and basic animals, but were clever with tools and communication, thinking it meant intelligence and a higher order in the animal kingdom?*

His mice had solved complex problems, such as navigation and puzzles, in short moments. They had built structures using simple items and tools. *They used tools! Tiny paws holding bits of wood! They assembled a stand to hang the cheese!*

He realised that the state of every kingdom and Government had set the idea of the Flock. Within the Flock, the society functioned, and chaos was in check. They had, he thought, though skewed the rule governing Chaos. The price to be paid for living in a flock was conformity. As with a Dinosaur flock of avian species, the flock was only as good as its weakest member. If the flock hadn't fled as one under a stone cave and hidden, they would have been discovered as one gave away their location and died from the massive terrorising bird above. If an avian member was weak, then it was pecked to death, and the flock was relieved of two things: Danger and the amount of food they would require. He realised the absolute danger of conformity, and the elixir defined the threat, setting it in his mind like an additive that filtered poison from a fresh water spring.

The wonderment of it wasn't so much the clarity it brought, but rather the assembly of the whole with fine, understood puzzle pieces. It was an understanding of the nature of things, not just knowing what they were, but also how they actually worked and why they were as they were in the first place. Like high distinction students, they understood the nature of what they were presenting in their answers and built upon that understanding because they knew the nature of it, not just what it was and what was required of them.

The human race had a grade of fail in his view on an imaginary scale of what was required. It was clear to him after taking the elixir that unless the human race understood the world in which they evolved and adapted to the environment without altering it unduly or destroying it, then the exam was lost. He knew instinctively that weapons would become more powerful in war and war would continue. He had watched as the Armistice in 1918 had fallen apart.

He had predicted that Germany would be severely punished if it had accepted it, and that another war would follow, a more devastating one. From the ashes of a seemingly completely defeated enemy always lies a seed—a seed deep within the ruined, smoking ashes of a fire of utter defeat. Like a fire in a forest, the seeds survived. After the rain and the light that the burnt trees no longer blocked, the seeds grew again. He was not surprised as the German hierarchy fought on; they too had realised.

He had watched the technological evolution of the Western Front's machines, including the larger guns, more powerful explosives, advances in ballistics, and the development of the tank. He had noticed terror weapons, like flamethrowers and air-burst shells, mines and dum-dum bullets, made to terrorise the enemy and create mayhem.

The modern soldier took little notice of the grub crawling over the cratered moonscape, with the trees gone and the butterflies absent after the use of terror weapons. Survival veneered all else, the sickness, cold, necrosis, trench-foot, wounds, infected cuts, gassed eyes, broken limbs, loss of sight, and the onset of the collapse of the nervous system that didn't understand constant shelling and the pounding concussion on the human skull and the beating penetrating the blood-brain barrier. It wasn't able to secure the human ape from such punishment in the course of evolution.

As evolution prepared a spider to trap its prey in a web and store it, wrapped for later eating, the horror of such a thing when considered on a human scale was a pure adaptation, not a cruel pastime. *"The Elephant does not converse with the tiger and says, Ok, it's my place to secure this forest for ourselves. Let's kill everything else within this plain, then it shall be ours. Only humans,"* he pondered, thinking things like that.

He understood that with the evolution of consciousness, humans began to overthink. Consciousness is the adaptation that enabled mammals to rise in dexterity and communication, and become the dominant species. Cave men fashioned effigies from grass and placed them on a stone shelf. These effigies became their blue blankets, a safety from the tempest outside, where the light flashed and the terrifying white lines struck the earth. It gave them hope and made them see

58

themselves as special, believing they would help mend a wound, hunt an animal, or find a mate. How can a human understand the Earth if they can't understand where they came from? The magic of the effigy's placebo effect grabbed a knot in the human brain, calming the nerves and providing a relaxing strategy of denial.

He understood this distinctly, but there were gaps he didn't understand, such as what happened to the fantastic beasts that roamed the earth, like the dinosaurs. Fossils had been found, incredible bones and erected skeletons pulled from sediment, washed, and assembled. They rose high within a museum's walls and looked down on him. He had travelled to America and visited the Philadelphia Academy of Natural Sciences, where he stood for some time looking up at the exhibits. The great Hadrosaurus Foulkii skeleton towered above at eight metres, dwarfing him. This experience made him understand a little more about the Earth and the nature of things.

He watched himself for side effects, but he found none. The wasps had somehow evolved. Something had happened, and they produced a chemical of sorts, a byproduct of their sap nests and acid stings. His wasps were in their specially prepared nest site, arrayed around in their attached paper saliva, and flew out the window from time to time to hunt for caterpillars for their young. His vegetable patch was within the greenhouse, and he discovered that the wasps had collected so many caterpillars that his capsicums had grown uneaten for the first time, turning red and delicious.

These wasps were different; however, they had stung him several times before he recognised and stopped. *We secured your Capsicum crop. Is that not enough?* He thought they might say it to him.

After he had been bitten, his foot swelled up, and he endured it, watching them instead. His back no longer ached, and his sinus issues improved; his vision became clearer, and he no longer needed his glasses. He experienced a reversal of his condition, something that diet and exercise couldn't achieve.

He walked long distances, changed his sparse diet, all to have the condition to sit in his lab late at night and study. He felt younger, as if his timeline was reversing, and he would awake one day in fifty-seven years and have to wear a diaper.

After the last nesting season, as summer and winter descended, he examined the dead workers that had exhausted themselves for the next generation and lay on the windowsill, yellow and black, their delicate wings reflecting the day's light in death. He distilled the wasp's acid poison and combined it with experimental substances, such as lemon juice, curry leaf, cardamom, and salt. He created a fine powder from several organic substances and discovered that their chemical composition did not affect their interactions with the venom. They were a placebo beside a catalyst.

The wasp venom, by itself in pure form, was a potent elixir. After the initial inflammation of the sting site, the venom was carried into the circulatory system, strengthening cell walls, he hypothesised. It was anti-microbial, anti-inflammatory and protected cells from decay, he hypothesised. The pure venom was a mixture of substances evolved over immense time, he hypothesised. It contained something else, though, a chemical that affected communication between nerve fibres in the brain, he hypothesised.

He set up his mouse laboratory and tested the elixir. Injected mice performed better at mental tasks, recovered from injury faster and spent less time on trial-and-error tasks. The chemical's effect was a mental awareness that transcended insight, bypassing the waiting. For a short duration, the chemical was clear to see the whole from the parts. When he was satisfied that the venom's effects were adverse for short duration, and beneficial for long duration, he trialled the venom on himself in a greater quantity. His mind relaxed and began to unwind, like a winding clock that understood its own workings and composition. He wrote a research paper and sent it to the Kaiser Wilhelm Society, the prestigious German research Institute in Berlin.

"Without proper verification and rigour of scientific cross-referencing, we cannot accept the paper on its current merit. You may..."

He continued the research and accepted that the institute was unlikely to take it seriously, and filed it away for the time being. Like a writer of fiction who knew what his ability was, and navigated a sea of subjective current and objective nonsensical reflection and rumination that had become popular and dragged his boat away from the central current of favour across a page-ripping reef and a forgotten narrative that was once just a good story.

He felt ill and strange after injecting the venom, and it was painful. His mind saw colours and textures, and his vision settled and sharpened as the venom made its way into his circulatory system and into his optic nerve. But then that subsided, and the clarity came like a meandering water flow across a parched ground, filling the cracks and seeping into him. Like a slight wind on a tree's canopy, a fluttering of initial breeze and atmospheric current. He noticed that his urine had become increasingly green, which alarmed him, although he felt fine, content, and intelligent. He reduced the dose, and it disappeared; then he increased the dose to see a darker shade of urine again.

He often thought about society far in the future and what it might become. *Would it become like the caveman, and instead of grass effigies on crude stone altars, construct terrible weapons that could destroy the Earth? All because they were frightened, and other humans disagreed with them? Yes, probably. Would humans start to reap, hoard resources, and multiply while disconnecting from the natural world? Yes, probably. Would, like the continents over evolutionary time, drift into isolated states, then amalgamate into allied states and then come together, their coasts greeting one another on the horizon when the species had died out? Yes, probably.*

"Wilhelm, have you had breakfast?" His wife had walked into the laboratory, and a beaker hid her, her head huge in proportion and her body a wavy ribbon. "Oh, no, my love, ah, I will come now," he awoke from his new clarity and suddenly felt hungry, smiling at his wife like a naughty child.

Over breakfast, he chatted to his wife about the seeds they had just planted. When their eating became the theme of the morning, he had already decided to get the Elixir, somehow, to the leaders of the German front. He also knew who to get it to: Paul von Hindenburg, the Chief of the General Staff of the High Command. *How,* was what he hoped the Elixir would tell him.

12

"If we abandon the forward trench line, we will have a good, clear five hundred metres before the Allied line," the Hauptmann said, looking at his Feldwebel to gauge his reaction, his finger on the terrain map. "It would allow better defence, at some time they will have to attack, it allows a better field of fire." "Yes," the Captain looked at the Sergeant-Major and nodded." "Once they realise we are in a defensive mode only, they must act." "What happened to our recruits?" "Three were captured in the raid," "Lucky them, back to school," the Captain said. "The blind spot?" "Yes" "Good, it worked then. The Australians, are we facing them again?" "Yes, Seventh Division, they are competent, clever, fearless and at times reckless." "Barn-Paler, yes, well, then our job is done for us. We are competent as well, but we will have the machine guns, they will have the five hundred metres." The Sergeant-Major nodded. "So, Captain, no more offensives?" "No, it is a waste of time, and men. If we hold the line across all battle-lines, then they will have to sue for an armistice in equal favour. And Sergeant-Major, you didn't hear that from me. "Jawohl, Herr Hauptmann."

§

Teddy Barnett sat crouched in the trench, hugging the wall. The artillery barrage was intense, the shells raining down; he deduced from experience that the massive detonations probably caused their two hundred and ten millimetre howitzers. There was no room for thinking in the barrage, the rain of steel permeated one's soul, and set them in place where nothing mattered anymore, and all life was on hold. He had survived his first barrage in terms of nerve, but that was different from fear, and he shook with the dread of being ripped apart. Every time was like an additional test that sought to seep into one's brain and infect a series of nerves and render the victim mad.

The air surrounding the trench was sucked away, and the concussive strikes detonated, dispersing flying metal shards everywhere; the sound of the shards in the air was a whisper of ragged atmospheric din. To be caught in the open meant being flayed alive. He knew after the bombardment, the Germans would lob their massive new mortar shells over and try to gain an overhead trajectory straight into the trench line from above.

The tactic had worked many times, and now, when it was thought imminent, the forward trenches were abandoned, and the line retreated to the second and third lines of the trench. Dugouts would become graves, and their flimsy tree-trunk roofs no longer held up under the new firepower. Sandbags under the siege mortars were like grains of sand that flew to bits in the wind. The Germans probably knew of the retreat to lines further back, but they no longer attacked with men; instead, they tried to adjust their fire.

He now knew the barrage no longer signalled a German attack, as it had in the past. It was simply a barrage. German tactics had changed wholly to harass and defend, and wait for costly charges or minor mistakes, which they exploited with severe repercussions as a theme. They also noted dinner-time, lobbing the odd shell over, and kept a vigilant lookout for officers, generals, and foolish men who looked above the trench line.

A shell coursed overhead and detonated close by, and his head shook like a watermelon full of painful spiky marbles. The concussive draw changed the pressure in his ears forever, and a large section of the trench blew away. The Sergeant couldn't blow the whistle for a retreat back to the line behind until they were sure there was an opportunity to move. The noise settled, and the haze from the impacts clouded the area.

The whistle finally blew, and the men charged like frenzied ants through the section trench back to the second line. The first motor round hit the first line trench, a mighty krump and thunder that shook the ground and threw an unimaginable

64

amount of detritus and soil into the air, spraying down on those fleeing in a shit rain hail.

In the second-line trench, he gazed down the line, saw Sam Cowan crouching beside him and Barney Hatter, and smiled. Everyone from the factory thought he had done away with the Foreman; he hadn't. Gerry Ateskew was the Foreman's name, and only he knew those two things. After roughing up Ateskew, he had walked down to the enlistment office and signed up. Mary had shown him her pierced hand the next week, telling him the Doctor had said she would have limited use of it forever.

He looked at it with controlled anger and walked to the factory after the shift had finished, during a half-hour break before the next shift of workers arrived. He knew Ateskew would be mixing the chemical something only he was allowed to do, the secret formula. *I'll give him a secret formula*, he had thought, but when he saw the Foreman face down in the liquid, he stood for a time and listened to make sure he was alone and slipped out into the evening.

Waiting to hear the news of Ateskew's death was in vain. Assuming the early shift would have found him, he inquired of Mary about the foreman. I don't know, he disappeared, I never saw him. I got some money, though.

He recalled the image of Ateskew in the vat, found it difficult to understand, and then realised he didn't know what had happened at all. He didn't feel guilty he hadn't helped him either, even though he may have been dead then anyway. *The guy was a brute but did he deserve that? I was too scared to hang around.*

He looked to see where the Sergeant was as another massive mortar round detonated and sucked the air out of his soul as if it was angry he was not concentrating on being dessicated in a meat-grinder. He kept his head tucked into his shoulder, his helmet secured, and smelled the dirt, and short wisps of burnt metal.

He rose, taking a chance. He had an image of casting a card in front of the Grim Reaper as they played, and crouched, running down to where Sam and Barney were getting their early taste of the folly of war. The Sergeant was still, with his head turned. A mortar round suddenly hit the second line and knocked them down, the blast wave evaporating several men further down. There was an evolutionary reckoning when a shell landed so close, like all time had been reassessed; a new animal had been born, a hostile, demented Earth-scouring hunter. He crouched beside Sam, and he turned, recognising him with a terrified look.

Barney suddenly realised as well, and he smiled grimly as the Sergeant blew the whistle to retreat to the third line. The Krauts hadn't cottoned on to that one and in the old days would've attacked, knowing the first two lines were there for the taking. The third line was shell-free, and the bombardment dropped off. Barney and Sam looked at him as they sat in the new trench.

"So, what do you think is better now, the Insecticide factory or this new European holiday destination?," he said, feeling like a shirt that had just been through the wringer. Sam was shaking, and Barney coughed. He could hear shouting down the trench, and the acrid fog drifted across the top of the parapet. "Look, Barnett, this is much better. What do you think, Sam?" Barney said tongue-in-cheek, looking at him. "Did you kill the foreman Barnett?" Sam said in a tremor-laden voice, to his surprise. They all started to laugh grimly. The Sergeant was yelling at the stretcher bearers who appeared at the end of the trench. "Ateskew" "What?" Barney looked at him as though he were mad. "Ateskew, that was his name, the foreman, Gerry Ateskew."

13

Harold Fich sat down at the high command's table, the table of all tables, hardwood and bulletproof. General Barn-Paler stood talking to General Jacob Riddle, the General in command of the Ninth British Army, deadlocked in Messines. Several new faces abounded; there had been several high-ranking casualties. The Australian Major-General Tamke had been shot by a German sniper the day before inspecting the front, and shell-fire South of the Ypres line killed the Welsh Lieutenant-General Tyler. Combat was now more lethal as the Germans enforced their new Sturmtruppen und Verteidigung, Stormtrooper and defence tactics. The German armies simply waited in defensive strength and attacked in small raiding parties in clinical sorties across no-man's land to kill officers and create havoc. Previously abandoned houses and sniper nests were reoccupied, and the men waited for targets to make mistakes, such as assuming they had gone.

"Gentlemen, let's begin," Riddle stood and approached the map. A German offensive plan has been acquired near the Seventh Australian Division's line, and we believe it is authentic. The Germans have pulled back, we believe, to regroup for the assault. They have, yes, been in defensive mode and advertised their intentions, but Edgar and I think this is the opportunity they have been waiting for. As such, we intend to pre-empt the assault and launch an attack on two fronts, using the Seventh Division here and the Eighth here."

The General pointed to the trenchline map with his batten, tapping the location on the board. "Edgar, can you elaborate?" "Yes, thanks, Arnold," Barn-Haler stood beside the map. He thought he had put on weight. The staff lunches continue, then? He thought, breathing in at the impending nightmare unfolding before him. "Gentlemen, this is it, the moment we have been waiting for. No amount of artillery or German technology will stop this attack, I say; *fortitude and rigour* will win the day here. There has been much discussion about tanks joining this attack, but we have seen their drawbacks in the field before. The First Australian Mechanised Division is arriving now at Calais, but it will be too late for this stouch anyway. We must be proud and aggressive, set and alert, this could be the defining attack of 1923, to swing the scales in our favour."

He reseated himself slightly and thought about his reply. Barn-Paler was set and was always going to waste lives. He wondered if he could devise a clever plan to elude the General or a master diversion. His men's faces clouded his memory, and he started to sweat slightly at the thought of their deaths. He decided to remain silent. If he questioned the plan, he was a goner at the meeting, already outranked and subordinate, and suspect for the rest of his tour. He had to remain with his men to give them the best chance. If he disagreed with the plan, then he would be replaced with a Barn-Paler-approved General, and that could be especially disastrous.

For some reason, the sight of his dog's face came to him, and it unsettled him —his sheepdog, *Clara*. The room smelled of methylated spirits and cigar smoke; outside, birds tweeted, and he thought that all of them must be at the Chalet, knowing it was a safe place where trees still grew.

Barn-Paler rattled on, and he swayed between standing and giving him a mouthful or sticking to his approach. The offensive tactics that the General was now prattling on about were stuff and nonsense, lines on maps, and he knew they would never get past the German first line. He knew the Germans had just brought into service the new machine guns, with a higher rate of fire, better ballistics, and cleaner, quicker kills. They had also perfected the twenty-five millimetre Minenwerfer saturation barrage designed to drop on an approaching attack from above. The farcical pincer manoeuvre that was suggested relied on breakthrough success, a fantasy conceived in the Roman Empire and used with disastrous consequences in 1915.

The Scottish Major-General, Douglas Campbell, sat grumpy and glanced at him with concise thought and read his mind. His Irish counterpart, Jim Sullivan, sat looking at the oak tabletop as if willing to burn it all down, the commander of what was left of the Irish Sixteenth Division, a single company. Ron Armstrong, the Eighth Division commander, a Gallipoli veteran, looked at Barn-Paler as if he was considering murder, then glanced out the window from time to time as if seeking an exit from danger. He was unarmed but glanced at the Staff Sergeant's pistol and holster by the door in a small moment of madness.

Jim Sullivan interrupted. "Edgar, you can't be serious? Fortitude and rigour? I think the plan is already arseways. I have one company left. What do you expect us to do?" Barn-Paler froze, and Riddle shuffled. "I mean, I'm happy to assist my Australian comrades, don't get me wrong, but for Jesus, Mary and Joseph's sake," Riddle motioned. "Jim, we have to take the offensive here. Edgar has a fine plan. Hear him out." "What, like the one at *Flurry*?" Barnpaler's face went red, he noticed. "Jim, please" Sullivan fell silent, and the others shuffled.

Jim Sullivan rose to the astonishment of the gathered. "No, sorry, Jacob, we have dispensed with bayonet attacks, have we not? So how do you propose to pull this one off? I thought the tanks were to be used in this." "A diversion will be created, and..." "Oh, grand, let me guess, artillery?" Sullivan shook his head and sat down as Barn-Paler continued unfazed, like an automaton that knew the future.

"I veto the plan," Ron Armstrong suddenly said, deadpan. "I take it it's another charge across five hundred metres of machine gun-flayed ground? Come on, Edgar. The Australian first is almost here; let us wait and send in the tanks." "I say that would be a disaster, the German plan kicks off within a week, " he said to Riddle.

"Sir, may I?" "Harold, yes. "The plan was found at the bottom of a deserted German forward line trench. My Officers consider it a plant. Besides, now knowing the plan is lost, would they continue with the same plan?" "Yes, Harold, and your intelligence officers don't, I note, consider it a plant" Barn-Paler was a little red-faced. Riddle shuffled. "Sir, may I continue?" "My company commanders have come up with a plan that may give us some advantage" "Ok, Harold, let's hear it" Riddle sat down across from him. "A coordinated attack with tanks and aircraft, the tanks shielding sections of soldiers. The aircraft will harass the mortar units from above, as the tanks cross the distance from the forward line, a relatively short distance for the tanks."

"Look, Harold, it's too late to alter this, the attack will go ahead." The others at the table shook their heads and he breathed out in resignation, falling silent. Riddle glanced at Barn-Paler, who looked intently at the strategy board. Even if they cancel their attack, which we believe is authentic, we don't think they will expect an attack from us. If we can pin this line in the front, we will have splintered two German divisions and isolated a third. Edgar will visit the Seventh's front today. If we think the plan has no merit, then we will reassess" Riddle looked at Barn-paler, and the room fell silent.

14

Greg Fieldlight read the day's dispatches given to him by his Batman, Tom Surrey. The Stringy Bark Times correspondent had won the ballot to become Australia's official war correspondent and had won over Pete Murdoch, the media mogul's son. *That went down like a lead balloon, but his Father is ultimately practical, I don't think he will hold it against me.*

"Is Barn-Paler on the seventh front today?" "Yes, he's there, I hear, to inspect the German recent withdrawal from the front line trenches. "Barn-Paler, what is he up to? We have to get there today, Tom. They have deliberately delayed giving us the dispatches. What time today?" "Ten fifteen" "Shit" He tapped his fingers in a fast tempo on the wooden desk. His typewriter stood silent and worn; a monument of a million words in one month of carnage and the loss of Australia's finest at Flurry and the withering of a generation.

"It's too far, it's nine-thirty now," Tom said, stopping to look at him. "How far?" "An hour's drive, if we could do it in a straight line, no more than fifteen minutes" "Shit, Tom" He stood and looked out of the dugout of the Eighth Division's frontline. He could hear the crack of distant gunfire and the sound of aircraft. A soldier looked at him, who was leaning against the trench wall, his sunken eyes the result of last week's brutal bombardments, the shelling relentless. "Mr Fieldlight, good morning" "Good morning, Sergeant. Another day in paradise." His nerves were shot like everyone else's, but many had succumbed to the shakes and the gibbering when their soul gave up, and the constant hell descended into their brain.

The trenches had taken such a beating that they were no longer as deep, and the trenchmen frantically worked to restore the life-giving cover, laying sandbags and digging them out again. Trenchmen could dig faster than anyone else, and the officers loved them. Dig, dig, dig. He dug too, and sheltered and covered his ears and cried out, everything but shoot and run out to no man's land at night on raids. A biplane coursed overhead, a British fighter, its markings clear on the underside on a clear day. The men looked up at the incredible machine and pointed at it. The German guns opened up immediately, and it climbed and buzzed away to the South.

He ran into the dugout again. "Tom, let's get back to the rear and get the staff car, Filly aerodrome, the First Australian aviation squadron owes me a favour." They walked down through the lines, past the trenchmen, sappers, and soldiers in the dugout, enjoying a rare morning free from shelling. Distant rattling of gunfire, the smell of tea brewing, and Australian accents with hard-tack biscuits and steel mugs, men shaving, washing and boot repair. The weather was getting warmer after the winter hell and the autumn rains, which had made the ground so thick that feet were useless.

He had his camera and his notebook, the pocket camera, released in 1912 and then remodelled in 1922, which was his constant companion. He had taken images of life in the trenches and death. His work, however, was heavily censored, and nine out of ten photographs never saw the light of day. Tom archived them for him and sent them back in secure boxes to the Stringy-Bark Times office. Photographs wives would never see, papers wouldn't, couldn't publish, dead men and lines of soldiers about to exit the trench into hell, explosions and Germans attacking in the distance, decayed corpses and vistas of hell and bodies in twisted wire.

The dugouts contained shovelled enclosures where the men slept, like holes in an Egyptian tomb where mummies had been placed for the afterlife; bandaged heads and covered, clothed limbs and white eyes peering on occasion to see who was passing their sacred place in the earth. Mirrors resting on the earth trench walls, for a future shaver, neat sandbags where certain men had made things ordered from the former perfected lives, smoking pots and billies, grenades and trench-knives, slouched hats and Australian rising sun badges on felt.

As he and Tom passed the men, they all looked; some recognised him as the War newspaperman. He felt guilty even walking to the rear, having connected his soul in the earth with the men and suffered as they did without a rifle. "Hey, Stringy-Bark Times, what about a photo?" A Corporal asked them as they approached. He stopped and smiled. "Where are you off to, Mr Fieldlight? Are you leaving us?" "No, to the Aerodrome, a story is brewing, but there is always time for a photo."

Their characters showed through without explanation, their resilience, humour, past lives in Australia, and their skills in crafting wood or casting stone. Tom got their names for the photograph, and he stepped up the pace. The inspection at the Seventh's front was an hour away, and the Aerodrome was a half-hour's rear-line road journey to the field. He knew the importance of considering the men at all times, even when he was in a hurry. Their companionship and their knowledge under fire had saved him many times. The Australians he saw as he looked back still swaggered as if the farm gate was only just up ahead, the train was waiting, or the billy had boiled.

§

The Fourth Australian Flying Corps airfield loomed in the distant plain, through the windscreen of their seconded staff car—part *of the Royal Flying Corps air-wing.* The parked aircraft in formation wing to wing, the biplanes arrayed in front of the main Headquarters wooden building, on top the observation platform and windsock. Stacks of wooden crates and enormous tent-hangers dominated the flat area, dirt roads and the hospital tent's red cross. A large pond dissected the buildings, and ducks were swimming around, a distant orchard in the distance, and rising plumes on the horizon. Several planes were being attended to by the ground crew, one taxiing to the runway.

"Fieldlight!," Captain Simpson" The Officer walked down the steps of the HQ, smiling. "Major, good to see you again. Recovered from the party?" "Ha! Yes, and by the way, I saw your story about us; thank you." "My Batman and Po Juggler, Tom Harris," he introduced Tom with a wave of his hand. "Tom," "Major," "I'm surprised they didn't censor it, but glad it went to print. "Well, so were we. Group Captain Tyler has the photo on the mess wall."

"So, time is the essence, I hear, "Forward line at the Seventh?" "Yes, General Barn-Paler and Riddle are visiting the front. All hush-hush, didn't hear it from me." "What time is he there?" "Ten fifteen" "Right, well, no problem, we can be there in fifteen minutes, which gives you ten minutes spare, the marvels of flight. Do you both need to be there? Only one spare seat, I'm afraid," Tom smiled. "No problem, I'll pick you up, the Sevenths rear?" "Yes, thanks, do you have your press pass?" "Yes, Sir"

Captain Simpson climbed up onto the plane and grabbed some items out of the crew seat. "Don that hat and glasses, and the jacket, it will get very cold as you know. You are in the rear and have machine gun duty as well, you remember?" "Yes, you taught me over Flanders," Simpson smiled remembering. "I can't stay, have to get cracking, will land and set you down, our non-official flight is being allowed by our generous Group Captain. There is a field that I use to get people into the Sevenths frontline, we'll sit down there and I'll be off." The crew helped him into the seat. The front man turned the screw, and the propeller started —a deafening machine. He checked the gun and the ammunition. *I would be sent home straight away if they knew I fired a weapon.* The Captain gave him the thumbs up and seated himself. The ground crew dispersed from the propeller, with one man keeping a close eye on the aircraft for faults.

The biplane rose into the air. He never got accustomed to the sensation of lifting off the ground. The wings tilted and adjusted with the captain's feet and hand on the stick. Rising over the terrain, the contours of the fields turned from green to grey and black as the landscape transitioned to the front, revealing a shell-torn moon, dotted with structures, abandoned farmhouses, riven tracks, and dugouts, as well as piles of detritus too small to make out, drifting smog, and distant clouds. The cold permeated his jacket, seeping into his trouser legs and the inside of his neckline. His wounded leg ached, having been shot in the thigh and having refused to leave the front. He had recovered in the field hospital and returned to the trenches. The bullet had ricocheted down from something, not giving him the full force of the round, but enough for him at the time to think that maybe that was that.

He adjusted the camera and began taking photos, knowing none would be published. The Captain pointed and motioned over the loud din of the engines, their destination ahead. The distant Seventh's trench lines became apparent, the German line so close from the air. He looked around for other aircraft, but the sky seemed clear. The wind was freezing and strong, casting a slipstream behind the Captain, his little glass window deflecting the wind. Below, roads stretched to the front lines in meandering stream-like patterns, the ground a brown and black oil-like pastel of ruined earth.

The Biplane shuddered, and the engine throttle wound down slightly; the Captain descended, and the lines became clearer. He could see they were still well behind the lines he had studied on the maps, and he could make out the Seventh Division headquarters and the supply depot to the East. He knew there was a supply airstrip somewhere below and figured that was where they would land, but the Captain flew on.

As they descended further, the terrain became clearer. Now, only a few hundred metres off the ground, the third line trenches stretched into the far right, and barrage balloons floated above. He saw a field ahead and thought that at any minute they would be mistaken for a German and shot down, but no bullets flew, and the Captain descended for landing in the dirt field by the river. The blurred lines of grass and distant trenches; he saw several men pointing. Then, the plane landed with a jolt and a thump, its wheels ripping up stones and grass flying in clouds from the rear.

The biplane shuddered and the Captain remained with the aircraft, craning his head indicating that he needed to take off again. He nodded and shook hands with the Captain, who smiled. Over the engine, he shouted. "See you, Fieldlight! Forward line, a mile to your left!" He jumped down and cleared the wing. The Captain turned the biplane and gunned the engine, lifting it again into the air on the flat field. Several Australian soldiers watched from the far side of the river. He saw a staff car and could make out several officers across the field. He took a moment to get his bearings, and the sound of artillery rose as a standard from the front line.

15

Barn-Paler was appalled that he was there, and his disdain emanated, but he didn't impose any restrictions on him. Riddle shook his hand, and they agreed to a photograph, only too aware of the public relations importance. Several other Military journalists took notes and milled around. A band of officers and men followed the procession, nervous and spread out in the field. Barn-Paler was in his element and excited, undoubtedly planning an attack, which he suspected.

They filed down the third line trench and across the supply trench after donning their private uniforms; the Generals were too aware of the risk. In the distance, an abandoned string of shelled-out houses within the Seventh's line littered the right side embankment, the ruins of a town called *Lucy*, beyond the second and first line trenches. "Major, can we get up into one of those houses? Then we can see beyond the first line," The Major hesitated, knowing what he risked. "Sir, it's inherently risky, the Krauts have it on their artillery maps" "When was it last shelled?" "Well, not in recent memory, but.." "Ok, then let's get in there, we have to see above the line otherwise it's a waste of time."

To *Lucy,* they went. The front was relatively quiet; the German pullout of their front-line trenches had quietened the fight. The day was clear, and the early summer weather was less variable, with scattered cloud cover. Artillery fire was the norm in the distance, among the bare, black-poled trees that stood still on the ruined plain. They crossed the small stream before Lucy, a meandering pebble-brackish water before a high embankment. Barn-Paler and Riddle struggled up with motivated rigour, carrying their portly stomachs within their private uniforms.

The ruined buildings rose above, wooden structures burnt to the ground and shells of stone and plaster. The Major sent a Sergeant forward to scout the ruins, and he ran crouched into the first ruin and disappeared. Barn-Paler and Riddle lay prone in the grass by the embankment, waiting. An artillery shell coursed in the distance and landed on the front line, spewing dirt into the skyline. The officers watched and assessed whether they had been seen.

He lay with the officers; the other reporters had been shuffled off, only he had access to the frontline. He heard the Major. "General, I recommend you go in one at a time." "Nonsense, we have to peruse the area together," Barn-Paler snorted. The Sergeant reappeared, crouching in the cover of the first building's wall, and gave the thumbs up. Paler and Riddle rose and crouched, running to the first wall and the waiting Sergeant. He rose and sprinted to the wall. The Major said something behind him. "Go back, Fieldlight, this is no place for you." Riddle looked at him, clear in his order."Sir," He rose and sprinted back. *Wait, wait until they are in, then no one will stop me; it's too dangerous.* He thought to himself, and waited. The Major looked at him as if to say, *I told you so.*

He rose and sprinted again to the wall. Barn-Paler and Riddle had entered the two-story ruin. "Fieldlight!" The Major shouted at him, but it was too late, and he entered the ruin and saw the Generals looking back, furious at him, but knowing they had to move on. The Sergeant knew he had the honourable rank of Journalist Captain, so he said nothing. Inside, a staircase still stood and zig-zagged up to the top floor, a charred wreck but still intact.

There were gaps where the outer wall sowed the distant plain, caved in from the shell-fire. He didn't follow, something his acquired frontline sixth-sense told him was not quite right. Scanning around, he saw the next house had crumbled, and the wall had slid; a massive pile of bricks and wood rose to what was left of the existing roof height. He scrambled to the slide of mortar and climbed up. He saw the Generals through the gap, and the Sergeant had seen him too, peering, the three crouched behind the remains of the top wall.

Gazing carefully above the last bricks through a convenient gap, he saw the front, a distant haze, and the abandoned German frontline, their new enclave, about two kilometres away. He ducked back down, thinking of snipers and shellfire and getting sent home for his discretion. He saw the map on the floor in front of the two generals through the gap in the adjoining house. They pointed and muttered, while the Sergeant sat with his back against the wall out of sight, a part of the exterior that had refused to crumble.

He gazed out through the gap again and saw several men taking cover in the shell craters of the abandoned German line. *Intelligence Unit?* Glancing over, the two Generals still perused the map on the floor. The Sergeant looked at him, smiling. He snuck another look and the men had gone, the shell craters empty.

Two fighters circled overhead, and he wondered if Captain Simpson was up in the sky fighting for his life without a machine gunner. He remembered the young Hanson, elated at the confirmation of his first kill as a fighter pilot. The Brits welcomed them into the base, and they had a party; many got drunk, and he and Tom were no exception. They threw Hanson into the pond, which was the Australian bases' right of passage; his welcome into No. 2 squadron. Laughter and frivolity ensued, he remembered the beer afterwards, a rare treat.

Minutes passed, he made sure he was concealed behind the bricks. In the distance he thought he caught a glimpse of a large man on their line, to the left of their position, some distance away, walking like he was off to the beach. *Who the hell is that?* Someone was smoking, he could smell the vapour. A shell burst in the sky out towards the German front line, puffing black, dispersing gently like a cloud.

There was a sudden distant crack, and he knew the sound instantly: a German sniper rifle. Barn-Paler was on the floor of the house, slippery was everywhere, and Riddle tried to stem it from his throat, and the Sergeant used a rag and stuffed it in his neck. Barn-Paler shook, then lay still. Riddle checked his pulse, and he assumed he had died. He didn't see Barn-Paler look above the ruined wall, but must have, the back of the house was a solid brick wall still standing. He grappled frantically for his camera and took a picture of the bloody scene.

Two more men came running up the steps, and they carried Barn-Paler down. He expected the sniper to let fly again, but no other shots were fired. The artillery opened up, and the German guns started to pepper the shelled ground in front of them in response. All hell broke loose as the Germans started lobbing mortar rounds. One detonated back further, shaking the houses, and his secret spy hole closed as the bricks fell. Riddle and the Sergeant struggled down the steps, manhandling a heavy Barn-Paler, and heaved the weight out from under the house. He scrambled down the brick pile. Stumbling on loose blocks like a stricken child.

In five minutes, the front was ablaze with artillery, and mighty concussive cracks bounded in like freight trains; the sky went dark as he saw two medical orderlies and the Major pointing frantically ahead, down the embankment to where they should go. His breathing started to get frantic and he was on the verge of panic as the shells landed and shook the ground.

The two orderlies and the Major were short a man and he took one end of the pole of the stretcher that Barn-Paler lay on his eyes wide, face white and deadened eyes and the red stain pooling through his bandaged neck. The orderlies looked at him, thinking all their Christmases had come at once. The major took the opposite pole, while Riddle was on the other side and was relieved by one of the orderlies. The Sergeant had the other. Shells coursed in, and they got knocked flat by a mighty explosion, which floored them and sent Barn-Paler flying off the stretcher and rolling down the embankment.

Riddle momentarily stood a little and caught some shrapnel in a lethal strike of steel at the exact moment that severed his head, which followed Barn-Paler down the grass gully like a footballer and a ball. The General's body wavered in its final stance, then collapsed as they all sat wide-eyed and horrified, slumped like a group of boys whose wooden glider had crashed and shattered on the ground, a tribe of contorted fallen.

The massive cracks from the artillery intensified, and he and the Sergeant looked at Barn-Paler's body, expecting to place him on the stretcher again, but he, too, lay close to Riddle, the two halves of his body a meter apart. The orderlies and the others crowded into the gully and prayed and covered their ears and opened their mouths as the concussions continued.

The rumbling tempest became a steel concerto, the sound so overpowering he thought his ears had burst. The Major and Sergeant, both experienced, lay prone under their helmets, with the orderlies following suit. There was no way to get to the close trench line; the steel forest whispered slaughter. Steel splinters whispered through the air, and the concussive strikes seemed to beat the air from the ground.

The gully was deep but wide, and he thought for sure that the time had come. The barrage lessened and then stopped. The smouldering ground choked everything, he ate the recently grown grass and lay still, not quite ready to move like a nine to five worker unwilling to rise to face the day. Glancing at the others, the Major looked at him as if to say, *"We live another day."* The orderlies were still under their helmets, alive and prone. The only sign of Barnpaler and Riddle was single raised dead arm just visible down the embankment, signalling the corpses positions in a macabre display.

§

Frank walked to the top of the crater, then crouched and lay down. The Australians knew they were there, but the Krauts didn't. In the distance were the ruined houses of Lucy. He saw the trench line and knew that somewhere Barn-Paler was visiting and perusing the frontline, checking his watch: 10:25.

81

Carter lay beside him, scratching the gravel. He breathed in hard, then out. "Carter, make your way back using the shell crater path, and get that report filed. I'll meet you back there.

"Ok, what are you going to do?" "I haven't looked at the German dugout yet, better check it," Carter's look told him he knew that was bullshit. "Time to myself then." Sergeant Carter scrambled backwards to leave. "Wait, hang on. Post this as well" He handed Carter a letter home. "Also," Carter waited. "You're a good man, Carter. For the record, I don't believe you were ever a Priest. Carter smiled. "Keep your head down." "Sergeant Carter crept away, and he looked around, and his man was gone.

He grabbed the German rifle and loaded it with the ammunition he had found near Adolf Hitler before Carter reached him in the shell-hole; within a runner's leather message satchel. The breach had dried, and he dropped the round and pulled back the bolt. Using the excellent scope, he scanned the trench line and then moved towards Lucy's ruined houses. The front was quiet as though the Germans were enjoying their breakfast longer than usual. The odd rifle crack and lobbed shell sounded as reminders of each side's temper. The wind swirled in his new crater, closer to the line. The bottom was devoid of corpses, but it still smelled the same, and he wondered what festering nightmare lay below the earth.

He figured Barn-Paler would want to look at the deserted German frontline and consider another foolish attack plan after discovering the satchel. Intelligence reports had him in the area, specifically this one, and he had a chance. His thoughts wandered from *What are you doing?* to *Stick to the plan.* He knew that he probably wouldn't make it to *Flurry*, not even out of the Seventh's area, but he had his Intelligence pass, and it would get him into places other men couldn't go, and he was an Intelligence officer; no one would question him until they knew he was missing, of course.

He still knew the chances of getting a look at Barn-Paler were extremely slim, even from the distance to the line, and he thought about occupying the ruined *Lucy* houses to gain height. He scanned the house line, looking through the sniper scope, the ruined structures devastated by shellfire.

He waited, and the ruins were silent and empty; his watch face: 10:45. The forward line was keeping good field practice; he hadn't seen any heads above the parapet. He had a German coat over him in the crater wall, and the brown stained cloak concealed him; he hoped to avoid friendly snipers and spotters.

A fighter biplane buzzed overhead, its view obscured by the clouds. He thought of his brother, Australia's official war correspondent, his only surviving relative. Greg would receive a letter. He returned to the scope, the crosshairs shifted past grass and the embankment that stretched down to the start of the line.

He saw a man run from the lower embankment and behind the first ruin. Then, two more, larger men. From a distance, he knew the Germans wouldn't be able to see the men because the embankment sloped down, making it visible from his position —a closer view of the crater. He saw a fourth man dash across, then shortly after, he returned. *That looks like Greg, fuck me.* He's unarmed as well, ok, this might be them. The unarmed man then dashed back and disappeared behind the houses. He waited and scanned the ruins.

The first building was a shell, and through the walls, he could see a blackened staircase. He saw a leg moving, then again through the next shell-hole gap. Well, the Germans will be able to see you now. He scanned the area with the excellent scope to see if any other soldiers were present; the other houses appeared empty. The house directly to the right of the blackened staircase house was a one-sided pile of bricks; the wall had collapsed. He panned left again and detected a non-brick form. He saw a man on a pile of bricks, his side just visible through the scope. *Greg, you devious trouble-maker you.* He panned left and saw a man bob up from behind the ruined wall of the next house. *Riddle, General Riddle, was he? For fucks sake they are both in the same house?*

He cringed, expecting to hear artillery at any moment; he knew from the reports that the Germans had the ruins explicitly sighted for this reason: to stop them from gaining an elevated position to spy on their trench line. I might not have to do anything here. He thought about abandoning the plan, his brother was there by some infinitesimal chance.

Then Barn-Paler's head appeared, lingering too long looking out towards the German lines. He ducked back down and sighted, keeping still and lowering his breathing. He scanned right again, and Greg was peering through the bricks. *Keep your head down brother.* Back left, he sighted again, and Barn Paler bobbed again, and he took half a second and fired. The bullet he saw struck him in the upper throat, and he wildly flailed backwards.

He couldn't see the result. He rose, left the rifle, and fled at a forty-five-degree angle toward the allied line, heading directly for the houses. The artillery started as he predicted, and the shells began to fall in front of him. Running, he crossed Adolf Hitler's shell-hole, making a beeline for the far row of Lucy houses, knowing the shellfire would concentrate on the other side. The mighty coursing flight of the shells sounded like trains shuddering along a railway in the sky. The ground shook with the first explosions; he didn't know if he had set it off or if the German spotters had seen the men in the Lucy house rows.

He ran like a possessed madman and saw Carter waving frantically at him past the last house away from the trench line. His throat had gone South and he coughed as he ran wildly. The thudding of the shellfire increased, and he stumbled up the far embankment where Carter had a dispatch motorbike, realising then that it would be harder to let Carter go than he thought. Mounting the bike, he almost fell in a slap-stick manner, Carter grabbing him with a free arm. The

84

bike gained momentum and all he could hear was the fire and ground shaking.

§

Johnathon read the after-action report of the disastrous events of the previous day; two Generals were killed on the same day trying to gather intelligence.

..killed by shell-fire. The Sergeant accompanying General Riddle and Barn-Paler was also a late casualty of the bombardment."Apparently, he was warned about the Lucy houses" Tom sat repairing his leggings in the dim, pale light from their candle. "Well, there goes any imminent attack for now, between you and me, thank god" "I hear you." Tom looked at the dugout entrance, listening for anyone outside. "Maybe they'll make him a Field Marshall. Our day could get better and better. In fact, I know it will." He held up the prize, a pilfered champagne bottle, complete and ready. Tom's eyes widened as he registered the find and smiled.

16

Sam watched the tanks roar over the first trench line. He hugged his rifle and watched the fine sand grains between the solidified blood on the trench wall. Barney had been superficially wounded in the hand the day before and got a reprieve from the assault, and he felt glad he was out of it and sad he wasn't with him. Pike-Pickard, he could see, was crouched with his men, ready to lead the assault. Somewhere down the line, Barnett crouched like him, a piece of meat for the skewer.

He couldn't stop shaking. The men were aligned down the trench line, their rifles pointed into the air like crosses for the dead. He thought of his chooks and said goodbye to them, sending a message through the magical communications channel he invented as a child up into the sky. He imagined that he would lie down beside them while he was dying and they would come and sit beside him and spread their wings over him as if they were having a sun-bath to say thank you and goodbye. He tried to imagine the feel of their feathers, their calmness, and their temperament, and set that in his soul like an elixir from a past age of avian comfort.

The man next to him had his head tucked into his neck much like his birds would do, his helmet strapped and fastened, a gallows prisoner like him, waiting for the Reaper's clock, the fall of rope and weight and broken crack of bone. The Sergeant's whistle was anticipated with a dread that superseded all else; a time bomb of life. The artillery rounds hadn't found their range, falling behind the second line with mighty cracks and thumping concussive bursts.

A body part of a horse careered overhead in bizarre cart-wheeling, flayed, circling motion; an animal exhumed from the early battles. The German siege mortars pounded the line, reducing the distant horizon to a blur. The acrid vapour whirled around, and bits of soil fell on his helmet, green flesh smelling, dirt congealing clumps; rotting hail. The concussion from the massive thumps of artillery sent him numb; he kept his mouth open to equalise the pressure in his ears. The ringing in his head obscured life and meaning, and the insanity of his situation focused and set him in some terrible mineralised conglomerate of fear, glued tension and high anxiety.

He thought that after Barnpaler had been killed, things would have been better. They worsened as some other deluded officers saw red and demanded a response. Pike-Pickard convinced them of a new approach, and they heard his plan, with Finch supporting him. Tanks and small groups of men followed, and planes bombarded the Germans from above. The carnage around him laughed at all else, and he thought they had little chance of getting past the parapet. It didn't seem possible that anything other than some small beetle under a rock would survive anything at all.

In the small bubble of time between waiting for a whistle and watching the earth near him, an attempt was made to reconcile the life that he had lived. All things seemed incredible that were not near the terminal trench, in this terrible place. The touch of felt or fibrous cloth, a butterfly wing, chicken feathers and falling rain, wind and sun. What would it be like to touch a woman's arm and feel the fine hairs on her soft skin? What would riding a salt sea wave be like?

Visions of the Australian bush filtered quickly through his thoughts. He saw the native animals crouching there and looking at him in his delirium: the small honey-eater birds with striated rumps and splendid colours, the fine fur of the wallabies, and the claws of the climbing koalas. He heard the wash of the creeks and the sound of the grass blowing in the wind. The beautiful microbats with their secret eyes and calm manner, flying with the dusk of the filtered light. The images calmed his mind, instinctual rather than emotional, and lost him for a few seconds on a rancid field.

The whistle blew, and they rose as one. He felt paralysed and rubbery, but his legs carried him forward. Pike-Pickard led the men on an angle up over the parapet, and they broke into small groups behind the second wave of tanks. Each section had a tank, and he followed Sergeant Morris and the other twelve men to their Hughes Destroyer tank, now grinding ahead. The steel monsters ground the earth and belched gas from the waste of their new diesel engines. Their guns fired at the German line, and the din of the tank tracks sounded like wounded dinosaurs. The machine gun fire was thick and struck the Hughes tanks, seething off the steel ahead in a scything alarm. Several bi-planes flew in circling contours above the increasing infernal noise and artillery dropping among them.

He couldn't see whether the Hughes's were hit or moved on, but they made headway through the steel fire. Several men got hit by flying steel shards of metal off the ricochets, but no one had yet been hit proper. His mouth was a dry inferno from the dust and risen earth; his shaking was unabated. The Hughes stopped, and they gathered behind like insects under a turned rock. He could see the German front trench ahead; several tanks had breached the line and were pushing their way through, destroying the sandbag parapet and sending several German soldiers scurrying. The tank to his right fired, and a machine gun position evaporated, sending the gun hurtling into the air, the chain of ammunition, a wounded line of umbilical.

As the right Hughes traversed the trench top, the men behind jumped into the trench, and he heard the retort of rifles. Further down, a man had a German flamethrower and scorched the trench downward, sending a plume of fire and black soot out of the trench. Keeping to the plan, the Sergeant led them forward into the German first line. Several diggers were already in the trench, and dead Germans lay around. The tanks continued forward over the trenches, grinding barbed wire behind them, leaving a distorted wooden pole and a tangled mess of string-like debris.

The feel of his rifle, the cold steel and the wood stock comforted him and he gripped it wide-eyes looking down momentarily at his now ragged boots. A grenade went off down the line, a digger yelled something, he could smell German coffee, and then saw the pot still placed on the stove by the trench wall; its maker had fled.

Two Germans came around the corner of the trench, surprised, and the diggers fired, and they fell like rag-dolls. He and the Sergeant continued down the line, the others behind. For the first time, he noticed how much deeper the German trenches were and how their concrete bunkers, covered in soil, provided superior protection from artillery fire. A stalled tank fiercely burned up ahead, having been hit by a shell. He heard German, and the Krauts came running across the gap between the second and third trench lines. They lay on the edge and fired, turning the tables as the Germans attacked their own line. Several got cut down by the rifle cracks; the others disappeared into the trench.

Artillery fire started to fall, and he realised that the Germans were shelling their own positions, now in full flight to the rear. They continued down the angled supply trench, and several dead men were arrayed on both sides of the bottom. Confusion and terror began to spread among them as the barrage intensified. Several men got left behind, and he found himself with the Sergeant at what seemed to be the end of the third line. No one from his section was there.

Sergeant Morris was shot and flung to the ground. A German rushed him and tackled him to the ground. The heavy man had him pinned, and he punched him in the face. The German grabbed him by the throat, trying to throttle him, his massive, firm grip suffocating him. His rifle was under him, bayonet attached, and he flailed, punched the man hard in the head several times with everything he had, which knocked the sense out of him, the strike hitting his temple. The man started to have a fit, shaking and trembling, then fell to the side as if he couldn't control his muscles.

The German shook himself to death and he watched horrified. He breathed in hard to clear his throat from the throttle and lifted the rifle again and checked the breach. The trench became momentarily silent. The german had injured his eye and wiped his eyes and tried to focus.

Rolling over, he rose and gasped for air as the next German came around the trench corner and raised his rifle. He crouched, running back down the trench, and the round missed. He heard a muffled explosion and saw two diggers running and throwing grenades down the trench. The German lay dead, and the two men continued down the line, not seeing him. He thought he could smell aftershave and noticed one of the diggers was carrying a shaving brush in his back pocket.

Slumping against the trench wall, his legs gave way a little; the exertion sapping his strength. A dead digger and a dead German lay entwined; a final embrace. Someone was shouting commands, an Australian. A bayonet was stuck into the trench wall opposite him as if marking a spot where hand to hand combat had occurred. Above, a severed arm hung over the trench wall, and he stared at it while his mind reconciled murder. He could hear boots at pace on the German trench boards, a distant thumping tempo.

Pike-Pickard came down the trench, a line of men behind him, and got him to his feet. He looked at him in amazement. "Come on, Sam, are you wounded?" Pike-Pickard looked at the now still German. Pike-Pickard motioned for a man to check Morris, who was unconscious and wounded. Pickard put his hand on his shoulder and had a good look at him for injuries, crouching down with him in the filth. "Don't think so," he said. "We've broken their line, I don't want you broken as well."

He looked around. He could hear Australians shouting, not in terror but in triumph. Several more diggers leaped over the trench line and he could hear the panicked cries of retreating Germans. He wanted to reply to Pickard but his throat held

90

him in amazement they might have achieved a breakthrough and that he had a moment to reflect on being alive.

"Sergeant, that way, get to the artillery emplacements. We are further back than I thought. Grenades and trench-knives. "Sir," the Sergeant and several men ran down the trench with captured German grenades. He steadied himself for the next chapter, controlling his laboured breath and looking at the stitching on his uniform sleeve.

A Sopwith Camel aircraft roared overhead, firing its Vickers machine guns at a low altitude. He raised himself, the men helped him, and they followed Pike-Pickard down the trench. In the distance, he could hear the screams of Germans and the thump of detonating grenades and the absence of artillery fire.

§

After a nervous twenty minutes, the trenchline deviated at a sharp angle away from the front; the supply trench. His neck was ablaze with the attempt at his life, and only his age stopped his physical exhaustion. Pike-Pickard moved above the last trenchline, and the men followed. Below were the German artillery section, and they yelled in alarm as the men started to shoot the gun operators down, having been totally surprised. They showed little mercy; artillery was a hated weapon and accounted for mates lost; every man had lost someone. The tanks had moved further down the line, and they must have thought the attack had been beaten off.

He shot a man running for the dugout, and he went down like a rag doll, the power of their rifles, sporting from the distance to the guns. Several Germans held their hands high and surrendered, knowing it was suicide to get their weapons, but several were shot anyway before Pike-Pickard stopped it. The Sergeant put them up against the trench wall, they started to panic, then realised it was to search them, not shoot them. All

91

the men searched them for souvenirs, the gold items to keep if they survived the war, or to send home. He searched the nearest German, a small bald man who repeatedly lamented, "Kamerad, Kamerad." He rummaged through his pockets, found a metal tin, put it in his pocket, and continued searching.

Pike-Pickard soon stopped that as well and got the men prepared for what was usually a predictable German counterattack in the days leading up to 1918. No such attack occurred, and the Germans stayed true to their defence strategy, not imagining how their line had been broken with the new tactics. They lay and waited just below the parapet. The closest German trench was the supply trench that ran to the rear, but they saw no one. He could smell the bizarre odour of popcorn and wondered if it was an artillery smell, the shells or the explosive.

Reinforcements arrived in the evening; Major Hobbs arrived with the rest of the company. The rustling of the new men he could hear behind, filtering into their positions. Pike-Pickard went looking for the tanks, taking a few men and leaving Hobbs to hold the line. He continued to peer down the old German rear line. Barton was examining a German rifle and Harris lit a cigarette and smiled as their glances met.

Hobbs relieved their battalion in small sections and rotated the positions of the old men and new arrivals. A man distant was having a coughing fit and the smell of someone brewing tea made him salivate. They crossed back down the German line back towards their trenches and watched as other groups of their Company filtered past and behind them, the same filthy, bloodstained, sunken-eyed kharki that had left. Almost all were wounded in some respect, bandaged arms, legs and faces. Several smiled, and there was banter about the rout. He fleetingly thought about football matches and cricket celebrations.

§

Late in the afternoon as an ominous orange sun filtered by the burning tanks started to set, the German Corps artillery started up, big guns, the mortars, and they had to stop and shelter in the excellent German concrete bunkers underground; a full half hour of murderous steel crashing above. Cantering across the broken and strewn discarded equipment and men with dead eyes open, they backtracked to the concrete emplacement set raised a little as if mocking the guns.

Their section sat inside and waited it out, rifling through the Germans' belongings, which included sausage and cheese, tins of shaving cream, and a magical find: a silver flask of Schnapps. They lit the lanterns the Germans had erected and played cards as the barrage beat down above, content that there was no need for a sentry; outside was death.

"Ok, Sam, what have ya got, me old China?" Harris, their Lewis-gun man, looked at him deadpan, then took a swig from the silver flask.

"More than you, I suspect, Harris," he replied.

Harris continued his deadpan stare, his mouth moving in pouting doubt. Barton looked at him with mocking friendliness.

"Harris never has anything — I know that," one of the men said in the gloom behind them, inspecting the Germans' shelves for more schnapps.

Harris turned his head slightly in response and fluttered his eyelids.

"A bird in the hand is worth two in the bush," he said.

"More like sticking to the Lewis gun instead of losing at cards," Barton uttered.

Several men laughed and murmured friendly jibes.

"Three aces" The men's faces went sour, and all groaned, and he collected the cards from the table, smiling. A round hit close, and the dugout shuddered. They all instinctively ducked down, and dirt from the concrete ceiling fell around them. "Luck of the Devil Cowan" "So you say, I say count of the cards" They all looked at him. He smiled and laughed silently. "Oh, Cowan, you almost had us there," Harris said, standing up and stretching. "Count of the cards, we could use a technique like that against Thomas's mob."

He suddenly reacted to the close call; his body went cold and started shaking like a leaf. The others hesitated, fell silent, and looked at him. "Sammy, it's ok mate" All his mates murmured encouragement.

"Th, Th, Thanks, I, I wa, wa, will be, ba be ok" He usually had the shakes after a bad engagement, but the action was always delayed like a vibration in a pool's water reaching the edge later. He turned away in embarrassment. "Don't worry, Sammy, it's ok. We thought we had lost you today when we got separated"

There was a pause in the artillery as if the Krauts had decided it was all too late, and Pike-Pickard scuttled down the steps of the dugout shortly after. All the men rose for their Captain, who had led the attack. "Ah, so the truth is revealed, Schnapps and sausage, " the men murmured, Sir and Captain. "Sammy, ok?" "Yeah, shakes again, but he just won a lugar at cards, so he's going to snap out of it in a minute and have a drink with us," Harris said deadpan. He tried to smile, but his body was jelly and he felt like a jumping jack child's toy.

"So am I, but not before some unfortunate gets sentry when our barrage ends. Their drink reserved, of course" Barton rose as always to do what others hesitated at, the Victoria Cross winner, the quietest man in the company. "No, Barty, my turn, you have done enough fine deeds for the season," Harris said, grabbing his Lewis gun and ascending the dugout steps.

94

"Don't do anything I wouldn't do!," Barton yelled after him. "No chance!," came the reply. Barton laughed silently.

Pike-Pickard sat next to him where Harris had vacated the seat. He grabbed the silver flask and drank then placed it in the middle of the card table. "Listen, Sammy, above and beyond today, mate." Pickard grabbed his shoulder to steady him.

"Look, while I'm here, there's something I want to try with your shakes." Johnaton squeezed his shoulder, Barton looked at him kindly and seriously. Hampton told me Jack Farmers got it as well, and it helped him"

"Wh, Wh, wa what's that?" "Really simple, you imagine a stop sign, then breathe in and out deeply, all the time telling yourself, Enough is enough. Sounds stupid, but it worked for him" St, St, St, stap sign?" "Yeah, O, O, O, O, O, Ok," He imagined the sign and breathed like Pickard told him. The others continued the card game, watching from time to time. He noticed Jothathon was wounded."Y, Y, Yo, Yo, You wounded, sir?" "Who isn't? Is it helping?" "Y, Y, Y, Y, yeah, it's ha, ha, ah, helping" Barton had moved behind him and crouched down placing a friendly hand on his back.The other man sat and listened silently as if they too were all in some way stuttering.

He kept the imaginary sign in his mind, the red oblong road sign, and added some grazing chooks around the pole and a vista of rolling hills where his land was. He imagined he was driving there and had stopped at the sign to look at his farm. He couldn't tell if it worked or if it just stopped, but he finished the game, had a swig from the flask and Barton nodded at him. Harris came back down and stared at him as though he were a lottery winner. Looking up, he realised Pike-Pickard had gone back out.

They spent the night in the bunker. Wrapped like pupae in their swag. Late into the night, the artillery faded and then an exhausted stupour descended on them in heavy breathing and tonal dreams.

The reinforcements filtered through in the morning. Outside and in the sun below the trenchline they cleaned their weapons and fingernails, brewed some tea and sat soaking up the light and warmth. He opened the pilfered German artilleryman's tin. Inside was a photograph of him and several chooks in a German backyard; the man smiled in front of the coop, holding a prize-winning hen, with the first prize wreath hanging below. He breathed in, and shook his head in disbelief and embarrassment. Harris, always alert to mood changes, stood behind him to see for himself. He turned and they said nothing but looked at each other in a moment of reflective understanding.

The next morning, they prepared for a counter-attack, shoring up the trench walls and waiting for the Krauts. The tank attack must have surprised the Germans, he thought, the furthest gain he had ever been part of. His shakes had abated, but his fear had not, and they waited and checked their weapons again and chewed the German sausage. A flock of small birds twitted by and they all lifted their heads and smiled at each other in amazement.

Major Hobbs arrived during the night with the rest of the Company, and the tanks had moved out of range of the artillery to be moved up in case of an attack. There were still planes in the sky, and the Krauts fired their machine guns at them, but they seemed too high.

He looked at the photograph of the German and his prize-winning hen and felt ashamed that he had pilfered it. He felt sorry for the man; instead of a picture of his wife, he had a chook. Then he thought that maybe the man was just like him, and he, like him, would kill to survive, chooks or no chooks.

§

Barney had rejoined the Company after his hand had been stitched up from the shell splinter, and he stood beside him, chewing on the Kraut sausage. "What was the hospital like?" "Heaven, for me at least. Lots of pandering nurses and fuss, good food and nights with sleep." "Jealous." "It needed to go another quarter inch, and that would have been it, my ticket home. I'm not complaining; the guy next to me had half a head, and the next guy on the other side was gasping and breathing like a fire bellows. I just hope if the Krauts get me, they get all of me."

He had hoped it was bad enough to get him out of it, but he was elated that he had returned anyway, his factory mate. Barton, the VC winner, stood talking to Harris, and Sergeant Morris, only wounded by the grazing bullet, checked their gear and waited like the rest of them. "So, Sammy, the tanks, what was that like?" "Barney stopped chewing and looked at him. Scary, but they stopped the machine gun fire, mostly. Some of the boys got hit by flying metal pieces. The fire was so heavy. The Krauts didn't like them at all; they got a right walloping." "What about you, mate? How did you go?" "Got the shakes, but after Pike-Pickard showed me a technique, it helped, I think" Barney looked at him to ask about the technique. "A stop sign, then thinking of other things, sounds silly, but I think it worked" "Stop sign, eh? Yeah, I hear that. This place needs a huge stop sign somewhere." Barney looked down the trench line and back at him.

"Hey Barton, is it true that you didn't show up for your Victoria Cross presentation the first time?" Sergeant Morris interrupted Barton and Harris, standing and looking at the Lewis gun. "Yep" "Why?" "To create an air of mystery, and sort of get on the King's nerves a little" The others laughed and shook their heads. "Actually, that was a newspaper story. I told them some lies to see what they would do; they didn't check the facts. I was there on time, King George and all the bells and whistles." "You're a story yourself, Barton" The Sergeant walked down the line smiling. "Yes, well, they sent me back here so that's the story that counts."

97

§

Johnathon spoke to the tank commander. The blackened beast was spewing black exhaust, and its metal armour was scarred with small-arms fire. On the side of the metal was the logo of the First Australian Mechanised Division: a sewer rat, showing its array of sharp teeth. "Outstanding, Lieutenant, Pull back to the old first German line and wait there, regroup and get your wounded to the station. Major Hobbs is bringing up more ammunition for you, via the supply trench. You will be our reinforcements if the Krauts try to counter-attack."

"Yes, Sir, we have lost six tanks, but we broke the line" The Commander smiled, with a blackened face and white teeth. A hatch opened, and the flagman started to wave the flag for Regroup at Rear Ensign. He kept himself behind the tank in case of snipers and crouched down, watching as the lumbering metal beasts started to move off towards their lines.

A front runner came into view, crouching low, not trusting the newly won ground. "Captain Pike-Pickard?" "Yes, what do you have?" "Message from Major-General Fich, Sir." The man handed him the message and crouched on one knee, waiting for a return message.

Johnathon, outstanding performance, you are now Colonel Pike-Pickard. The Germans have retreated again, almost eight kilometres, right back to their fortified line and the Corps Artillery positions. Aerial spotters confirm that three artillery fire positions have been bombed and severely damaged. Colonel Hobbs will reinforce overnight, assisted by Armstrong's Eighth Division. Scottish eighth and Irish sixteenth on the left flank. What is your intention? Your scotch and ice await.

He and the runner crouched down in a shell-hole. He scribbled a note from his filthy notepad while the runner scanned the ground at the top of the crater in an experienced field-craft manner. "Here, return message"

Will occupy German trenches and hold the line. Expect a German counter-attack despite their defensive posture. We need ammunition from Hobbs, and the tanks require resupply. The German supply trench is intact and can be used.

Hold off on Scotch and ice indefinitely.

17

Gunter entered the palatial room in the Belgium Chateau that was his high command workplace. Drapes of grand designs and large hatched windows, a smell of musty wood and the slight hint of cheese and aftershave. He set his character, the obedient servant. *Schieße, my leg hurts.* He approached expertly as always to attend to the two men.

Paul Von Hindenburg sat with his deputy, General Ludendorff, at the breakfast table, adorned as usual at nine sharp. He watched as the two friends and the Generals discussed the day's events, while he placed the candelabra on the white tablecloth and set the centre of the cool water on the fine-grained oak table. The clock showed fifteen minutes past nine; the General's day had started, his four hours old. Hindenburg was immaculately dressed as always, and Lundendorff's medal glistened on his chest as he sipped his morning tea. He heard snippets of the front's news: the success of the new defensive lines, their new tactics. The Generals were in the best of moods.

His role as personal adjutant to the Generals had been finely crafted over a long period. Gunter Scumarterschwartzer, was now seated alongside the most powerful men in Germany, the German high command, at breakfast. He selected the food that was procured from Bulgaria and the Eastern provinces, where shortages were not as severe as in Germany. The crisis, food shortages, and an increase in the price of bread, along with malnutrition, were now rife in a Country at war. But not at this table. The table of the revered Paul Von Hindenberg.

Tea, cakes, eggs, wine, fruit, schnapps, sausage, cheese and bacon. All shipped in to secure the over-weight General's plans, poring over maps of dead men and men yet to die. Hindenburg had a sense of humour and didn't fuss about making fun of himself; First Quartermaster General Ludendorff was a contrasting worried man. His stern look betrayed worry and the burden of Generalship. He had no concern for the men he sent to their deaths, only the Social Darwinist outcomes. War was Ludendorff's life, and he saw war as the right of passage for men; women didn't figure in his thinking, except as boilers for the next generation thrust into the cauldron. A man who worshipped Odin, the Nordic god. *That fits. Where else can one be received after death by the Valkyries?* Ludendorff was at odds with religion; he saw it as an impediment to war. How wrong was he about that one? The Church is with the State! He mused, placing the canter on the table as the two war-chiefs chortled at some joke over the Western Front map.

"Thank you, Gunter. Did you enjoy your day off?" Hindenberg momentarily looked at him. "Yes, thank you, Field Marshall" He fakely smiled. He was mostly invisible, and that was the extent of the conversation as he had predicted. He had secured the job because he was a former stormtrooper and now an invalid, tolerated. Ludendorff said nothing and may as well have been in some Nordic Valhalla, as he fingered the map in concerted concentration. One hour a night, that's all he gets from his sleep; he is destined for a breakdown. He had heard the Doctor talking to him one morning. He looked at Ludendorff's sad face and eyes, a weary portent of black rings and impending staff meetings and orders. He smiled and thought of how long Hindenburg and Ludendorff would last on a trench raid. They wouldn't even have the stamina to get over the trench parapet. What a target Hindenburg would be!

He now had the full effect of the elixir, and his clarity came to him in a long, sustained train of powerful thought. He watched the two men in short glances as he served the breakfast, procured on this occasion from the local home owners of the surrounding countryside, much to their disbelief. They have little understanding of others, but a great sense of themselves, as if they were two Kings that people love and like to give their food to. He did not relish his role in asking locals to give up their larder. Hindenburg and Ludendorff just saw it as what was right and chortled at any disagreement. Their outdated behaviour behind the front reflected their management style.

The lack of personal regard for their soldiers was staggering—cogs *in the Prussian war-wheel.* Ludendorff had gone on and on about the wounded on the front line after their recent visit, as they were getting in the way of the able troops. The outdated minds of these two reflect a Prussian arrogance that defies description. He knew they were always on the lookout for that one offensive that would solve everything, finish the war, and allow them to mount horses or ride in elaborate carts down a Berlin street victorious. The Michael offensive earlier in the war was one such catalyst of hope. They shall end the war in two weeks, where have I heard that before?

He realised the same thinking reflected their misunderstanding of the civilian population and the possible ripple effect from the home front. Mothers had sons, and people were starving. Politicians in opposition had friends as well; the monarchy was blind to the mood of the people, expecting a pious benevolence. Master and servant. Hunger, he thought, rules much of the discontent. Hunger and a growing weariness that the war had gone on now for an infernal amount of time. Conscription, another generation into the fire. Europe was almost done economically.

He, being wounded and sent back unfit for the front, worked his way into the General staff's employment, first as a telegraph operator, then a Master-Sergeant's assistant, then a kitchen cook, now a waiter for the two fat men, as he called them. The Elixir had guided him as a potion, allowing him to make decisions that he would not usually make and align his behaviour accordingly. Patience, calmness, and an ability to be a puzzle piece waiting for a jigsaw puzzle person's hand to grab him and slot him where he needed to go. As a puzzle-piece, he watched from below as the hands of the ruler placed the pieces, and he waited.

His jigsaw was completed, almost. The last harrah was his Father's elixir, and this fine morning was the morning. He had opened the metal tin and shaken the fine powder into the

General's milk for his tea. The elixir was set, and the two men had already ingested the contents, utterly unaware of the future effect. A Local Walloon's milk was what they might have thought if they actually thought about the milk on the table and where it came from; oblivious and equally unconcerned with what effect taking that milk actually meant. Milk on a table, the ultimate covert messenger. Mother's milk for two sons.

The Field Marshall and his chief of staff didn't know it, but this was his last day. He had a berth booked on a ship to Australia after he arrived in Sweden. Yes, after being the keyword, if I make it. The Elixir will show me the way, as I hope will show these two hippopotamuses the way.

§

After breakfast, he felt a bit odd. He had felt odd many times in his prestigious career. Paul von Hindenburg, I am a legend of the Russian Front. Ah, Tannenberg - what a great victory it was. His friend and operational confidant, Erich, sat across from him. He glanced at the waiter, the former storm-trooper Scumarterschwartzer, who was already preparing cutlery for the lead and taking items away to the kitchen. A good man, but alas, now no longer of use in the most crucial role. He glanced at the map, Erich sipped his tea and continued to finger a place on the paper.

He rose with the discomfort and walked to the window and gazed out of the chateau's grounds. He felt a bit light-headed and sipped his tea, so Erich had no suspicions about his health. Perhaps it is Belgian bacon. *Ha! Yes, a Flemish plot! He He.* Erich Ludendorff rose and continued to stare at the map. "Paul, I must get to the telegraph and question these new maneuvers; you will excuse me." "Of course, Erich, I shall follow shortly. We can make the adjustments to the orders" His friend and confidant turned and left the room.

103

Together, we are the German hope, their lifeblood. We shall secure victory, I am sure. I am sure, I..."His mind started to wander, and his sight glazed over momentarily, like a fishbowl view of the room and then cleared. He walked over to the map and stared at the trench lines and the terrain, thinking for the first time about the blood-lines lost, the sons lost, and the cost. The cost. He wondered how many men had died in each spot and asked what he was doing, there in the room, the great Field-Marshall of Germany.

We made plans for the conquest of Europe. Did we really do that? Could we annex France, Belgium, and subjugate England? What on earth were we thinking? He placed his tea on the oak tabletop and looked at the clock, which showed ten sharp. Great gods, what is wrong with me? Casualties are a side-effect of war, you fool; we must accept the cost. Have I finally gone soft, like a Russian? The Grandfather clock ticked an echoing, clunking tick that reverberated within the wood-panelled room. The waiter had gone, and he was now alone. He breathed in and sat back and lit his pipe, the vapour rising as a curl to the ceiling.

I am an opportunist, that's what I am. Erich is a good friend, but would I sacrifice the man for Germany? Of course I would. People like my rule; I am powerful and guiding. And this war? Will it help Germany or destroy it? End the war? How? How? It has gone on too long; we have regained our bargaining power with the defence strategy, and the allies cannot win.

The Chancellery awaits the head of Germany. I must avoid a full return to Monarchy, but keep the Kaiser as a continued head of state and rule with continued Authoritarianism. The people demand this: a firm, experienced hand—an iron fist of kindness—is what is required. The Communists must also be placated, then pigeon-holed, create some strawmen and then burn them all down. What of the far right? There are many options, but too many far-right options, and no leader with my level of experience.

The Grandfather clock continued its tune, and he looked at the wood veneer on the wall and then at his reflection in the clock glass. *I am Germany's future, with the Kaiser's support, a return to a modified monarchy, but really, absolute power centralised. The other right-wing parties will be forced to toe my line in this new Germany; the people will see to that. The only way to stop this war is to negotiate with the British and the foolhardy Australians sacrificing their youth here. We shall withdraw from Belgium if they return to England and Australia. Both sides shall pay equal reparations to Belgium and France. Who shall be the neutral party in these negotiations? Spain? Perhaps.*

In the latter afternoon, Erich returned through the door and sat down, his manner much like a child coming to him to confess something terrible. He had already decided, he had worked through his changed thoughts and his hand was now ready to act. "What is it, Erich?" Erich Ludendorff, the Quartermaster General, looked at him; his demeanour had changed entirely. "I er, I have an idea" "An idea?" "Yes, I think we should end the war, make plans, I have realised that it has been the wrong thing to do, I feel ashamed, actually" "Ashamed, Erich?" "Yes, what have we done, Paul?" Ludendorff looked out the window and back at him and swept his hand across the Western Front map. "The loss of life, the carnage, the war was not meant to progress past a few weeks!"

"Has it been for anything other than to sue for a negotiated peace?" Ludendorff raised his hand as if to say *Hear me out.* "I can't explain this. I have changed tack; the wind blows against me. No one can win this war; we are now at the stage where our defensive strength has given us the chance to sue for a mutually agreed-upon armistice. We must act while you are still in favour of the German people. We can no longer avoid domestic discontent; the Communist parties are gathering political momentum in Berlin. There, now you may fire me if you see fit."

"Well, Erich, I must say I agree" "You do?" "Yes, I have a plan. A plan for a negotiated end to the war, as you do. The Allies know they cannot win. Britain is on its knees after eight years of war, and both sides will pay reparations; they will sign an agreement of peace. We must embrace the people of Germany and start an era of peace and prosperity. The parties are disorganised and leaderless; we must build on your Deutschvolkische Reichspartei Party, with both of us at the helm." "Thank god, then let us begin," the two men said, and he saw Ludendorff smile for the first time in living memory.

Gunter Scumarterschwartzer read the letter from his Father. His beloved greenhouse and his capsicums, his seeds and his wasps. His Father was a brilliant Scientist, who knew that bordered on the slightly touched mad scientist side. An Alchemist, a riddle and a man convinced of the power of the unknown that could be unlocked through science. *What's this with his wasps? A discovery? He has sent a letter to the Institute very well. Goodness Father, wasps and capsicums, your world is slightly different to my world, Bombs and gas.*

They prepared for an attack, the first attack for a year. He was frightened, which was normal, but as a Sturmtruppen, he was among the select few in small teams of tough, motivated men skilled at killing the enemy. They perfected infiltration into the enemy's trenches, bypassing strong points and creating havoc in weaker areas, leaving the strong points to the following waves. They carried flamethrowers, grenades, and light machine guns, and were physically fit and strong.

Physically fit and strong, until an artillery barrage tears us to bits. What is this, Father? You know how to stop the war? Alright, you really have gone mad. Powder that is made from wasp venom, very well. Clarity of mind, an elixir of sorts. His Father ended the letter. 'I have sent you a tin of the powder; you must take some yourself, then you will understand that I am not mad.' Ha, you read my mind, Father. It couldn't hurt; it might give me a gentle death. Maybe he has become touched.
His Mother took over, discussing the war and what she had sent him: socks, a mirror and a shaving brush.

He glanced at his Sergeant, who was preparing the flame-thrower while the tank was set on the ground. The Sergeant had used the flame to incinerate many British soldiers, and they nicknamed it the *Tommy-Cooker*. He was the frontman, the man who led the way. He had relished killing with his grenades and his club and showed no mercy, but too many of the Allied shells had taken their toll. His specialty was command dugouts; if he could reach them, he flung in his grenades and torched the officers, a main prize. He did not really care who was winning the war or what else had happened; he kept himself within his own little group of elite soldiers and fought for the sake of fighting. It had struck him in the mind, like an imaginary shell that set him in stone and made him into an automaton.

It was better, he thought, to stay alert and hostile, never thinking too much about his almost inevitable demise and just fight. He felt as little as possible; only practical thoughts pervaded his mind. Rumination and emotional diatribe had no place in his soul. He never thought about a wife, a family; he was sure that he would die in some stinking hole. He was a living example of a machine that killed, no feeling, just reaped and got back to their lines. He had survived too long and was practised, yet still fearful—a necessary trait to survive—but now he had a sixth sense. He instinctively knew where to go at certain times, which is why he had the perfect job. Once he had moved during a night raid, the spot didn't quite feel right; a shell landed after and blew the position to bits.

Their first forays had taken a toll on the British line in the old days; they had not accounted for the new tactics. Now it was the Australians, and they were a little different, clever and hard-nosed like they were, and he thought that this time it might be the time, his end. The Australians didn't shy from using the bayonet and fought till the end, like them. In the old days, the Australians had raided with considerable success; he remembered being constantly on edge as a young recruit.

Their successful tank attack had left them stunned. These tanks were faster and a new variety to the old clunkers that had been deployed in the past. Their guns were also accurate. Usually, the artillery had taken care of them, but the tanks had reached them quickly, and the guns had no time to centre their targets. Three trench lines and nearly eight kilometres had been taken, spurring the command to action. Another tank attack may secure more ground for them, preempting the possible incursion.

18

"Cowan! Hatter!" the Sergeant-Major shouted at them and waved his hand for them to come over. The Sergeant-Major, Gerrard Tyler, was standing next to the dug-out periscope, a huge man who towered over all of them. Sam thought his arms were bigger than his legs and thought about his chances in a fight every time he met him; every time he lost easily. They saluted the Sergeant-Major as they approached. "Now listen, you two, get back in the rear with Harris and Barton and the rest of your section.

The Canadian liaison officer is there to teach you idiots how to fight hand-to-hand. "Hand to hand, Sergeant-Major?" "Close Quarter Combat Hatter, without weapons. Refresher course to add to the bayonet thrusts you learned in basic training. The Canadians were good at it. Boxing, jujitsu, that sort of thing. The Germans are good at it as well, and it's only a matter of time before they raid our line"

They watched as the Canadian Lieutenant stood and bore the brunt of the two men's best attempts at knocking him down. As a group, he noticed they still spread out, fearful of shellfire but knowing they were well out of range. "So, gentlemen, I want two of you to give it your best, try and knock me down. It will give you some idea of what I am trying to teach you," he had said, standing in the dirt circle. Harris, their most capable man and a boxer, was selected and Barton because he was, or seemed to be, fearless like a Willy Wagtail that waited for the last moment to get out of harm's way.

Harris approached with his arms raised and swung, using his feet as leverage. The Officer grabbed Harris's arm during the swing and grappled him to the ground, holding him in a pinned pose. The men gasped, joked, and whooped, showing interest in how easily Harris was put out of action. Harris smiled, was released by the Canadian officer, and returned to the circle of men, embarrassed but smiling, receiving pats on the back and the usual jibes. Barton was next and rushed the man, and he was easily tackled to the ground, using Barton's weight, and he went down on the dirt, and the officer grabbed him and was on top of him, holding him down. Barton too rejoined the circle, nodding, covered with dirt, placated. Someone murmured down the line: *"Old Victoria didn't help you there Barton"* The men laughed.

"Men, in the limited confines of a trench, this may help you get out of strife. I know many of you have beaten Germans to death already." Some men chuckled, some showed no emotion. "But you can see, ah, Corporal, what's your name?" "Harris, sir" "Harris, he is what, a fair bit bigger than I am. Did that make any difference? So, if you are in close contact and no weapons are allowed, these holds and pinning moves, using their weight, may give you an edge."

"So, some background about me. I was with the Canadian Second Division in 1916-1917. We conducted many trench raids and made a good account of ourselves. Your older First Division was also adept at this sort of thing. One of the things about close-quarter combat is the shock of contact, whether you are attacking or being attacked. Getting hit in the face suddenly is shocking. So, Corporal Harris, a boxer, would be used to that more than most of you. However, for the rest of us, we need to be aware of how to avoid that if possible and react, get our opponent to the ground, and deal with them. We took trench knives, clubs, grenades and Lewis guns into the raids. Lewis guns were light to carry and pack a punch for their weight. We have supplied a new shipment of these for you. Have I grappled with a German? Yes, I have. Killed a German? Yes, many."

The Lieutenant showed them several moves, including how to use a club and get out of holds, as well as how to utilise their weight. He got a man to use a knife and feint at him, and showed how to avoid contact and grapple the knife away. Every man had a turn, and every time the Lieutenant sent them on some twisting fall or pinned them to the ground. "Ok, Sam, is it?" "Yes, sir" "Raise the knife and come at me hard, don't worry, neither of us will get hurt, we have to try these moves and get them as real as possible in the time we have" Rushing

111

the Lieutenant, he raised the bayonet as if to strike the officer and found himself suddenly pivoted forward, the knife wrenched out of his hand as the officer twisted his arm and then he was in the dirt face-down. The Canadian helped him up, smiling, then showed him the move in slow motion, holding the knife above him, being the attacker.

After the training, they took the rare opportunity to have some rear-line lunch and brewed tea, sitting and talking to the Canadian veteran. He could hear the distant shellfire, and the afternoon was almost a pleasant treat as the pioneers in the distance unloaded supplies from the carts, their horses milling around the bombed-out farmhouse. "Remember, the bolder you are, the better your chances. Don't hesitate." The Lieutenant stood again alone in the dirt circle, like a Roman emperor, and discussed the German trench raiders and their tactics. The Germans employ the same tactics, but also utilise flame-throwers. He showed them the device, a captured tank and a pole.

He showed them helpful small tips, such as how to quickly unjam a Lewis gun and how to position themselves when raiding as a party, each man having a specific job to do. He showed them how to use a boot to clout someone effectively, how to best treat trauma wounds, and concluded with a final sentence in French. Veux-tu coucher avec moi? The Lieutenant smiled, and the men looked at him deadpan. "If you happen to meet a nice French or Belgian lass, *will you sleep with me?*" Cat-calls followed, and smiles abounded.

"No mercy," the Lieutenant looked at them in a return to seriousness, and hesitated, looking around at the motley group of Australians. "The Germans will try and kill you first, one hesitation and you are dead" He noticed for the first time the officer had a nasty scar around his neck as if he had been decapitated and his head had been put back on. His tunic was lowered a little, and he glanced at the scar. *How did he survive that?*

He glanced at Barney, who was looking at the Canadian like a stricken sea Captain. Harris was looking at a plane in the sky, and Barton's eyes glistened in the fading afternoon light.

The Sergeant-Major gave them a reprieve, and they spent the night in the bombed-out farmhouse out of range from the artillery fire. Pioneers gave them fresh tunics and made some soup with some captured ham in it, and they sat silent and ate like famished children. One of the Pioneers lifted a box, looked around as if he was stealing something, placed the box with them, and nodded. They opened the crate, saw it was full of apples, and stashed them for their mates, eating one each, core and all.

He lay with his section like worms on the bare dirt ground, watching the stars come out as flashes of shell bursts reflected off the brick wall, momentarily lighting up the sky. The Canadian Officer stayed with them, and when he got up to use the toilet, he saw the man still awake, sitting on the low brick wall in the moonlight, and nodded. His shadow was reflected on the single standing brick wall by the rising moon, casting him in a grotesque shape as though it were revealing some clue to his continued life on Earth. The man's scar highlighted white in the moon's glare. When he returned, the Canadian Lieutenant had gone.

19

Carter gunned the motorbike through the Irish rear area, lines of horse-drawn carriages with supplies, ruined past piles of wood, soldiers discarded clothes, dead donkeys, and shell casings stacked like abacuses of the body count. The rail junction was three miles distant, where the port's supplies terminated on land-based supply routes and where machines generally failed, where horses and donkeys ruled the soft ground.

They passed over a bridge being rebuilt by Engineers, men arrayed, lifting wood beams and stone blocks like ants in a forest. Bodies still were piled on the side of the road from time to time, some not yet moved from their places of death, where front lines became rear lines and old trenches became pits for mass graves. Shell casings lined the road, small child-like mini-trains that transported the ammunition from the railway junction were stopped at the roadside, men unloading and in the background, under a stand of trees, a pile of discarded shells in high mounds of steel.

He thought about how far he might get, what he would do and say to Carter as he held the corporal's waist as the bike veered over ruts and swerved to avoid supply trucks and men on the road. They passed a field Hospital, where women in long skirts tended to men on stretchers outside the tents. A wounded overflow spilled onto the rare grass behind the lines. Several men wandered, bandaged heads, crutches and slings of bandage, bandanered eyes, broken legs, one-armed gassed men, blind and sitting, the sun shining that they couldn't see but felt. The red crosses highlighted the canvas, and Doctors milled in a meeting to the side of one of the tents.

In the distance, he could see a low suspicious cloud, over Carter's shoulder, the front ablaze on the sunny day. They caught up to an ambulance column, the canvas back of the last truck flapping to reveal a medic tending to a wounded soldier, reminiscent of an old animation movie with its shutter-like fabric flap. Carter overtook, and the line of trucks filtered by, ahead, a narrowing of the road and a treeline on either side of the track. The road widened, and then they came to a crossroads, with four dirt, nondescript roads and a four-sign pole, like a propeller, in the middle directing traffic. The junction gave way to more British vehicles, and several trucks carried more soldiers in the direction of the front. Carter slowed and stopped at the Military Police checkpoint.

A small wooden hut sat on the side of the crossroads. The Sergeant was directing traffic; soldiers one way, supplies the other. The Sergeant approached, an older man holding a cup of tea and scanning the traffic movements. "Sergeant, Seventh Australian Division intelligence, we need to get to the rail junction at Pilarry." Carter rested his leg to steady the bike, and he got off to address the Sergeant. The Sergeant looked at them, smiled, and pointed to the eastern road, then took a sip of his tea before walking further away from them. He thought he noticed the Fifteenth Division's logo on his sleeve, then dismissed the idea. His hut was full of souvenirs: a German pickle-helmet and a Phonograph record player that was playing the popular twenties tune, Wheezer on the Whizzbang. Carter moved off, the Sergeant a man of few words, smiling at him with the tin mug steaming in the day's sunlight.

They traversed the road East, past a sentry gate to an airfield, the biplanes in the distance lined up in a row among the hangar tents and winding dirt roads. Cows crossed the road ahead, a Belgian farmer guiding them across; their sides were black and white, like the map of France. Blocking the road was an injured cow, revealed as the Farmer passed and heralded his herd through a gate, then returned to the cow prostrate on the ground.

Carter pulled over, and they got off. There was no other traffic, which he thought was odd. "Qu'est-ce qui ne va pas chez elle?" Carter asked the Farmer. "Je ne peux pas le dire, elle vient de s'effondrer," he replied, obviously upset. "He says she just collapsed; he can't tell what's wrong with her." He nodded to the Farmer and crouched down, looking at the

115

beast. She snorted, and her eyes closed and opened again. He couldn't see any injury. "Can you see anything, any injury?" Carter shook his head, scanning the bovines' rear. He placed his hand on the cow's rump, feeling the massive beast's breath.

The coarse hair rose with the laboured breaths. Feeling the rump of the cow, inspecting the eyes and the legs, he saw nothing of note. Carter raised his eyes in apparent bemusement. The Farmer looked at Carter, then at him as if they were secret veterinarians. He crabbed over to the cow's head; the bovine had its head resting on the dirt, one eye glazed and looking at him suspiciously.

"What's wrong then, old girl?" A gust of wind momentarily crossed the road, raising some dust and turning their heads as a dead branch cracked off a tree by the side of the road and hit the ground with a thud. He felt his blood pressure drop, and a strange sensation came over him, his hand still upon the beast. The clouds raced in the sky overhead, and his skin tingled with a cold paresthesia.

He daydreamed, imagining what might be wrong with the bovine. His mind set within the beast. He followed the arteries and multiple hearts, through the chambers and valves, wondering why he was thinking like he was. Carter crouched down beside him and helped him inspect the cow as if he had seen a tool that would help. His hand, splayed on the rump; the feel of the cow's coarse hair, the heartbeat within. Time slowed, and the wind played across them, Carter and him and the French Farmer on the road.

He glanced at the roadside and saw the plant. *Digitalis Purpurea.* "It's *Foxglove,* that plant" He pointed and Carter looked puzzled. "Poisonous" The Farmer suddenly realised and walked to the plant and confirmed his suspicion, muttering and pulling the plant out by the roots.

The bovine suddenly rose slightly, snorting and blinking. Carter stepped away, and she rose using her hind legs, the three of them moving away to avoid a collision. "Wow, elle a l'air bien. Je vais devoir avoir plus d'Australiens sur ma ferme!"

Carter looked at him inquiringly. "What did you do?" "Nothing, anyway she seems fine now," The cow snorted and bellowed a nasal tune, then started to eat the grass beside the road. "Merci, merci" The man smiled and led his cow over to the gate, looking back at them. Carter looked puzzled. "Merci, bonne chance!" Carter waved at the man, who continued to smile at them as if they were a visiting monarch, still clutching the *foxglove* plant. "Let's go," they said. They moved off, the road widened, and several more trucks pulled up alongside the road.

The sign to *Pilarry* loomed ahead. As they passed, all the men in the trucks were looking at them, and he wondered with trepidation what was so interesting. Carter looked to the side as if trying to discern why. He yelled in Carter's ear. "What's so interesting!?" Carter shook his head in reply. They passed, and the fifty or so white faces that still stared as they turned the corner and disappeared behind the treeline. A pig farm loomed on the left, the porkers milling in several stalls; several raised their heads and stared as they passed, the engine purring across the dirt.

The outskirts of Pilarry came into view: a ruined, bombed-out house from the earlier conflicts, with piles of rubble and a church spire standing on a few sections of brick raised to the sky. Beyond the rail junction settled ahead, a hive of activity, several trains were being offloaded, carrying precious supplies that had got through the U-Boat blockade. Trucks lined the train at right angles. He watched as they traversed the line and headed to the fuel depot to get the bike more petrol.

A train parked alongside the depot was pumping fuel directly into the ground via a pipeline that ran to the front. Two civilian men supervised the flow. They parked the bike. He looked around. There were two hand-cranked petrol pumps nearby, and soldiers and a Master Sergeant were filling several

117

trucks, to the sound of clanking metal and wafting plumes of petrol haze.

"Listen, Carter, it's the end of the road for you; you have to go back. Classified from here," Carter smiled at him. "What?" Carter looked in the know. "You're dead" "What?" "They think you're dead, on the old German line, they think you copped it from the artillery" "You put that in the report?" Carter smiled. "Also, Barn-Paler was killed by artillery as was Riddle, which pretty much takes care of that" "And what are *you* supposed to be doing?" "Leave, two weeks, Boulogne, got permission to drive to the port myself. I'm off to see my former boss, Cardinal Rufus. To resign actually." "Good grief, so you were a Priest" "Not anymore."

He looked at the ground, nodding, his Corporal as always one step ahead. "Look, Frank, you could come. What are they going to do? Kill the war hero?" "You'd be surprised. No, I have to get to Flurry," he said, looking at Carter, who nodded. "Gotcha, I get it. Carter stood looking at him nodding. "See you, mate" They embraced; a set combat relationship, a crucible of steel. Carter turned and walked in the direction of the rail junction past the trucks and was gone.

He watched his man leave, and then saw the Master Sergeant walking towards him. "What do we have here, ah, intelligence section. Where are you off to, Sergeant?" "Can't actually say, Master-Sergeant" "Ha!, indeed, but you need some of my fuel?" "That would be appreciated."

"What about Chess? A game with me in return for your fuel," The Master-Sergeant narrowed his eyes, waiting for his response, sweeping his hand in the direction of a small table planted in the dirt. "Oh, yes, I see. That's your board over there, isn't it?" He pointed to the table by the depot office, where the pieces lay out on the board in the sun. The Master-Sergeant looked up to the sky and over to the trucks, then back at him.

118

§

The depot Sergeant watched as he held out his two arms, a pawn in each closed hand. The Sergeant pointed, revealing the black pawn. "You are black then?" "It suits me well," he replied. Frank thought he must have been an intelligence officer or a member of the Military Police, but neither of those roles sat right with him. Since Flurry, he thought he had no fear, but as he sat in front of this man, it welled up within—options for saving his life beyond the chess game filtered through his consciousness.

The game commenced. Trucks were idling, and men were calling somewhere within the depot. A private stood filling his motorbike tank. A large bird was perched upon a tree on the other side of the railway cutting, watching the match. The two pondered and ruminated. The Sergeant had hands like weaved straw, watching the depot Sergeant rub his skin and move a pawn one space. The chessboard was carved from wood, a master's craft. The chess pieces told him that the person who had made them played as well, although he wasn't sure why. In time, the man took his knight as he thought, his clever trap.

He looked at the Master-Sergeant, and he smiled. "Your right-hand man, Corporal Carter, you are not going to accompany him if you win?" "Why do you ask?" "No reason," "Check," he said. He glanced over to a truck and saw it wasn't a tanker, full of soldiers, idling by the road. It slowly moved off down the road to the North.

The Depot Sergeant seemed thin and plump at the same time. The man had a round face, but wiry legs, grey eyes, and a pockmarked left cheek, with some scars from acne or shotgun pellets. Moving his Queen one space, the second move in the master-plan to feint an attack, but really to secure the Sergeant's rook; a left-hand assault. The bird was still perched, and still, thoughts of home permeated the mind—a poem formed within the thoughts, a between-move tapping of an imaginary finger.

119

Through the ankle-high wallaby grass and barbed-wire stalks,
walking alone under a day-breaking sky.
Buzz of bees and native drum, the acacia tree and beating sun.
To a shade canopy and a sweet smell, the flowers of
Eucalyptus and a rough-barked tree.
The slight whisper of wind through a standing pine, the
mailman's horse and the distant shine.
The waning crescent above in the clear blue sky, Rufus
Whistler, Wattle fly.

"I would protect your King" "Isn't that the idea" "I am very
good at this game, you understand" "Yes, you are very
rehearsed," the Master Sergeant stared at him momentarily.
"Being the Master-Sergent I am a little pressed for time as
well as you can imagine, the Dep... "I see, but we shall finish
the game?" "Of course."

A gust of wind blew half the pieces off the board, and a small
dust devil whipped the area around them. "Oh dear, how is
that for an answer?" "What do we do?" The Master-Sergeant
hesitated and looked across the road. "I have to go, Frank
Fieldlight, maybe we will finish our game another time."

The Master-Sergeant picked up the pieces and stared at him.
He rose, walked to the pump, cranked the handle, and set the
fuel pipe into the motorcycle tank. When he looked up again,
the Master-Sergeant was gone, and another truck full of
soldiers trundled off the road to the North. He engaged the
motorcycle and turned down the port road that would
eventually lead him to the town of Flurry. Glancing at the tree,
the bird was gone.

20

As he waited, he grew more unsettled. Barney was beside him in the darkness, smelling of German sausage and tobacco. His section aligned down the trench; there was no turning in unless a barrage eventuated. They expected a German raid. He could smell the permeating clay soil and the distinct horror of decaying human flesh intermingled with the musty soil. The dark shapes on the new-moon night vignetted dark upon dark, puzzle blocks that hid things that stuck up in no-man's land, like barbed-wire posts and the shape of a bombed-out tank, dead men's severed heads, he thought, but probably helmets and the scuttle of rats through carcasses.

He had gone down to the Quarter-Masters' office and handed in the German's photograph of him and his prize-winning hen. *"It will be sent to the rear with his personal effects; he may retrieve it again,"* he had been told. He felt odd keeping it—a man's love of chooks, his trophy—not a photo of his wife or lover, but his hen.

I will die a terrible death if I keep it. Harris cleaned his Lewis gun for the umpteenth time in the darkness, hearing the ratcheting of the ammunition drum. He went over the Canadian Sergeant's moves again and again; Barney and he had practised what they had been taught. They had reached the stage where they could execute the moves in real-time, with fast flings at one another and quick counter-moves.

"Hey Sam, we get leave soon, do you want to go to *Flurry*? They have a brothel there. "Ah, yeah, I guess, I don't want to get the crabs though. Barney stifled his laugh; the Sergeant-Major was strict with noise. "We have to have sex, otherwise we might die and then..." "Yeah, but remember Mick Blanchard's experience" "We'll have a better one, I promise" "You promise?" he said sarcastically. "Yeah, I'll work on it" "Ah ha."

Their conversation was rudely interrupted by an artillery barrage. The shells flew over in a concentrated thumping and churning of the Earth, then the distinctive hiss. The thunderous concerto made the night darker, and they fled down into the dugouts to escape the steel and whispering savagery of splinters and powder. He and Barney scuttled into cover, their small dugout holes in the side of the trench. The Germans wanted their trenches back, and at night, they no longer had the advantage of their tanks.

"Gas! Gas!" The relayed alarm he just heard above the artillery. The gas ratchet sounder was turning; the gas sentry had sounded the alarm. He reached for his mask, the suffocating bellows and donned the mask, his breathing already more laboured. The barrage continued, the gas shells falling like rain. He heard firing from their machine gun down the line. "Attack! hold the line!" He heard the Sergeant-Major yelling, and several of the men lined the parapet and were firing off.

The artillery had stopped, and he rushed to the top line of sandbags and saw the Germans approaching in small groups across no-man's land. The Germans had their gas masks on as well and looked like alien monsters. Down the trench line, there was a breach, and a flame-thrower lit the area with a terrible spew of flame, torching two men in the line. The night had revealed the approaching storm-troopers, and the creeping gas barrage had hidden them from view. A flare was fired and cast down an eerie light on no-man's land, and he could see the forms moving across from his two inadequate glass eye-pieces.

He sighted to fire, but the Germans had retreated, or so it seemed, then reappeared further down the line, crossing an unmanned part of the trench. The darkness and the mask heightened his confusion, limiting his view. He, along with Barney and several other men, cautiously moved down the trench in pursuit of the German team. The trench lit up again, and the Germans let fly with the flame-thrower, scouring the trench in anticipation of their contact. Two grenades fell ahead and blew out the side of the trench in a mighty explosion. The first German rushed him through the dark, and he fired, already having the rifle to his shoulder. The man dropped, and he realised the other Germans had no gas masks on.

He ripped his mask off. Barney was struggling with a second man on top of him. The third German knifed the man in front of him and turned to face him. The German lunged and tried to drive the knife into his head, but he grabbed the man's arm and used his weight to make him stumble forward. Barney, having dealt with the man on top of him, fired from the ground and collected the German with the flame-thrower, who slipped back and fell like a stone. His floored German rose, but he swung his rifle and butted him in the head, cracking his jaw, and the man went down cold. He heard the retort of the Lewis gun and saw Harris firing from above the parapet at the German team. Several Germans cried out, one screaming in pain.

Barney was on his feet, and Harris was still firing down the trench line. Running forward up the trench wall, he saw why Harris was firing madly; the Germans had breached the trench line further and were running across no-man's land in greater numbers. Pike-Pickard suddenly appeared, alert to the danger and ran down the other side of the trench. Bullets were whispering above, and he didn't understand why Jothathon didn't get hit. Pickard threw a grenade down the line and then threw himself to the ground, and he disappeared from view. The section must have noticed the incursion as more men ran towards the Germans from behind the trench line. Barney regained his feet, and he saw Harris go down in a hail of fire from the Germans. Barton, just behind him, picked up the Lewis gun and continued Harris's work.

They continued down the trench where the two groups were milling together in close-combat fury. Dark confusion reigned, guttural sounds and the thudding of flesh and struggling, grappling; terror and life snuffed out. Several diggers, bayonets fixed, charged the German team. Both sides met as if equal threats and matched boxers, confident of victory.

One German had a club and was dealing menace with it, landing a blow on one of the soldiers. Barton was prone on top of the trench parapet and firing at the Germans trying to cross no-man's land with devastating effect. He saw several go down by the light of the flare. The trench was lit by the fire started by the flame-thrower, casting a hellish light on the wood-lined trench. Pike-Pickard charged across the trench in a wild leap, and he and Barton ran towards the filtering Germans firing. Barney joined them, and he followed closely behind. He could hear the gas shells in the dirt hissing, but there was no gas as far as he could tell.

The four of them charged through the darkness toward the German line. Small groups of Germans yelled out in alarm as Pike-Pickard threw another grenade and sent several Germans running the other way. Barton reloaded and started to cut down the fleeing men. Behind him, he could hear terrified shrieks and muffled struggling. He saw a German soldier rise under the failing flare light, and he fired, hitting the man and twisting him down.

Dawn began to rise, and the cold air lightened slightly, making the definition more straightforward. Ahead, the land rose to the German positions. He and Barney took cover in the closest shellhole to try to determine what Pike-Pickard intended. Barton dived into a shellhole closest to them, and Pickard continued up the slope. The Germans were trying to set up a machine gun, but were too slow, and Pickard shot them down with what he realised was a trench shotgun with a bayonet affixed. Barton rose and sprinted towards Pickard's position. Barney looked at him in terror, and they both rose and followed the two madmen.

As they topped the rise, he saw the Germans running in full retreat and Barton charging at them, firing from the hip. Two Germans were hit, one was thumped to the ground, the other held his thigh and managed to scuttle over the parapet with the others. Pike-Pickard yelled for him to stop as heavy fire began from the forward German trench. Barton took cover in a shell-hole about twenty metres ahead, and Pike-Pickard lay prone with them in the forward machine gun position. "Fuck! Sammy, give me a hand with this gun. We might be able to give Barton some covering fire" Johnathon grabbed the Kraut gun and carried the heavy beast over to the opposite side of the trench. He and Barney helped with the bipod. A fury of machine gun fire was whispering overhead, and they ducked and tried to get the gun in the correct firing position.

As if in response, the artillery opened up again, and all hell broke loose, the shells landing far to the rear on their lines. With the gun set, Pike-Pickard let the gun fire at the German forward line, the heavy rounds tearing the top of the trench. Barton, possessed, didn't hesitate and charged the front line. They watched as the VC winner began firing into the trench, where their previous fire had kept the German heads down. German screams abounded, and several came out, with their hands up, lamenting, "Kamerad, Kamerad!" Ten German soldiers exited the trench, and Barton turned to them, smiling, before hurriedly leading them back into the trench line.

They rose and approached the German frontline trench. He could hear the Germans in the rear trenches shouting and regrouping. "Barton, leave it. They are coming; we have to leave." Barton turned to his temporary prisoners and waved his finger at them. They made their way back as the Germans started to reclaim their front line. The German prisoners were disarmed and threatened with the threat of being taken to the rear of their trenches. For good measure, Barton rigged a grenade for them to trigger as they came into the forward trench, which exploded as they ran back through the shell holes, accompanied by shouting and screaming. "That was for Harris," he said, smiling.

The progression through the shell holes took some time, as they knew the enemy would have a line of sight back to their own line. Barton started to falter, and he looked over at Barton as they rested in the second hole and saw that he was wounded, his arm crimson. "Barton, for fucks sake" Pike-Pickard and Barney saw his dilemma, and they helped him lie on the ground. "Ah, fuck and fuck all, and dithery fuck," Barton uttered. "Take it easy, Barton. By the way, does anyone know your first name?"

"No, but maybe I should tell you now,... It's Victoria." "Fuck you, Barton" Barney couldn't help laughing momentarily, and Johnathon smiled. He helped Barney take his shirt off, and they wound the bandage around him, his armpit a bloody mess. "Barney, you know some medicine, any ideas?" "I think it's his auxiliary artery, I think, we have to stop the bleeding." Barney used more fabric and made a makeshift pad, then wound the bandage around again, which immediately became crimson.

While Barney worked on Barton, he put his helmet on the end of his bayonet and raised the rifle above the shell hole to gauge whether the Germans knew where they were. Pike-Pickard looked carefully over to their lines, thirty or forty metres distant. He could hear some withering fire behind, but the Germans hadn't opened up at them. "I'll go," he said, looking at Pike-Pickard, who stared back at him grimly. "No way, Sammy, this is my baby."

Barney continued to set the bandage on Barton, barely conscious. "Ok, look, this is how we will do it," Pike-Pickard crawled back down the shellhole side."I am going to run at right angles over to the next hole, it's about ten metres away. Sammy, Barney, grab Barton and run like hell for our front line. The boys will know we have men coming back; they will hesitate with their fire." I will then get back on my own. They looked at him and nodded. They set themselves up, prepared Barton, and discarded the Lewis gun. He breathed in and settled himself. Barney was grim-faced, and Pike-Pickard lay on the shell-hole side, poised like a cat.

"Ready? See you both back there," Johnathon smiled, and they knelt and held Barton, the task harder as they had to bandage his arm to his side. He held Barton around the waist, and Barney took his other arm around his shoulder. The VC man was a dead weight, heavy. Pike-Pickard sprinted out of the hole, and the Germans opened up. He and Barney walked as

126

fast as they could and stumbled over to the next hole, ten metres distant. He waited for the rounds to hit him, but they seemed to be firing too high, getting their aim wrong. "Colonel! Are you ok?" A distant muffled reply had Pickard in the shell hole."Alright! Keep going, that's an order!"

The Germans opened up again and found their mark, he assumed, peppering Pike-Pickard's hole. They lifted Barton and carried him, the three upright. Barney looked at him as if to say Fuck it. Rounds whispered past; he could hear the bullets in the air, which told him they had passed them and weren't for them. He struggled with Barton's weight and looked at the Australian front-line trench. Several men knew who they were, he summed up, and he could see the trench periscope binoculars move, indicating that they were being watched.

As they reached their forward line, he waited for the rounds to hit him, but the Germans were crap shots in that small moment, and they shuffled down the trench face. Several men came and helped them. Barton collapsed, still smiling. He and Barney got him down the trench and checked his wound. He knelt and saw the bandage; blood was pumping out. "Sammy, press here hard," Barney hollered for a medic and got some more bandages from the trench kit. Barton's skin went cold, and his skin turned white.

Barney tried his technique of pumping the heart after feeling for a pulse, but he died with a small breath and went white, and they stood as the medics came and looked at him, then took him away. Barney was crying, and he was exhausted with the effort. He grabbed Barney and hugged him, and they sat down, sobbing and listening to the sound of the artillery cracking in the distance. He looked up at a shredded tree in no man's land and saw that a small bird was perched upon it, looking at them, including Harris, whose body was yet to be taken away, lying on top of the trench line where he had fallen.

The Sergeant-Major came over, half an hour later, pointing at someone to do something behind him. "Sergeant-Major, the Colonel is still out there about thirty metres away," he said. They waited, and the man on the periscope scanned the area they thought their Colonel might be. As the day progressed, they assumed Pike-Pickard would return during the cover of darkness. They returned to their holes like spent wash-clothes in the side of the trench; the men had tidied it for them, and exhausted and spent, they slept. He thought something was odd and couldn't quite place it, then realised he wasn't shaking. He thought of Jonathon in the shell hole and knew that if anyone could get back, it was their Colonel. It would be suicide to try now; the Germans have a line of sight.

The news of Barton's and Harris's deaths filtered down the line, and there were whispered laments and the odd Fuck uttered. Someone was humming Wheezer on the Whizzbang by Colly Harper, the Australian show-woman, her Twenties hit. Exhausted men lay against the trench walls and slept. Someone was awake, sharpening their bayonet, the rasps of steel a trench poem. He heard that the gas attack was a fake, the shells filled with an inert gas.

"Tricky Kraut's. Not that it did much good for them," someone said in the distance. Someone down the line farted loudly, and they all laughed at the gesture. Night fell, and he and Barney had some soup the cooks brought up. Johnny, the machine gunner, gave them his tin of beef, and Jack, the sixteen-year-old rear runner, attempted to provide them with his prized apple, which they refused.

The mail came up for the first time in a month, and he had three letters from his Mum. She had sent him a tin of shaving cream, a pair of woollen socks and a pair of woollen gloves. Inside the parcel was a photo of his chooks, milling in the coop. Another small parcel was inside, and he gingerly opened it, his fingers stiff from the fight. A perfectly folded letter was inside, along with a small pocket knife, a wooden handle, and a glistening steel blade.

Sam, take my lucky knife; it got me back home, and it will bring you back home too.
May all your desired fucks come true.
Yours, Major Thomas Farrington.

He smiled—major, good to know, older man still kicking against the pricks. Barney read his mail from his Sister and glanced over from his dark dirt hole. The two considered each other with exhausted contemplation. Barney held up a comb to the moonlight that was in the parcel and laughed silently. They returned to their reading. His mood wavered like a sine wave. At the lower sine, he felt like running down to the rear; at the height, he lay and read the letters like some planetary alien, the idea almost inconceivable in his dirt hole. He controlled his breathing. Some medical orderlies came and worked on them, and the Sergeant-Major walked down the trench and looked through the binoculars and told the men to check their fire in case Pike-Pickard came back.

Pickard didn't return, and for several hours they hoped and waited. The Sergeant-Major and Major Hobbs met down the trench line. The Sergeant-Major and Hobbs turned to the men, barking instructions. "Tom, periscope thirty metres to your left, try and locate the Colonel's hole. "Sir! "Jacobs! Get that machine gun down the line ready for firing for a diversion. I'm going out. "Sir!" The Sergeant Major looked at Hobbs and objected. "Listen, Sergeant-Major, this is my task for the evening" "No way, Sir. I am responsible for the men's safety; it's my area. Respectfully, Sir, we don't need to lose both of you" The Sergeant Major looked at Hobbs with deadpan eyes. Hobbs relented, knowing his Sergeant-Major was right and effectively had veto power. The stress on his face showed in the darkness. Through his exhaustion, he waited as did the rest of them as the Sergeant-Major got ready. The front was relatively quiet, and they eventually decided to dispense with the diversion in case all hell broke loose.

The man on the periscope binoculars narrated the desperate path of their Sergeant-Major as he traversed the distance to Johnathon's shell-hole. "Made it, he's just in the next hole.

129

Hang on, yep, he's raised his helmet." There was encouraged murmuring from the men in the trench line. He and Barney watched the periscope man and waited for the next update. He looked up at the small sliver of moon that was lighting the periscope man's narrative.

The sniper, Templeton, came up and positioned himself on the parapet and watched the German line for any unfortunates. "Three metres," he said after a while. "Three metres away from Pickard's hole, I'd say, raised his helmet," Tempelton whispered. There was an interminable wait. "Coming in, he's got Pickard." The Sergeant-Major returned, scrambling down the trench with Pike-Pickard. The men helped them down. He soon realised his friend was dead, his Colonel. They found a bullet wound in his leg and his attempt to stem the flow. A letter was found, hastily written on paper, streaked dirt and a stamp of blood-fingerprints to his girlfriend and a paragraph for them.

Hobbs, you rogue, you were no doubt cleverer than me. Keep the boys safe as much as you can. Finch, that's just the way the Company Commanders go. Goodbye, my friend, have a Scotch for me. There is a letter for Mary enclosed; perhaps you can translate it onto clean paper. I hope Sammy, you, Barney, and Barton made it back. I'm afraid I caught one. Barton deserves another VC and Harris his first. Then, a short poem that Pickard always wrote before every engagement and usually left on the dugout wall, and read out aloud when he returned.

Fear not, what is unknown, but what is known.
Temper your souls.
A fine warm wind across Wallaby grass,
The fading light of Eucalypt day, an hourglass,
Shallow creek and milling water-beetle past
Where the roads cross and bridge spans
A thousand handshakes and smiles like fans
The Farm-gate fire-fly and best held plan,
To open again with an invited hand.

130

Johnathon Pike-Pickard, Colonel, A Company, Seventh Division, AIF.

21

Frank continued down the dirt road; the railroad wound away to the East. Beyond the Pillary depot, lines of trucks fed from the Port, carrying supplies going in the opposite direction. The motorbike thrummed its tune, a reliable mechanical sound like his thoughts and memories of Flurry, which started to appear more often. It was rare that the Germans let anyone live to show them mercy. They would just have to fight them again, but they had already done so. He thought about Donny and wondered if it was he who had saved them, ironically. Did the German Sergeant see that he was so young? Why would he care? His dead mates surrounded him at all times, and every man was a mate; every one of the five thousand, five hundred and fifty-three.

The river loomed ahead, the flow that ran to the sea from the Alps, way away in countries that were neutral and whose sons were still alive. He passed the sign that identified the bridge: *Pont De Lumiere*. The treeline bordered the river, and a large span bridge that he could see was in the distance. Several trucks were queued, and some traversed the span coming his way, their rattling planks and bridge nails a soldier's musical tune. He waited for the convoy to pass. The men looked at him as they passed, none waved as if they were jealous that he was going, not coming.

The Military Policeman approached him with a look of interest. The man had no shirt, a police cap, kharki pants, red hair and a broad smile. He noticed he had a big, muscular nose, giving him a strong appearance. He bizarrely carried a boat oar over his shoulder. "Good afternoon, Sergeant, " the man continued to smile as if he had found some ancient treasure. The last truck trundled off the bridge, and the road became empty. "Afternoon, Seventh Division Intelligence, I" "Yes, Sergeant, I was forewarned, you want to cross into Elysee province" *Forewarned?* He tried to temper his surprise.

"Yes, business in *Flurry*" The man looked at him still with a treasure-like smile. He twisted side to side, and the boat oar moved side to side with him. "Most of our traffic comes the other way, you know?" "I dare say," he replied, getting a little annoyed at the small talk.

He thought about the Sergeant being forewarned and slowly calculated that it was his chess partner with a high probability. "There is, however, a fee, a tax of sorts to cross the other way" "Ok" "If the tax is paid, well then I might forget that you crossed, completely forget" "Oh, yes and what if I decide to throw you in the river?" "Hah! I do not recommend it" The Sergeant pointed to the bridge span where he was taken aback and noticed a man with a sniper rifle perched like a bird.

"Lieutenant Griffiths is back from the front; he seldom misses," he said. He looked up at the man perched on the span. *A sniper on a bridge in the rear, who are these guys?* "I have always wanted a motorcycle," he said. He parked the bike, and the man grinned as he looked at the machine. The Sergeant placed the oar against the bridge and rummaged in his tunic. "Smoke?" The Sergeant offered him the packet. "No. I don't smoke"

"You know, there is some medical research that says smoking is a healthy pastime" "Is there?" The bridge sergeant swayed the oar side to side. He glanced up at the sniper whose white face was looking at him like some drained corpse, his rifle barrel pointing upwards by his side. "You are free to cross, minus the bike, of course. Can you ride?" "Ride?" "A horse?" "Yes, I can ride." "There is a corral at the other side, some horses from the front waiting to be shipped back home. You are welcome to commandeer one, saddles in the stable. Don't take the Major-General's horse, behind the red door."

He nodded; the Sergeant continued to grin and stood the oars' heavy wood beside the bridge span, looking at his new prize. He walked across the span, the sniper gazed down as he walked across the rattling lumber, and the traffic was now absent. The lieutenant's emotionless, white face contrasted with the aged bridge wood, as if he were a termite on an oak beam. A light wind blew in short gusts from the left side of the

133

bridge, a mixture of clover and musty swamp. He looked up at the spans and wondered how difficult it had been to build the bridge, with its massive beams, the effort, and the driven, bolted-through hardwood, rough-grain, and tar-caulked crossbeams on the road. A trail of tiny ants coursed up a beam he noticed as he passed; an insect highway, their pace indicating rain.

The large river milled below in rapid flow, the water swirling black and brown, with leaves, sticks, and a floating bough drifting under. A body floated under, and he gazed to make sure he had seen it right, then another, and another. A further pile of bloated corpses floated under in a mass, then milled away with the flow. The wind carried the stench, and he held his breath momentarily as the miasma passed. He looked out to the Western side and saw a farmer on the riverbank sowing some crops, alone in the sun.

The horses milled in a small paddock, someone was looking after them, hay was piled, and a water trough was the centrepiece of the small field. Some past bombardment had partly demolished the stables, but the end of the brick enclosure had held, and four stalls lined up down the corridor. The Major-General's horse stood behind the red door. A stroke of the forehead of the black and white mottled warrior, its eyes with just as many stories as he; two veterans meeting one another. The horse snorted and seemed calmed by his presence.

A barrel of partly rotten apples was welcome, one of which she devoured whole. He checked her water and hay, gave her a final pat, and walked out to see the other horses. The horses came running over, betting on a treat. Carried the apple bin out and fed each of them their due. Checked the saddles and decided then he wouldn't take a horse. Not back to the front. "Going home, girls, good deal," they whinied and nodded. Their tails swished from side to side as he turned towards the road.

Shouldering his pack from the motorcycle, the road wound in the distance through the sidelined trees. He could hear the fire from the front in Flurry. The positions had not changed from when his Division engaged the Germans. The Germans had Flurry, or what was left of it, and they controlled the southern edge of the province. The sign for the ruined town was in the distance, which read ten kilometres. Walking down the silver reflecting path as the dusk started to send colours into the sky and small birds hopped from branch to branch in the trees beside the road, shadowing him.

22

The Generals met in a grassy field that belied the carnage that was a distinct contrast from beyond the tree line. Dead horses and sludge, broken bones and an earth *Davey Jones* locker that contained a thousand hearts of boys killed and discarded souls. Harold-Finch walked to the erected tent, a general's meeting house. Beside the tent was a German staff officer and an Australian Corporal talking as though the war had never started and they were on holiday. It struck him as odd that there were no weapons, as they were part of the peace meeting. He looked at the green grass between his feet as he walked and felt increasingly guilty as if his part in the terrible tempest of war was an immature child's play. A game gone terribly wrong - *my God, what have we done?* His thoughts swirled and hammered lightly inside his brain as he assessed the generation of males that had been decimated, the maiming, the future walking dead.

Any idea of *Country* and *Empire* had vanished from his mind. He thought that having the Union Jack on Australia's flag was a bad idea. He kept these thoughts to himself; he would be demoted or deemed mad otherwise. He thought about how Australia was a young country and could continue to progress in the future decades. *The Aboriginal people, the unique landscape, and Australia's geographical position are significant aspects of the country. Does all this change the relationship with Britain? It should. We need to be independent now, not dragged into more futile wars.*

The news of Pike-Pickard had struck him numb and staring in the mirror on the morning of the news, and then he read Pickard's note, crumpled and torn. He folded the poem and the writing away in a small tin, neatly and expertly folding the red blood-celled paper, like an Egyptian priest securing a library for the dead. The tick of the Grandfather clock in the echoing hallway of the Headquarters permeated the wooden room and haunted the still dawn. He imagined, like a child, that Pickard would appear, or that the news was false. His Sergeant had left the latest dispatches on his table, and he opened the first to discover he had been promoted to Brigadier-General. The order was signed by his friend and commanding General, General Arllingfaller.

His mind had gotten clearer for some reason a month before the scheduled peace talks. He understood things as a collected whole with precise clarity, as if a cleansing tide had swept through his consciousness. People seemed different: his staff Sergeant, his Batman, his men. There was no doubt that the talks would succeed; no argument could be made against it. The Kaiser outlined the German terms, and the Allies had all but accepted them. The stalemate raised new questions about Europe, as well as Australia and Britain, while France, Belgium, and Russia looked on from the outside, licking their wounds and collating responses. The United States encouraged the process but took little else; the isolationist policy was firmly established within the new administration.

The Canadians had pitched in, sending several more hospital ships to help evacuate the wounded to get the Australians home, anticipating the acute shortage of vessels; their delay after pulling out getting home was still a wound for them. Able to ship only five thousand to Canada at a time, the wait was a sore point; many waited months after their disengagement, leading to riots and brewing trouble.

Ludendorff and Paul Hindenburg sat at the far end of the massive table. Hindenburg was enjoying a joke with General Arlingfaller, who smiled in his direction as he noticed him enter the tent. Emile Fayolle and Ferdinand Foch sat and hesitated in conversation with Arlingfaller, the French Generals wizened by war and weary from the morning lines, eating fresh eggs for breakfast—the two Frenchmen, now Government appointees for French negotiations, the warriors of Verdun and the Somme.

Both German and Allied Military police officers he saw were armed and dispelled his anxiety about the talks. Douglas Campbell, Jim Sullivan, and Ron Armstrong were seated together in a tired threesome, chatting. A waiter was serving

137

water and crackers on a silver plate with some type of cheese. The air was one of gruffness and certain optimism; a collected herd of overweight leaders and play-makers. Tobacco odour filled the tent. Ron Armstrong had his pipe, and several of the German staff Officers were smoking. Riddles' replacement, General Harris, sat on the other side of Ludendorff, the English General with a finger raised and uttering broken German.

"Harold-Finch," Ron Armstrong stood and held out his hand, the two Australians shaking hands. "Congratulations, Brigadier-General" "Thanks, Ron, Douglas, Jim" He nodded in their direction. "That's grand, Finchy, now you're one of us, fortunate or not, sweet Mary and Joseph, welcome to our sorry club." Jim Sullivan smiled, and Campbell shook his hand. "A we Brigadier, G'aun Yersal" He noticed Hindenberg was glancing at him. Ludendorff sat smiling and regal as Arlingfaller discussed grafting fruit trees.

There was muttering with the Military Policeman. Allingfaller whispered in his ear, then turned to glance at the other members seated, now in contemplation of what was to come, anticipating an announcement. "Gentlemen," Arllingfaller stood and swept his gaze across the waiting parties. A bee had become trapped in the tent; he could hear the din, then the insect escaped through the open tent door. Arlingfaller hesitated and tracked the path of the bee, then glanced back at the waiting members. Hindenburg stared at the seated soldiers as if he suspected more insects to emerge from the table. A long wisp of pipe cloud curled into the air, and Ludendorff looked like a schoolboy who had seen a beautiful girl.

"Hostilities will cease today at precisely midday; that is an hour from now." The palpable relief was silent within the confines of the tent. The German translator buzzed off an incessant stream of German in an echoing reply. "I would like to say that we are experiencing today the most significant historical decision of this century. The agreeing armies of Germany, Britain, Australia and France will now put in place the ten-step plan to demobilise. The Chancellor of Germany,

Chancellor Strausmann, will address the German public tonight. Prime Minister Baldwin will meet with the Kaiser on Sunday to sign the agreement. Reparations will be paid by all parties to Belgium and France, and the work will begin to bring home our soldiers."

He glanced at the table and thought of Pike-Pickard and how he was yet to transcribe the last words of his friend onto clean paper for his wife, Mary.

23

The road was empty, which struck him as odd; the sign, covered in moss, read FLURRY 5. The trees on the side of the road whispered to the wind and shook leaves that were abrasions in the stillness. The day was closing, and darkness encroached, setting the pebbles on the road silver and the running pools of water leaden and seeping. He couldn't hear gunfire, and the little birds had begun their last call for insects in the trees and flitted past and shadowed him in interest.

The grass by the side of the road wilted to the breeze, the rivers lament, and he could hear down the grass embankment, stone and wash. A crack rang out, and he instinctively leapt down the grass embankment; a single rifle shot. Crawling, he peered up at the bridge through the long stalks of grass to see the sniper slump, then slip and fall from the bridge span, a single dot that crashed into the water below. He watched as the Sergeant controlling the bridge ran from a building and was cut down by another retort of the rifle. The sound of the round echoed across the river in the stillness, then was consumed in the river wash.

German sniper? I would be dead by now. No, this is something else. Not understanding he rose and crouched, ran through the grass, and used the terrain of the riverbank to shield himself from the direction of the bridge. After a few hundred metres, he again walked up to the road and continued, the quiet and approaching dusk belying the violence behind him.

As the sun set on the land, he walked into the ruins of Flurry, an abandoned outskirt and shell-shocked brick hollowed-out houses where boys and girls had grown up, and Farmers had come and gone, now similar to a beehive burnt out. Still, no humans roamed; the smell of charred, wet wood was like an urban forest fire. The sky lit up in shards of streaking lines, like the emblem on his diggers' slouch hats, and cast purple and green on the exosphere to the west, where his mates were buried. The town was most certainly deserted, and he wondered if the Germans had retaken it or if they had withdrawn. He scanned the ruins for piked helmets and grey coats, but found nothing. The river ran through the town, washing a constant lament. His boots crunched sand, and the whisper did the talking for him in contentment.

At the outskirts where he supposed the Allied line ended, he saw in the distance, as the last light faded, the German line, in the same position as it had been when he had run in that terrible direction: barbed wire and stinking, blood and bone. There was no sound, still, and the guns were silent. Expecting to be cut down by the sniper, he glanced around, but only inanimate objects stared back, and he sort of knew. *I should be dead by now. I don't get it.* The last house was a three-wall crumpled mess, but a beam had refused to fall and was propped securely by the stone. He settled inside on the earth in the corner and unshouldered his motorcycle satchel, ate a rotten apple and then retired to the smell of the wood beam and the familiar scent from the wind that was blowing across no-man's land that contained his mates' souls.

§

Awaking to the sun, he found the day bright, with puffy clouds sweeping across his view above the wooden beam. He waited and didn't move, knowing he had passed out entirely for the first time in several months and had slept straight through the early morning, a time when he was usually most alert. No dangerous sounds like men walking and searching, the clinking of a rifle on a water canteen or German voices. The gunfire was also absent. Breathing, he tasted the air as if to test for some unknown allergen, the senses alive now and waiting for action. Although on the dirt ground, his body found rest, and the feel of the satchel under his head was a leather discomfort that comforted. In the distance, music emanated across the plain. Sitting up, he tried to determine its distance and origin. The sound carried into the air. *A woman*

singing, a twenties tune, no doubt, German, Berlin, something
contemporary.

Gazing from the side of the ruined wall. A small crack, visible
in the distance, was on the front line where the woman's
singing seemed to come from. The German line was dead
quiet, no movement, just the singer in the wind. The letter was
inside the waterproof box, ensuring it was secure. He set the
satchel down at the entrance of the ruined house wall. Placing
the pistol on the ground beside the satchel, he made sure his
hat was set right. The warm sun hit his back, and the wind set
at a steady pace into his face, the smell of rosemary and thyme
still within the plain somewhere after all that had been
corrupted and torn apart. His mates whispered to him from the
German line, and he imagined a bush creek and the smell of
eucalyptus on a wet morning after rain.

He walked out to the start of no-man's land past some tangled
wire and a rusty field gun, its barrel splayed after the sappers
had blown it up to prevent capture. Rags of uniform still
littered the ground, discarded cloth and shell casings from the
artillery, a pile of stone, a canteen jagged and torn apart, tilting
to tempo from the wind on a rock and beating a geological
tune. As he neared the first line of German wire, a skeleton
greeted him, its arms splayed either side, holding the frame of
the long, rotted torso up in a kneeling position as if a
gatekeeper to the dead.

He swallowed hard, and he began to sweat. He controlled his
breathing and calmed himself as he passed the bones. The
skeleton stared straight ahead and let him pass and danced to
the movement of the wire in the whisper of the wind as he
stretched the strands, much as he would do when navigating a
barbed wire farm fence.

A burnt-out tank loomed ahead. From a hatch long fired like a
molten forge, a white, burnt skull was propped out as if the
driver had refused to accept the loss of control in death and
stared straight ahead, wishing for the engine to start. The
metal was scorched and torn; a metal shard, hung by a single

rivet, softly grazed the side of the now-rusting armour in a metallic scrape and haunting tune. The behemoth revealed its massive form as he passed in the shadow of the hulk like the moon blocking the sun in a steel eclipse. He walked and turned to watch the skull, expecting it to turn in a macabre display of frightening conversation. The white bone caught the wind, and a faint whistle emanated from the bone through the teeth grinning out towards the German line.

He was sure of the outcome and happy with it. He expected a shot and was surprised to find the Germans still napping. The German line revealed nothing, and the continued tune of the skeleton tank driver whispered in the wind.

He walked through the line, this time the other way, without Donny, the same field, the same small rosemary bushes, some having survived the slaughter. A glance around as if he would see his mates still, but the earth was set, grey, molten red and reflecting the sun.

Ahead of the German line, the first line trench slowly loomed about a hundred metres distant. Well within sniper range. He waited and hoped the man would shoot straight when the time came. The wind buffeted across the plain and sent pieces of cloth scuttling across the earth. To the right, a horse stood in the middle of no-man's land, a pile of straw on the ground. The horse ate and glanced at him momentarily, then devoured the hay, desiccating in rotating jaw movements, then looked at him again at the same time. The quiet din was deafening; his ears rang with the sound of reverse artillery. He stepped roughly across the dirt, shell holes and churned stone.

Fifty metres. The parapet was defined, and a man he could see watched him as he approached. Not long now. He then heard the woman's voice again; her tune recommenced as if she had been watching him approach. The music had halted on the plain of the dead. *Twenty metres.* The man he saw wore a German pike helmet, like the one the sergeant had saved Donny's life with. Another man joined the group wearing a pike helmet, and they watched as he approached. He saw other

143

German soldiers carrying items into a truck and glanced at him, clearly visible from behind the trench. To the rear, he saw the origin of the tune, a pile of wooden artillery crates and a gramophone perched like a god on an altar. Several men gathered around the device, all watching his approach, glasses in hand.

Two Germans waited as if they had located a lost desert dweller that had emerged from a mirage on a heated plain. It seemed odd that no one was armed, and he stopped five metres from the Sergeant. A German staff officer was watching him with a pair of binoculars further back; they had known he was unarmed. The German smiled and held up a sausage as if to invite him to dinner.

He had practised his German for this moment."Wirst du mich nicht erschießen?" The German Sergeant roared with laughter, his companion smiled, showing an array of yellow teeth. "Ha! Die Zeit dafur ist vorbei" *He never intended to shoot me; it's him, it's him.* The German offered his hand, a strong, filthy appendage with a rye smile attached. The other man bent down behind the trench and pulled a bottle of schnapps from the earth, it seemed, and held it up as an offering. The Sergeant held the sausage, and the Corporal he saw had the bottle like two alley drunks. They smiled and blinked in understanding as he shook the Sergeant's hand. They walked down into the trench-line in the sunshine and the quiet of the day, as the gramophone scratched as another record was placed on the table.

"Nein, wir können Sie nicht erschießen," the officer said, glancing at the Sergeant with a smile. The German translator spoke in perfect English and explained that the war had ended, translating, "We cannot shoot you" "Unsterblich" The Sergeant smiled. The translator smiled. "Immortal, you are immortal, we have been unable to kill you" All the Germans laughed. His second glass of Schnapps had gone to his hungry head, and the Sergeant smiled, and the other men showed him their quarters and pictures of their wives and children.

Digested the news, his plan had failed, his mates in the ground now bones and dust.

"Can you translate for me?" "Certainly, " the translator waited for his message. He turned to the Captain. "Captain, when your division repelled the attack on May 15th, the Fifteenth Australian Division, were the bodies buried?" The translator talked to the Captain, who listened intently. He nodded, turned to the Sergeant, and inquired. The Sergeant replied with a certain nodding.

"He says yes, the Captain was not here, but Sergeant Muller and his men were part of the effort to bury the men. They are in two mass graves, still in no-man's land; Germans and Australians are buried in the same graves. The Sergeant continued and added something to the translator. "He can show you the location if you wish, but there are no markings, only the ground"

§

He and the Sergeant stood at the spot. The ground was like any other piece of no-man's land. To their left, the land sloped a little towards the previous allied line; he could see the house he had slept in about a hundred metres distant. The brilliant day was at its zenith, casting little shadow, and the warm dust wind swept post-apocalyptic odours across the plain. Sergeant Muller stood looking around, then back at his counterpart. They both raised their heads in concerted field-craft training.

A figure loomed from the allied line, and a lone walker approached through the sunshine and the rusted wire. A man who looked like he was walking down to a beach on a summer's day. They both instinctively crouched and saw what the other had done, then burst out laughing. They watched as the man strode through the first line of wire with a pistol at his side. Müller mumbled at the sight, his demeanour changed and his alarm flag flew red. The armed man made them nervous. He continued to move towards them; both now running for cover. They searched for fallen weapons, but the ordinance was long gone, only cloth and dead men's skeletons. The man was closer, and an attempt to run for the German line would be suicide, he judged. Muller glanced around for a weapon, and they looked at each other. Language was unnecessary; a plan had to be made.

Muller crawled over to a long discarded pole on the ground. He waited and wondered. He snuck a look and saw the man was smiling as he approached. The Sergeant raised the pole, attaching a flag with a red and yellow four-square design. He raised the flag, and he heard the approaching man laugh. He had reached the shell-hole, and he had stopped, they judged, as not to expose himself to them.

"Gentlemen, Depot Master-Sergeant Thanatos at your service. I suggest you alight the dirt hole, hands on your heads" The German had placed the flag in the ground, and the top of the ensign flew above the shell-crater. The Depot Sergeant seemed unconcerned and waited for a response. They waited. "Very well, if I have to come into the hole then."

He turned to the German and held out his hand for him to wait, and ascended the hole. The Master-Sergeant stood grinning at him as he stopped at the edge of the crater. "Mr Fieldlight?" He glanced out towards the German line. Sergeant Muller remained in the hole. "A splendid day, Mr Fieldlight, is it not?" "I reckon," he replied. "Our game of chess was a slight reprieve, as advised, there is more to discuss." He realised it was indeed the Master Sergeant from the Depot. "Another game then?" "Ha, I am afraid not," Thanatos patted the pistol on his thigh. "It's the high Command decision I am afraid" "I see. Well, I have arrived at my destination. Anyway, my mates are here, so it was either the Germans or you."

He looked up into the blue sky. Thanatos looked at him, still smiling in final resolution. He slowly crouched down on his haunches, watching Thanatos, and felt the sand that was covering his mates and tried to calm his mind, letting the sand filter through his rough trigger digits and back to the source, tried to settle his side of the transaction, feel the wind and

146

keep calm under the sky. In no-man's land where there was no law, no care or regard, just the instinct of a vicious biped, or some unknown law of life itself.

He waited and looked up at the German line beyond, sure it would soon be over. Just visible, he noticed the German Captain looking at the scene unfolding with his glasses. He glanced behind him at Thanatos, who had the pistol raised, ready to fire at his head, the man smiling in final resolution.

The crack was a delayed sound. The noise preceded the thud of the round that took off the side of the Master-Sergeant's head and splayed it on the ground in a spattered geyser. The echo of the rifle retort loudly cascaded over the field and reverberated through the line and through the quiet ghost town of *Flurry*; the only gun not silent.

The emaciated Thanatos hesitated in his stance, then fell like a stone in a crumpled heap, the rest of his pressurised circulation expiring on the dirt in a crimson spray; turning, one leg farcically flaying to the side and falling in a grotesque position, half hunched, half lying on his back, wide-eyed, then stone-dead. He instinctively fell flat, shocked, and watched the Allied line, then turned and watched the German line, searching for the gunman.

Muller alighted from the shell hole, eyes wide, his look above the edge telling him to get down in the hole. He shuffled down. Sergeant Muller smiled and looked at his line and pointed at the German parapet as if to indicate the shot had come from that direction. He squinted in the direction of Bombed *Flurry*. The stark, bright sunlit allied line revealed nothing."This idea of mine just isn't working, is it?" Müller, still smiling, looked at him, puzzled and not understanding. He rose and motioned for him to crouch and follow him back to their line.

24

So, my boy. I trust you have taken the Elixir. I await your final judgment. Am I mad? Am I at an age where I no longer see the world through the eyes of the younger generation, and therefore considered dated and wrong? Is it because I disagree with twelve others, so also deemed wrong, perhaps I am!? I also trust you have taken the solution as prescribed, four equal doses, three hours apart, for maximum effect. The initial effect should be clarity. Clarity is the essence of the drug, clarity. Clarity in all things, so as in the fullness of time to interconnect with all other things. This ends in a sharpness of thinking, apart from our evolutionary brains. Something to match the dexterity of man, something evolution excelled in. Rumination is demolished, procrastination is ripped apart, and worry becomes a rudimentary construct. Sadness, desire, humour, anger and contentment remain, and other things I cannot mention in a dispatch...

Gunter Scumarterschwartzer read his Fathers letter. He had already decided to die or remove himself from the war. There was no middle grey ground; he either went into combat and survived and got injured and discharged, or died aware of the elixir in his chemistry as he imagined lying on the cold trench ground. That was the plan, his Fathers and his. The path was set: success or death. His Father had concocted a chemical he could not quite fathom.

He had raised an ancient chest of treasure from the sea floor, encrusted with silver jewels and sparkling rubies. Within, the key to man and woman, biped and Homo sapiens. From somewhere within time, he had distilled a chemical amalgam, a protein synthesis, a potion clock. It wouldn't matter if he were mad or not; he had located the key to the human instinct that lay within the mammalian consciousness. Combined, they unlocked the evolutionary door to ascendancy, an apex of life. The wasps had evolved into an apex insect, suggesting a mutualistic relationship might have occurred. *What, though, is the wasp's benefit?*

His Father had been investigating that question, convinced it was the case. He read a long research paper in the letter itself.

The host (Human subjects) have remarkable new cerebral abilities as described. It is unclear whether there is an outcome for the wasp species that has been exposed to the chemical, as it has yet to exhibit changes in what to date has been observed as normal wasp life-cycle behaviour.

Is the chemical a naturally occurring anomaly? A substance that reacts not with insect physiology but has found a path through a mammal's one by chance? A human Hybrid!? This is possible and has been observed in many cross-species studies. The relatively short duration of contact with the elixir through human chemical pathways has not yet yielded any new insights. Has the elixir itself been the catalyst for the chemicals' potent effects? This seems unlikely given the relatively benign contents that make the elixir potion drinkable.

He knew things, or rather, knew different things. He was able to piece the new information together with a better brain. He was like a finely crafted clock, its wheels within turning with precision. He dreamed of machines that moved like humans, solved problems, swam like fish in a primordial sea, and walked onto an untouched shore. Colourful, fine detailed dreams, wondrous creatures and flying monsters, delicate scaled fish that silvered through shoals and crusted reefs.

The animals and machines he became, night after night. His nightmares were replaced as if they were inconsequential. Lumbering monsters eating plants, he was once a box atop a desk that was marvellous in its thinking. He was a running meat-flayer, *Oh, the speed.* He was a ground bird, a running, seven-foot-tall speedster. Through the grass he ran, like a bullet, a steam car, a cloud. Last night, he strode to a tree line, the wondrous conifers were weird and weeping. A figure emerged —a man in a silver and gold-green suit. *A robot?*

Like that chess-playing machine, his Father had alerted him to 1912. *But it is like a man!*

The man disappeared into the forest, and he awoke. The night was still, and the line was quiet as if his comrades had left him. He lay there content; he had another hour before dawn. The dream tremored within him as he lay in the filth, in the hole in the side of the trench, and quivered knowledge like an extra cerebellum; a core of time and chemicals. *My god, what is this? Is there a god? Was the robot a god?; this is different, this is from time. This is within me, I feel its pull like a tide.* In the time he spent before his watch at dawn, he knew how plants respired and ants colonised.

He knew how the weather moved with the pressurised sky in specific patterns and interacted with the sea and the land. He understood that political demographics and leaders of nations were yet to face more terrible choices and actions than the war, the war that had defined him and killed his friends. He fell asleep again, a feat he had never accomplished before, not even just before dawn.

His blood pressure dropped. He quivered and descended. He slowly fell as if he were a piece of heavy paper in a viscous mixture. The sum of all fears permeated his mind, not combat or slaughter, penetrated flesh or horror-laden fields of decomposing bodies. He had seen all of those and was horrified enough. It paled, though, like cloudy water at the top of a small sea. Then, as if he had been dropped like a stone through the depths, he descended, and the darkness had become a clear lament of warning. At the bottom were not dead men's skulls or lost friends, broken dreams, nor lost family, cherished children or beloved pets.

At the bottom was an evolutionary lament, a chemical brain that chanted a neurological tune. It connected him to everything past, setting an imprint and connecting puzzle pieces, drawing connecting dots and best-laid plans like a planetary carpet that had form and intelligence. He was frightened as he was a plant and a mollusc, a ribbon kelp and a

150

crawling anthropod; all at the same time. The connections were clear, and the transitions, all at once, were both troubling and wonderful. He was fearful because he was in an unfamiliar place, yet a strange one —a chemical-like substance. A substance his Father had discovered from the wasps, a substance far more potent than the thinking man and woman, the thinking General or Chancellor, Scientist or deep sea fish. A substance of life itself; the earth, time and billions of years of mastery.

Within him, it swam over his anatomical reef of bone and carbon, revealing his evolutionary soul in memories of being an aquatic creature, a plant, and a protein within a warm pool. Fusion of gas and protein synthesis of a chemical cocktail. It disconnected him from and placed him within other things, like he was trapped, and he panicked, like he was buried alive. Then he set his mind strong, to combat the terror, with sure breaths, with his combat skills tempering his nerve on sharpened steel.

Settling and drifting with the chemical current and then lying content in the warm mire. He awakened afresh, feeling the warm wind down the retched trench graze his skin lightly and watching as his comrades smiled at the Gunter Schmarterschwarzer, who had slept in for the only time in four long years.

25

Greg Fieldlight tossed with the bouncing of the staff car as Tom navigated the deep rutted road towards the Seventh Australian Field hospital. The village called *Chanty* consisted of two remaining bombed-out brick houses and a single tree that had somehow survived past artillery barrages. To put a *cherry* on the picture he thought, a small bird perched atop the highest branch, as if in a final placing in the savagery against the natural world. The area was a large, open grass field, with large white tents and red crosses marking the canvas. The gate guard let them through, eyeing his press card with a smile and his rank of Captain. Wounded and patched broken men wandered around the tents.

A group of three doctors discussed something beside a green tent, their white clothes stained like butchers. The surgeons eyed them as they parked, alert to something beyond the usual trucks carrying the wounded. The Doctors looked at them as they approached, waiting for some news. The men were tall and worn out; their eyes showed little sleep, and the same look he knew from the front —a thousand-yard stare.

"Gentlemen, Captain Fieldlight, Stringy Bark Times, this is Tom Surrey, my Batman." He saluted as best he could. "Well, well, the press, I am surprised. This is Captain John Morris, and our commanding Colonel Whittaker." "Captain, er, Colonel," he saluted, surprised that the commanding officer was there, but then checked his simple thinking. *All hands on deck, it must be overwhelming.*

"Mr Fieldlight, Mr Surrey." Tom saluted awkwardly. "What can we do for you? You have caught us on our sacred break, you know" The Colonel looked at him with still a hint of humour in his soul. "Sir, sorry to barge in, but by any chance do you have a Mickey Tempelton here? He is an old friend, wounded." "We may, we may. The Colonel turned his head in an inquiring fashion, eyes wide at his butcher-like Major. "John, can you get Sergeant Bollard to show these fine men around and see if they have a Tempelton?" "No problem"

"So, gentlemen, what sort of story can we expect?" The Colonel smiled. A nurse was waiting for them by their side with a look that said," "*It's time*". Tom, he felt, was eyeing him. "Well, Colonel, what would you like?" The two officers beamed smiles as if they had topped a sunny rise from a relentless hell.

§

Tempelton, the Sergeant said, lay in the last bed in the row of twenty beds, the recovery ward. The Sergeant walked briskly away, pointing to the tent entrance, already with other things on his mind. He crossed the grass gap between the tents with a strident gait as two nurses approached him, holding pieces of paper in their hands in quiet demand.

He shifted the ward tent-flap aside and entered the dim canvas cave. Several men eyed them, one-legged and gassed, burnt and in post-traumatic pain and in crippled rest. The gravity of the place descended upon him instantly; the men who lay maimed in the dark musty canvas place, as if he had moved from delightful sun to portentous shadow.

He walked down an aisle like he had stumbled on a secret meeting. The weight of the union cried out for an explanation or a hidden password. Then he realised it was a sacred place, somewhere in between life and death, a chance of dying and cards, where men had survived, and a death was still somewhere waiting to pull them back down into a hell-hole.

The room was imbued with a mixture of lament and forgotten dreams—a dash of humility and resignation. The ward smelled of serum and ether and the acrid cordite that seemed to be part of the earth after ten years of artillery. In contrast, he caught a whiff of brill-cream and rosemary, which partly stunned him and set his mind further to the mood of the tent. A human cocktail poured within a steel world of shrapnel, shell, blade, round, wire and barbed salt. He saw a menacing mannequin in

153

the corner, which made him jump. A doctor's dummy for some reference, he assumed and imagined a chef in a dark corner, sharpening two blades like a mad Doctor who had come to finish them off.

The nurses had no blades, only soiled cloths. They eyed them, smiling, checking their credentials non-verbally as they worked, turning a groaning man and washing his burns. *There are no priests here, just the particular smell of war,* he thought. Some men slept, others were sitting bandaged, raw, ghostly.—coughs, gurgles, wheezing and shifting of feet under the sheet.A flood-gate opened without warning, an emotional flood-gate, something he didn't expect, a wake-up call.

He had fallen into a trap of sorts. He felt as if he had entered a members-only area, and a price was to be paid if he didn't leave. Continuing the walk, his legs grew heavier and uncertain, unlike the measured crouch of a gait within a trench on the front. This was different; it was the result —a brand for life and a legacy not seen before. He nodded at them, and some replied, others nodded back. He felt he was there to say something specific; that they expected a speech, but he had nothing to say to them.

No one saluted the Press Captain, and he was glad. Australia's finest were on display. One man was holding a photograph, while another noticed his slouch hat on a table next to him. Another attempted to shave one-armed. There were boys, a sixteen-year-old, he surmised, too young for a place like this. Most of them stared at him as if he approached it would be his last. He knew that wasn't what they thought, though; they were thinking of things he didn't understand. He couldn't cope with the sinking feeling, the realisation of the place he had entered.

As he walked between the slightly rusted and bent steel bed frames, worn from the erosion of human writhing, he grew increasingly upset for his broken fellow comrades and tried to temper his feelings for their sake. He didn't deserve to be there, he thought; it was a secret, terrible club. The grip of the

154

infection. His previously considered temperament was extinguished, and the sheen of sweat that now banded across his forehead confirmed the change. He thought because he was always on the front and saw death daily, that he was now immune. *This is a different hell.* He didn't know such a scene would have such an effect, but physiologically, he was waning, and psychologically, he was horrified.

He glanced back at Tom, two steps behind him, who was also clearly upset, and the look between them confirmed their mutual view, which teared them up. Then he stared straight ahead, like a schoolboy trying to avoid crying in front of his peers. He stopped at an empty bed, three beds from the man Templeton, who was watching their approach like a cat.

He began to shake a little. He grabbed the end of the bed steel frame to settle himself, and Tom caught up to him and wiped the tears from his eyes and put his hand on his shoulder. The men he had passed watched and said nothing; a line of resting sheeted worms, like pupa on a leaf. He looked at Templeton, who still stared with silver eyes, his bandaged shoulder and bruised side of his face set like weathered and broken grey stone. He walked the last two beds and stood at Tempelton's bedside. Templeton said nothing, as if he knew why he had come and was waiting, like a slot machine, to be activated.

26

"Could Ateskew swim?" "Who?" "Ateskew, the foreman," Barney slowly, non-verbally determined what he was saying. "No idea, never saw him outside of the place" "So he probably fell in while he was stirring the insecticide" "Maybe, ask Barnett again would be my advice" He looked across the gap between the sandbags; the German line was almost five hundred metres away; a lifetime to run in war. "Careful, Sammy, Tyrell copped it doing what you are doing at the moment" Barney's look told him the truth, and he bent down further behind the parapet wall. It seemed almost impossible for a round to hit him, let alone kill him. "Snipers don't miss Sammy"

"The attack is tomorrow, Sergeant Major has told everyone to get ready, the *heads* have some more madness planned." Tempelton, the lean fit sniper, crouched past at a trot and offered the news in an opportune moment. Looking at them as he passed with a grim face and the stone silver eyes that held torn men and lost sons trapped within. Tempelton made his way down the trenchline and disappeared among groups of men coming out of the supply trench; the wolf among friendly sheep.

§

Sam fell flat into the trench; the shell had landed close, and he was in flight for a while, he thought. Barney lay a few metres away, contorted and smoking, his tunic smouldering. The line of men was gone, and he remembered only hopping the bags and walking out onto a steel plain of fire. Checking, there didn't seem to be any wounds; it was whole. Rolling Barney into the wet ground extinguished the heat. Barney's shoulder was shattered and looked detached from his body. Another shell landed nearby but didn't explode and sank into the mud with a strange suction sound. The slight depression probably saved him from the murderous machine-gun fire.

The sky was a black cloak, glowing with a red haze like hell itself. Other dead men lay around in pieces, bits of flesh and body parts littered the field in smoking, heated steam on the cold ground. Steel helmets bobbed with the wind that eddied down the depression. A dead man was kneeling at the top of the depression as if in prayer, who had slumped in death and become a statue. German artillery was dropping gas shells dispersed with high explosive behind them; the distinctive pop of the shells alerted him to the danger. He checked the wind and saw that the gas was flowing back to the Australian line behind him. He looked at Barney's wound and grabbed a man's tunic that had been flung in the hole and wrapped it around his shoulder. The crimson flow had somehow already been affected by the heat. He crawled to the crater rim and gazed at the German line. Up ahead, behind a mound of shelled earth, were three men sheltering from the fire, backs against the wall staring back to the Australian line.

One of the men noticed him, and they stared at each other like men on two drifting stricken rafts on a sea of cordite. Several men he saw were crawling back across no-man's land, back to their line, wounded. The fire from the German line seemed to temper as though they had realised the attack had failed. An abandoned and burning tank was about fifty metres to his rear. Pulling Barney across the flayed dirt, machine gun fire was still flying over in bursts.

Barney's gas mask was fitted, but he took it off again, worried about his breathing. The gas seemed to be dispersing behind the Australian line. Deciding to shoulder Barney, raising himself and walking as fast as he could to the burning tank, rounds whizzed by him, but he didn't get hit. Twenty metres out, machine gun rounds were hitting the tank and bouncing off the metal. Lowering Barney and dragging him required all he had. Behind the tank, they sheltered from the fire. The Australian line was not more than twenty metres away. Using the tank as shelter, he shouldered Barney and walked back. Several men were in front of him, reaching for the bags.

The sky grew dark, and swirling masses of shell impact dust eddied and flowed over the muddy flat ground. Resting, he watched high in the sky a plane whirling around with the wind among clouds that seemed to be friendlier, puffy and white. For a farcical moment, he wondered how his chooks would fare on this hell-ground and thought that maybe they would be better than them, more instinctual.

He remembered his Mum telling him about Auntie Gladys's chooks; they survived a bushfire. The worst fire in living memory. She said she expected cooked chook, but they came running, from where she couldn't imagine, across the burnt ground; like this, he thought, just like this. Then it went dark.

27

The Elixir was distributed as a powder. Wilhelm Scumarterschwartzer tested the powder in many solutions, and it had neither a smell nor a taste. *What about the Cardamon? It is tasteless!* He was surprised. His small glass bottles, which he sold, were named the *Elixir of Vigour*. The changes he observed were permanent; he remained lucid, aware, and clever. The war had been halted as if someone had awoken from a bad dream and told all the players in the terrible nightmare that their roles were over. He didn't know why the Allies had agreed so readily, either, but he suspected Gunter had been successful. Both sides exhibited the same clever, considered actions that held them apart from fundamentally human groupthink processes.

There was little fumbling over the terms; those who were thought to be hardliners became more thoughtful and considered about the repercussions for everyone after the post-geopolitical war map changed. Rumours surfaced of a plan that had been discovered by a German servant in Ludendorff's office. The German high command had apparently drawn up a plan of European domination before the conflict.

The servant had subsequently fled to Sweden with the intelligence. *Gunter, you have been creating havoc even when you are not on the front!* The Swedes wouldn't confirm or deny, but the Swedish press did, embarrassing the Government with a full front-page story. The German plan for the annexation of France and Eastern European states aimed to acquire agricultural and living space after victory. The Allies were to pay reparations for the cost of World War I.

Ludendorff and Hindenburg, to their credit, didn't deny it and regretted the plan, but added that the British, French, and their allies would have done the same, albeit in reparations in dollars. They would have crippled Germany for years thereafter.

He thought the French Generals, such as Foch, and the Australian Prime Minister, Hughes, would seek harsh terms for Germany's aggression. Still, they had remained silent and worked in the background of politics, seeking what was right for their respective nations. Germany had to relinquish its colonial rights to West Papua anyway; France would benefit from the shift in German politics to the left. *Has Europe realised that the right of politics doesn't work?*

Ludendorff, his smile captured in the newspaper photograph, shaking hands with General Arlingfaller, the King, and the assembled German High Command, spoke volumes about his personality. *Gunter, my son, you managed it. That, my son, is your most incredible legacy, alive or dead.* The report was a bonus, providing insight into the thinking that preceded the Elixir. He gazed out at the sea as the freighter surged through the Indonesian islands, and in the distance, the Son of Krakatoa smouldered, contemplating its next explosive move.

The sea cast a green and salty hue, and flying fish darted across the side of the ship; their silver wings shimmered in the reflection of the cracked sea. The smell of diesel, marine oil, and grease permeated the deck, the rust shaping but patched in places where the eroding wind and spray had cracked the paint. The heavy swell mist from the motion of the ship cast upward, and he saw the half-moon in the blue sky. The ship was a sea Zeppelin, the heavy steel behemoth surged through the cast blue-silver sea, its beam low and weight set within the tide. Such a blue sky, the Southern Hemisphere, Australia, soon.

Gelda was grabbing the rail further down, his wife of twenty years, her hair twirling with the wind like a calm *Medusa*. Her tall, wiry frame seemed to slice through the wind and salt. She glanced at him, smiling; her blue eyes and altered elixir demeanour reflected for a moment, then she looked out to sea again, just like him.

Germany, he thought, was going to take a long time to recover from the war. He thought two generations had actually died, almost two. Details were emerging of several German battalions, each consisting of fifteen-year-old soldiers, that had been sent into major battles. Changes were already apparent; Hindenburg and Ludendorff no longer enjoyed the reverence they once commanded. Casualty lists saw to that in 1923.

The return to the left and rejection of the right in recent German politics led Russia to soften its stance on the once-enemy. Efforts in reparations and the rebuilding of Belgium and France saw Germany become an ally, rather than an aggressor. He heard the clink of glasses and turned to see a waiter setting some tables for the night's dance on the deck above through the railings. The man had one arm, the other sleeve pinned to his shirt, and he wondered if he, too, had left the war behind.

28

Sam couldn't talk about the war. Not to civilians. Only those who had been in an artillery barrage or a bayonet charge knew the nature of man; in his opinion, there were certainly no gods of any sort, not the ones willing to help anyway. He knew he was on his own and had always been that way. There were no hands of help reaching down unjudgmental, only hands of opportunity. Only men and probably, he thought, women, and people's aggression and their fumbling, and underhandedness and the insular perspective that could wage horror and war. They were the same people who were managers, clerks, and Government officials, vulnerable until the next conflict brewed, making them Generals and dead men and widows of women.

Like most of the Generals that had commanded them, their out of sight, out of mind approach was the key to feeding in mince into a meat-grinder. The war had been an inventive technological process; it wasn't until 1916 that they realised massed infantry charges wouldn't work, most of them. Then the Australian high command began to work together with tanks, aircraft, and men, achieving some victories. Almost all the Gallipoli veterans were now dead, killed in Belgium and France.

A further three divisions had been raised through conscription, and the eight, nearly nine divisions fought until 1923. Australia lost 180,000 men. The Australians, New Zealanders and Canadians had been used as the striking force throughout the three years 1918 -1920 and had been decimated. The Germans fought fanatically, throwing every available man into the cauldron of the ages, fifteen to fifty into the fight.

There had been talk of an Armistice in 1918, but the Germans reviewed the reparations demands they had drafted in case of victory over the Allies. They surmised that the cost to Germany would be virtual slavery and the sacking of the German homeland. The confirmation lay in the direct knowledge of secured documents that their agents had found in a Belgian chalet late in 1918. A high-ranking clerk had left a satchel of papers behind, leaning against a fireplace; the stone and satchel colours were almost identical. If not for a drunken German staff sergeant, the satchel would have never been discovered. The British high command's temporary headquarters had hosted a meeting with the British and Australian Prime Ministers to outline an unconditional surrender demand to Germany. The Germans fought on, knowing the cost of war and the cost of peace.

The maimed returned home in Australian and Canadian ships and entered the civilian world, where things in Australia had changed. He was surprised but glad. The Government set up mandatory service at home for a year, so the men had a purpose and a source of pay. Like a cooling-off period, the men lived on established military bases, talking about the war, settling in with their mates, and enjoying the quiet and the sway of gum trees as magpies called. The bases provided free medical care, shell-shock care, clean, warm beds, clean water, and hot meals, all free from the contamination of decaying bodies. The men were allowed to visit their families every weekend but had to return to the *safety* of the barracks.

Men filtered out after the years of secondment, and women helped them to return to civilian life. Some immediately committed suicide, others talked about the vacuum, the banality of civilian life, the boredom. War was hell, but it put you at the edge of life, and nothing compared to that in a safe, dirty city.

He did his time in the return camp with the others; it worked. They wound down, took a long breath, and talked to the dead men that slept next to them. He visited the Circus and bought some of a Professor's Elixir, the *Elixir of Vigour*. He put it in his tea and offered it to his mates, and then realised over time that those who drank it became different. They seemed more straightforward, and he initially dismissed it as a superstition. It was a silly thing to be involved in, he thought, in superstition and mystical nonsense. He lay one night in his bunk and thought about the Elixir afterwards. The Professor had experimented, though, on mice at the Circus, and the elixir seemed to work on them too.

The purchase of the Elixir sent him on another path, one he didn't expect. The next tin of Elixir he had been given was a beauty product, part of a mix-up of tins. He revisited the Circus and found the woman who had made the product, a beauty cream. He was struck by her kindness and her attractive, easy-going way, and he really liked her. Candice Thompson.

He gazed out towards his Eastern boundary, his land, all four hundred hectares of bush. He understood the local ecosystem. He knew that the insects in the ground were fundamentally linked to the eagles in the sky, and chopping trees down would alter that. A living tree was an eternal gift to the wildlife, and so he harvested some young trees for firewood, leaving the dead ones when he saw that birds nested in them. There were some open patches where rocks had stopped growing, and he planned his farm within these areas to control bushfires, imagining greenhouses on the site where his crops would be.

There were some Aboriginal men and women still living off the land near the Western boundary, and he visited them, sitting by the fire, all of whom were like warriors, and they made some tea. They looked at him, expecting trouble, but then they noticed his stare and demeanour, and he noticed their distinct, calm way. They cancelled each other out. He made it clear he wanted them to teach him a bit about the bush. They sat for some time, the wind blowing through the eucalypt canopy, while several honeyeaters fed on the flowers, dropping fine nettle seeds on them. The men showed him their crafted tools, and the women offered him some native honey. The older woman laughed, and the men smiled. He left them the tea metal box, painted with a logo of a white man in a slouch hat sipping from a mug.

The morning rain had stopped, and he walked in the dripping softness through the Acacias, the spotted gums towering above. Small birds followed him through the undergrowth, watching and shadowing him. Have they seen a human before? He wondered—the small green feathered birds, tiny one-grammers, no bigger than a large spider. The native grasses swept his feet, and he marvelled at the wet strands that covered the ground like a straw mat. Insects flew off the disturbed grass stalks as he walked, crickets, praying mantis, and coloured bees. The different grass seed stuck in his woollen socks, the needle grass he could feel and the soft wallaby grass buds. So long in soft ground in France, he had developed a sort of sway like someone who had been at sea to the heft of the swells. His feet found solid ground, and he had to learn to walk again.

For a moment, he wondered how he had survived the war and thought maybe he hadn't; this was a dream while he lay dying somewhere. *No, this is real enough.* He remembered waking near the trench line, given up for dead. Somehow, he was ok; he had passed out and then awakened. The bullet had struck him he knew. The men were shocked to see him, thinking he had copped it.

Forgotten how good clean air was, not particle-ridden, cordite, decaying flesh and the stink of the trenchline. Some men found him and Barney and got them back down the line. Then, the news came that afternoon: the war was over, just like that. His mate was shipped back on a hospital ship, and he saw him again at the military hospital. They sat staring at one another for a while, then started laughing because he was beaten up from a fight in the Circus bar and looked worse than Barney.

Past the tree line, the creek washes water on stone. In the stirring water, beetles were grazing below the murky surface, where water-spiders strode in the reflection of the sky. The wind had picked up a little and grazed the nearest gums, the wind a calming portent. Sitting and listening. The violent past and memories cascaded and dammed against the wall of nature, sitting like a protected beast. Wattle flowers had been dispersed by the wind and covered the surface of the creek and transited like yellow broken strands down the course. The Acacia trees stood out in yellow against the olive green, casting a warm sheen on the ground as the sun struck them, reflecting their hue.

A sense of needing to look for cover and select spots where one might need to run. Fussy about what water to drink; too many shell-holes full of decaying men and poisonous gas shells and tepid, stinking pools of water. Still got the shakes. They had a service for the last Gallipoli men who passed away, the previous three killed in *Pozieres*. Stood together, what was left of the Seventh, under the parade ground gum, silent and arrayed like broken puppets as the Australian flag was raised and the trumpet echoed through the bush. A flock of little Corellas flew over at the same time and screeched their tune, and the men looked skyward with approval. He knew it meant nothing to the dead men. They were gone, extinguished, but the birds, they meant something, wild, free.

It was all ritual, like a civilian saying there would never be another war or *everything would be okay. The dead are dead. Atoms that would return to the stars.* He had begun to realise how the world worked and what the Earth had produced through its incredible thin chance of time and evolution. The Elixir told him that they were lucky to be within the Universe, the infinitesimal chance of life. The cost to a consciousness was aggression, their survival tool beneath the feet of the Dinosaurs. The evolution of the ape was marked by anger, a steel-like chemical composition, and diabolical dexterity.

And endurance. That's why we don't give in, and fight and die like flies for a cause, and why we torture and rape and burn down people's houses and create monstrous weapons and scour the landscape, poison the water so nothing living but man exists. That's why we deceive and plot, plunder and trick. To survive and take what we think we deserve. Because we are conditioned to be aggressive, not defensive, we are all vicious cuties, faces of smiles and minds of murder.

166

And when I awake at night, and I can't hear the animals of the night because we've cut down all the trees, flattened the grass, dug up, chopped down, and desiccated everything, then burned it into carbon, my chemical composition alerts me to that terrible occurrence. A signal, an evolutionary beacon. A terrible warning. A terrible portent, because we are part of the Earth, not from some deity, some magical cloud nine where we are forgiven and protected. Perhaps now, the elixir will give us the key to the Evolutionary door, not a door, but a key—an evolutionary mind.

The memories of war were healing, somehow. In contrast, his thirst for excitement and terror was an embarrassed monster that waited in the earth for the next conflict. Part of him wanted to continue fighting when he was at peace, and part of him wanted to flee when he was in war and horror. Put it down to taking the Elixir of Vigour. It was his secret, a superstition. The nature of nature pervaded him, and the connection of things was wondrous and ancient. The creek ran and was a habitat for billions of creatures, including bugs, flies, beetles, yabbies, slugs, ants, and scorpions. The beauty of things was now within more than ever, like it had been squeezed out by the war and the contrasting horror and set within him like a mould or a cast of memories of natural time.

Candice Thompson, the beauty therapist at the Circus, had taken the tin of beauty powder from him and given him a tin of the Elixir. The tins had been mixed up, and she had received the wrong box. Dr Schmarterschwartzer's box was delivered to her. She offered to treat his weeping wound from the bar fight. Her tent was light and organised, with a chair and a small table to treat her clients. She inspected the wound and applied a light powder to it, sprinkling the powder over the gash. The hair on the back of his neck stood up, and he watched her as politely as he could, inside, wanting to kiss her with every fibre in his being. *Barney and I never did visit that French place.* The powder dried the wound and lapsed him into a relaxed state, sitting there like a child, content that he had been seen to.

Intimacy, that's what it was. I just can't remember the last time I felt any intimacy. Someone showing it, receiving it. It felt electric.

"So, Sam, that should make it dry up a bit. She smiled and dusted the powder from his shirt, and it electrified him. "Thanks, that's kind of you" "What do I owe you?" "Owe me, Sam?" She looked at him with a rye grin. "No, I think we all owe you, don't you? By the way, you can keep the powder if you like, great for dry skin." Scanning the wound, it felt strange, like some third appendage; a tingling furry haze across his skin. "Thanks, that may give me an excuse to come and get some more," he said with a smile, placing the powder down. She tied her hair back, and looked at him smiling.

"You run this business by yourself?" "Yes, just me with some help from the Circus crew, I don't travel with them though, just set up when they are here. Dr Schmarterschwarzter and I have an arrangement, we share the cost of the packaging and moving our products." Looking around, Candice rose and walked to one of the stacked crates nearby.

"So, I have fifty tins of the Professor's elixir, and since you have paid for it," Candice walked back smiling and sat, offering the tin, hand outstretched. "Thanks, you sure he won't mind?" "No, he's a nice man, clever, I suspect he wasn't the one that shipped the crates to different tents... anyway, " trying not to stare at her, looking around and examining the inside of her tent, his emotions stirred. Candice also looked around, and their gazes again focused on each other. "Want to stay for tea, soldier?" Candice smiled, and he repositioned himself in the wooden chair, smiling back.

29

Tempelton gazed at the flow of the silver river washing through his scope, where he was sure the sniper fell. His wounded shoulder was hurting, but he stayed still. He made himself believe that he was an inanimate object, like a stone or a fallen log, and became a part of the local ecosystem he was lying on. The man had fallen, the white-faced sniper had dropped thirty feet from the top of the bridge span. He had been too visible, and he wondered if the man was a sniper at all. Maybe a guy with a rifle on top of the bridge.

His position in the trees beyond the bridge, elevated on a small hill, was perfectly concealed, and he had looked through his scope at Fieldlight walking down the road and changing his direction as he realised there was firing. He then hit the bridge Sergeant in the head as he rounded the corner, wondering what had happened to his bridge man. The bridge was silent; a small boat moored on the lower embankment wafted with the breeze, reflecting the late afternoon light in ripples and small wakes.

The light was failing through the trees, and his leaf-bourne abode was a mottled grey and brown lament. A small spider crawled across his hand, and he watched it still as it looked up at the human monster momentarily, as they both watched warrior to warrior, and then as the eight legs scuttled back under the leaf litter.

For some reason, he knew that the spider was a part of him, a small fraction of chemical time. In the hospital, he had been given a small vial of medicine. The nurse said it was called *B-Aspirin*. After that, the dreams about the planet were like he was in an armchair, rotating the large gas cloud and dust that was circling in an enormous vacuum around a dazzling, bright star. Watching as the accretion of dust and gas took an eternity to mould into a sphere.

Then the dreams began to feature animals and plants. An anchored plant in the sea, at one stage, a kelp.

He swayed to the current and drank the detritus that milled in the warm sea around the rocks and the coral. Small fish and crabs were there, large predator shapes too, in the distance where the continental shelf dropped into the deep sea. Swam as a type of lizard, he thought afterwards, and emerged from the shallow sea on sand and watched the mica grains, knowing that the rocks had taken eons to erode into that bed of grain. His silver eyes cleared, the lens of the liquid salt. Strange shapes appeared. Liquid lungs cleared, and he started to heave with gas. A moment of panic subsided as he seemed to drown in the oxygen-rich air and walked up into the sea grass, watching as the star overhead warmed his form.

The air was moist with the warmth of the day; still and musty within the small forest. The smell of fungus and flower, musty decay of leaf litter and some sort of sap or amber. The forest floor was warm from the day's soil, and the sniper rifle's scope ensured that no one had seen his position; he was another sniper. Waiting as always. Smelt, evaluated, and used his sixth sense of combat to absorb his surroundings and discern movement or a smell of cigarettes, wafting tea from a boiling billy or the aftershave of an officer. He knew when officers were around, they simply smelled different. Using cigarette smell, paths of a soldier's demise could be chased, and the wind was determined. Reflection could mean death for a lazy *Landser* or another sniper, his covert prey. Talk carried with certain winds better than others as the eddies swirled invisible with the waves and presented him with information.

He smelt different too, he thought, as he had lain there in the white Hospital sheets watching the man up from him, gasping for air and not gas. His inner core of strength returned, but now it was different, and he couldn't figure out how. He felt still vulnerable in bed, and he wanted to sneak into a concealed position and be safe from an imaginary artillery shell.

170

Shadows cast on the leaf carpet, he saw shapes of dead men, men that he had shot down across the trench-line. The red leaves cast reflections of crimson pattern, and the brown leaves, cadavers and dead, skinned men. A fine sheen of mist wafted down from the trees and settled like an ominous spirit, it seemed. Some past soul had placed a sheet on his body in the mistaken belief he was dead.

Fieldlight had dropped down the river water-course to get lower into cover and make his way towards Flurry by the river's wash. His fieldcraft had made him now invisible. He smiled at the Sergeant's training, rose slowly, held his rifle, crouched for a moment to assess the area for any dangers, and then scuttled down the embankment towards *Flurry.*

§

Stopping and crouching on one knee from time to time to listen for a possible hunter, he made his way following the river into the forest beside the embankment. The woods allowed him to hear for the enemy in case they were in the town, but the intelligence indicated that the Germans would be behind their own lines.

A snipers climb up the stone tower, what was left of Flurry's spire. The German artillery had severed its head, but it still had about ten metres of height; enough for him to keep an eye on Fieldlight, where he had settled for the night in the ruined house. The oak beams had stayed true, and he climbed over the shattered stairs and across the gaps to what was remaining of a small, unbroken wood floor. At the top, he could gaze at the German line with concealment and had an unbroken field of fire. Two half skeletons lay at the bottom, partly decayed and smelling like hell, but he liked that as well; it would deter most from the space.

171

The town in the dusk gloom looked like some Medieval hovel harbouring the Black Death. The shattered buildings rose like grey fingers to the leaden sky, and across the Horizon, a red strand of sky completed the hellscape. To the South, he could see the river winding silver and across the German distant line, the wire entanglements spread like patches of broken dark across the soaked sand of no-man's land.

Detritus land-based flotsam lay across the allied line, disabled cannons and strewn equipment, helmets and discarded unrecognisable clothing, piles of artillery shell casings, and he could see white dots in no-man's land reflecting the moonlight and looked wondering for a time and then realised they were skulls of the decayed dead; beacons of the lost. The skulls shone white, like lighthouse beacons warning of the fragility of life; the entrance to a treacherous harbour. Scanning the contrasting no-man's land earth as a reminder of the transition between awareness and darkness, the skulls were scattered here and there like schoolboy footballs, waiting for practice, as the dirt had given them up and they had rolled down small gullies, oval sails of bone.

Back to the stars in death or a chemical reaction, synthesis of proteins and carbon, gases and the photosynthesis of the sun, to bring life. Why do I know that? Why do I see how the Earth was formed, through the accretion of gas and dust, and the influence of gravity? How do I know things about the Earth and its past? The dreams! How wonderful, the images of the creatures! The sea, the forests, the rivers, the volcanoes, the splitting of the continents and the darkening of the sun. The endless waves and moss-covered lakes, plains of red and mountains of white.

Fantastic shaped trees and strange shells arrayed among the million conches on mineralised shores of 10×7.5^{18} sand grains. Sweeping clouds and fuming geysers, oxygen-rich flying insects as big as cows and dogs and dark shapes in the endless sea.

Have I gone mad? All the death, fighting, loss, and torment? No. Not mad. It's clear to me that my mind can still reason and understand with clarity and intelligence. My kit is always in top shape so that I can survive, I can tie my bootlaces, clean my teeth, shave and dispose of my shit. I still get a hardon in the morning. My eyesight is clearer, literally. I can hit a target at one mile with cross-wind with accuracy. I can walk for twenty miles without feeling it. Lie down for eight hours in complete stillness. Adjust a sight, load a breach, no. Not mad. Different.

Different. Funerals, churches, priests lamenting over dug holes and tears of soldiers. Men standing still in the dawn darkness over men in the earth. The human consciousness is trying to make sense of loss. How many of those gatherings have I seen through my scope? Even the Germans. During those times, I stayed still, and the breach remained cold. If there had been a General standing above a grave, it would have been different, I suppose. Would it have been different? I wonder. They may as well have been cloth dummies on wooden poles for all it means to me now. Carbon, Hydrogen, Nitrogen and calcium stick men are unable to comprehend what they were doing as creatures of the Earth. What do I think about death now? Life ends, and I am alive, that's it. That's it. Yes, old boy, life ends, and I am alive.

Later, a sliver of moon rose above the blue horizon, hoping to cast the field in silver despite the light. He then wondered about the total stillness of the German line and the abandoned town. It must be over; it's too quiet. They said it would happen soon and fast: the Armistice.

He sat silent and listened to the town; the absence of guns a din in his ringing ears. Thanatos, he knew, would be somewhere there; the Greek was like a ship at night; he seemed to appear near your shoulder unexpectedly at Intelligence operations.

He knew it was all over when he saw the Germans exposing themselves on their line. Some soldiers were drunk and

173

gathering around a stack of crates and a gramophone. His instinct was to cut them all down, but he was also elated that the war he thought was almost certainly over. *The Germans typically do not hold tea parties in the open.* No doubt they had tried to find him. He was glad they hadn't, though, if they could, Thanatos could.

Fieldlight and the German sergeant stood a distance away in no man's land and stared at the ground there. He waited. Thanatos revealed himself, emerging from the treeline and strolling towards no-man's land. Through his scope, he confirmed the Greek, his thick-set figure and deadpan face. His revolver was in his hand by his side as he walked, and he shifted the bolt and steadied himself in his watch-tower.

§

He waited until Fieldlight and the German soldier he was with had gone back to the German line. Under darkness, he crept out to where he surmised Thanatos's body's rough location would be, but there was no body he could find. In the spot where fresh injury and brains lay, also lay Thanatos's clothing. He crouched and thought whoever removed the body was very good at concealment, as he had been watching from time to time but had missed the event through his scope. Possibly, they dragged it and buried it roughly, I suppose. It would make sense, the stench of it in the coming days.

He had heard the single shot and realised a version of him was on the line. The moon had set, and he was an expert at getting from position to position, having spent countless nights in no man's land among the dead and dying. He had secured a small tin, a pair of pocket binoculars and what had felt like three photographs, the paper thicker and rougher to his touch. The German line was a din of music and voices; he could discern light from a fire and smell wood burning. Content that Thanatos had given up his worldly possessions, he shuttled back in careful steps, feeling slightly foolish now the war had ended, but making sure he wasn't the last casualty.

He arrayed the items before him in the morning stillness. His ears were ringing, and his small patch of sun had been carefully selected so he could watch around him for death and danger as he had always done. What remained of the town's church battlements surrounded the remnants of a small stone balcony. Sitting, he surveyed the surrounding distant German line and the forest to the South where he had infiltrated. He could no longer smell the scent of combat. However, he could still detect the aromas of people, their shaving cream, and the wood stoves, as well as the lingering scent of thyme that still grew in the cordite earth of no-man's land, unconcerned with war and death, only driven by photosynthesis.

There was sound and movement on the German line. Using Thanatos's binoculars, he looked at a small party of British officers walking from a lorry to the German line. A group of German counterparts stood waiting in the centre of no man's land, not far from Thanatos's spattered body; of Fieldlight, there was no sign.

I will have to exit here soon; this place is about to become a hive of peaceful activity. Taking off his shirt, he rested the sniper rifle in an easy-access position against the wall. But he confirmed that his trench knife was sure, strapped against his leg. Several casualties of his knife flashed past his memory like a picture show, as if to confirm his ability and practice with the blade. Usually, they tried to deal with snipers using artillery, but on one occasion, they sent two men, and he was waiting for them.

He listened intently for any other activity in the ruins, but his senses assured him it was still a ghost town; just him and the small red-rumped birds, the insects alive to the coming of the sun, and the flies awakening to the heat and anticipating fresh flesh.

Feeling the scar down his shoulder, the wound was still red and sore; the shrapnel had sliced him open like a tuna can. The sun warmed the wound, allowing him to close his eyes for just a moment as the warmth and tingling sensation covered the site like the velvet fingers of an invisible nurse. His ears were still on sentry, and still, the all-clear was the news of the day.

The small tin was worn. The metal, once a red can, has flaked red patches, the record of a well-used item. Three photographs pinned together, two he recognised. The backs of the paper were scrawled with the names of the men. Frank Fieldlight, some civilian, German, a Wilhelm Scumarterschwartzer, and Cardinal Rufus, *oh dear, he knows Rufus.* Before each name, the word Instar was pencilled. Instar? What's that?

30

Carter entered the oak-lined cavern that was the religious retreat of numerous past cardinals. Heavy office dew greeted his senses of past theological rigour and a constant temperament atmosphere.

"You wish to leave the clergy?" "Yes, my Eminence, I er" "You can't be serious, Harry Carter, have you lost your faith?" "I have your Eminence, completely" Cardinal Rufus turned with a scowl and rummaged through the documents upon the oak table. "So you enlisted as a priest and now what? You are an atheist soldier? "An atheist Intelligence serviceman, Cardinal" "What of your faith, Harry? He shook his head in reply to the Cardinal's stare of apprehension. "You helped men dying on the front?" "Many" "And the cause of this loss of faith?" "There was never any faith to be lost, I have realised, artillery barrages will teach you that" The Cardinal's face dropped further into despair.

Outside, he noticed a Raven perched upon a tree branch swaying with the strong wind blowing outside. The black bird held firm on the strong bough, gazing at the window as the leaves drew fluttering in gusty sweeps, some detaching and striking the window pane with force. The Raven still stared and seemed unfazed by the tempest. He was calm, returning the bird's stare, aware of its evolutionary chain, and stole a smile, thinking that a more religious figure might consider it a sign of some superstitious nature.

"When did you have these thoughts?" Rufus leaned forward in an examining pose. "For some time, my Eminence." "You realise you will lose your residence, your standing in the community, your commitments to the Lord?" "Yes, my Eminence, I have already lost my faith; that's why I am here." "Harry, I cannot allow it" Cardinal Rufus stared at him with a screwed up face, half-annoyed, half flummoxed. The Cardinal's gold pen shook a little between his slightly trembling fingers.

He smiled, knowing it was the worst time, but he couldn't help himself. "You find this amusing, Carter? Rufus barked, lowering his eyes in headmaster fashion. "Are you on something? Tell me you have taken that white substance, er, what is it?" "Cocaine, my Eminence?" "Yes, cocaine, do you have an addiction?" "No, my Eminence"

"Stop calling me Your Eminence! and sit down for the Father's sake!" The Cardinal leaned back on his throne-like purple velvet chair and exhaled. He could see the signs of heart disease within the man, his red face, the overweight form mirroring cup-cakes and port with the other Priests. *Not to mention that duck fat they pour on their roast on Sundays.* The raven was still perched as if waiting for the outcome of the meeting. Cardinal Rufus was a good man, and he was one of the few who had a sense of humour.

"I have also taken the Elixir of Vigour, your Eminence" The Cardinal stared barbs at him. "The potion? The heathen potion? You have taken it!" "I am afraid so" "And you took it despite a direct order from the Pontiff?" "Yes, Derrick," "Cardinal Rufus will do fine," "Cardinal"

"And poof! Just like that, you have no god" The Cardinal stared at him with a smile, his hands splayed like a magician. "There are no gods" Their stares met, and the Cardinal narrowed his gaze. The Raven he saw was now holding the branch and facing the wind to steady itself. The gusts were increasing, and large rain droplets were horizontally striking the ancient glass more frequently.

"Oh, I see, and what else does the Elixir say?" The Cardinal folded his arms, nodding in fake agreement and looked at him with a bit of contempt mixed with humour. He looked out at the Raven riding the tempest and contemplated the Cardinal's desktop, pulling focus to consider his answer."It narrates the Earth's past in dreams and hints at the future, all the while ironically enlightening you of how things work"

178

"Good lord, Harry," the Cardinal turned and looked outside at the beating rain. The Raven had departed, he noticed. "You realise this is some sort of new illegal drug, a criminal money-making enterprise?" "I wasn't charged for it," he looked at the Cardinal deadpan."Who gave it to you?" "A German soldier with nothing to lose" "Oh, my great Pontiff, Harry the enemy? You have gone mad!" He stared at the Cardinal, amused by his state.

The Cardinal rose and shuffled to the window, the rain now a driving force, the droplets streaking the lead-lined window and tempering the lead-lined Jesus Christ's face in distorted lines. He looked at the Cardinal's robe, the blue tasselled velvet reminded him of a type of caterpillar he had seen in a nursery rhyme book when he was young. The window continued to spatter rain, sending droplets to distort the view of God. *Christ is smiling. I haven't seen that in a while.*

"You have commitments, Harry, commitments!" "No longer Cardinal, my decision is final" "And what of the word of God?" "There are no gods," the Cardinal blew out with distinct disdain as if he had tasted a hot chilli. "So the Elixir says there are no gods? I see. And what does it say to you specifically to confirm this belief?" "Nothing, it doesn't work like that. It's not a debate; after taking it, you just know other things." "Give me some examples" The Cardinal blinked at him, waiting.

"Well, let's see. I know that in billions of years, the Earth's continents will be in different places on the globe than they are now. "Different places? Are you mad, Harry?" "They will drift very slowly and eventually, in millions of years, form a gigantic continent, all connected again. Australia, for example, is closely tied to India, Africa, and South America." The Cardinal looked at him with growing alarm.

"I see. And what does that have to do with the non-existence of gods?" "Well, for one, if God created the Earth as we are led to believe, why is there no mention of this occurrence? Why did god intend to make an Earth that had a molten core

179

and magma under the surface of the Earth? Indeed, why include an atmosphere?" Rufus frowned in puzzlement. "Why not make a solid ball of perfectly livable dimensions for the inhabitants and monitor it in his powerful ways? Why the need for moving continents and volcanoes?"

"Then the Earth wouldn't need a molten core at its centre and a magnetic field. Moreover, I know that the Earth took billions of years to form from gases and dust in space, moulded by gravity and heat. God says it took seven days." "God's ways are infinitely sent to test us, Harry. Who can know his creation intimately?"

"The *Olduvai* postulate…" "Who?" "The Olduvai, the secret society that embraces the Elixir." "Oh, Harry, for goodness' sake," he continued unfazed. "Oh, I know what they postulate-nonsense!" He continued unfazed, "From an increasingly zero long-term effect militaristic energy consuming society to the adoption of an agrarian lifestyle culture, preceding a stone-age society; Social Anthropological history in reverse."

"War and the wielding of power will achieve nothing in their view but short-term geo-political changes and regime alterations, whether they be Nationalist or Communist, Totalitarian or Democratic, accompanied, of course, by untold suffering and or death of the masses in almost all cases either by war, famine, genocide or a slow death by taxes. The key to the human race's continued existence is the immersion of itself within a balanced ecological footprint."

The Cardinal folded his arms and bowed his head, all the while looking at him, chin resting on his velvet robe, eyes blinking in patience and intent listening. Rufus looked at the cloth covering his table, then rubbed his hands together like a baker preparing flour. "Harry, could you imagine for just a moment that maybe this magic Elixir will make things worse? You seem to be flummoxed with certain untested theory"

He stared at the Cardinal and continued, pausing momentarily as the Cardinal's clock struck nine and gonged with a reverent reverberation against the wooden walls.

"Humans…" He waited until the reverberation subsided. "See themselves as warriors competing for resources when in reality they are a highly effective evolutionary survivor; the two are distinctly different. It is in this misinterpretation of the duality where their misdirection lies, and where, forgive me, Cardinal, Religion intercedes with disastrous consequences." The Cardinal raised one eye but remained silent.

"The apex animal has forgotten where he, and she, may I add, came from. The inability to be an integral part of the Earth is a catalyst for the future destruction of the human species, whether through natural disasters or political oblivion. One only has to look at the Dinosaurs that lived for one hundred and sixty million years as an integral part of the Earth, despite being hostile; the only thing that stopped their presence today on the Earth came from outer space." The Cardinal's eyes widened in surprise, with a look of fundamental doubt about his sanity and puzzlement, adding, "Harry, I can help you, this, whatever has occurred, I"

He continued unfazed. "Man is a Monarch's courtier, playing the game and plotting its course at the same time, always to the weighted detriment of others and the natural world that created him. When placed in a framework of societal control, anxiety is the outcome above all else, toxic anxiety that becomes power, aggression, fear and ultimately destruction."

The Cardinals pen rolled off the desk and landed on the rug beneath it. He watched as his Eminence bent down and tried to reach the golden pen, which was just beyond his reach. "For pity's sake," he muttered. Getting off the chair, he stumbled embarrassingly but recovered and grabbed it, returning to his lofted position. Then he slid off the chair and landed buttocks first on the floor, red faced and furious. "Great thousand Pontiffs, I!" He waited until he was seated again properly, then continued, much to the Cardinals' embarrassed disdain.

"Man would like to see Utopia, and as a consequence holds on to dreams and the *Goodness* of man and woman, when in reality we are all cunning deceivers out for ourselves. Look at the mirror and you see yourself, but behind the mirror is where the cunning lurks. The powers that be are a good example; they control dissent through obligation and strict rules, but forgive the flock their sins anyway, thus maintaining power while keeping the followers in line." The Cardinal closed and opened his eyes in silent disagreement. "Harry, can't you see that..."

"Despite technology, no matter how advanced, the descent of man is assured due to this outlook upon the Universe. After the seemingly terminal end, whether by natural or artificial causes, the Earth will slowly recover, and the seas, plains, and forests will replenish and return. The cities will be silent and crumbling; humans will be extinguished. All that will remain is a giant continental mass, where new apex creatures will surely inhabit. The Earth, formed from the Universe, will continue to orbit the stars until its final descent into the sun."

"Stand in a forest after taking the Elixir and one realises something as simple as the life span of a small bird is all that is needed to understand life in totality; an avian lifespan of two to five years."

"The prediction from the *Olduvai* is, unless the thinking I have outlined is altered, that is: The warrior in competition for resources; the outcome I have described is sure. They are still sceptical that humans could alter such an evolutionary reaction to society, but are sure of one thing: The Elixir aligns human thinking to optimal survival within a society, so they postulate that it may succeed."

"Beyond a movement trying to bring change, the Elixir is so much more. One can only explain it to others who have experienced it. So much is discarded, and the little that remains is the most potent chemical ever known, linking the mind to an Evolutionary past in instinctual genetics and ancient catalysts. Therefore, most behaviour initially takes a back seat to knowledge, and then the synthesis of knowledge is transformed into optimal behaviour." He stopped and sat blinking at the Cardinal; the page of his book turned.

"For god's sake, Harry, you will need to give me a moment to reply to that one. And Christ on Earth, I haven't even had my port yet. For pities sake Harry, moving continents and ape men, you can't be serious" Cardinal Rufus covered his head with his hands, then rose and walked, staring out the stained-glass window at the elaborately coloured image of Christ, with a magellanic cloud littered with appointed angels flying above. "No doubt you believe in this nonsense, but what I ask is about its validity?"

"What of your God? To its validity, time will tell; it's a theory, but the effect of the Elixir cannot be ignored." The Cardinal shook his head, turning to him in disdain."May I ask the Cardinal, do you have dreams of Christ?" "All the time, Harry, especially in moments like these" In a brief moment of humour, both smiled for different reasons as the Cardinal turned to look at him. The robed man turned and stared once again out the stained window to the rainy gardens below, turning his back on him, hands on his hips.

Seeing the Cardinal's glass of port, he quickly unscrewed the small glass vial's cap and poured the Elixir into the red current and pocketed the vial. In perfect timing, the Cardinal, his back turned, suddenly swivelled again to look at him. "So, Harry, how can we move forward here? I cannot let you walk out that door, not with the Pontiff's visit only a week away. "Perhaps we have moved forward already?" The Cardinal furrowed his brow, trying to detect his meaning, then returned to stare out the glass, beyond which, perched what he assumed to be the same Raven on the same branch.

"Here is what is required of me in these circumstances. Rufus raised his finger, his back still turned toward the tempest. Firstly, you will take a period of laicization, a period where you can release yourself from your Priestly duties and reflect on the loss of your faith and perhaps repair and restore your thoughts." The Cardinal paused, turned, and seated himself again while talking, watching the port glass reflect the light of the yellow desk lamp, the Elixir invisible.

"Oh, by the way, would you like a Port?" "No, thank you, Cardinal," he said, genuinely smiling at the Cardinal's candour. Rufus picked up his glass and drained it in a gulp. He followed the path of the port glass upwards as Rufus tilted his head back and down again to rest on the table. "Mmm, interesting one that, aged more, I think" He watched and tried to look as deadpan as possible, disguising his slight humorous look for fascination at what Rufus was saying. Cardinal Rufus looked at the desk top and slid the fingers of his right hand across the oak grain of the table. In apparent resignation, the Cardinal looked at him as his fingers met the edge of the table; eyes in unison, in contemplation.

"Well, then, your period of Laicization will be a little different to what I had in mind, not to mention how far ahead you are of me in this matter. We still have some time to change your mind, don't we? Cardinal Rufus smiled with optimism. You leave?" "Three days, Cardinal, duty calls. I'm afraid there will be no Laicization." "And what of your theory of war, Harry? Are you not joining the very regime that man is perpetuating? What will your Olduvai mind do on the front?"

He continued to look into the Cardinal's eyes as the man shifted slightly, his demeanour from one of godly administration to a hint of change in his thoughts. He remained silent, as the Cardinal had probed to the edge of his cliff of information, and beyond the edge lay a secret he was unable to reveal. The two gazed at one another for some moments, and in that time, he thought he saw a small tear of fear and understanding in the Cardinal's glistening eyes.

31

Giannis Thanatos felt the round and immediately got angrier. Now he would have to lie there dead and wait for the first moult to take effect. As he lay in a state of shutdown, he recalled the meeting with the Grand Wizard, the other Monarchists, Aristocrats, Politicians, Generals, and Senior Executives from several large Companies. All seated at the secret table, in the secret underground cellar in the nondescript town nestled before the Bavarian Alps, rose to dominate the sky. *There are so many secrets that I sometimes get lost as to what is occurring.* Recalling the conversation, his mind wandered.

"So, Gentlemen. This development is quite disturbing. We have an Elixir created by someone who has managed to distribute the solution to certain members of the High Command, notably Carl Hindenburg and Erich Ludendorff. They have now brought the Allies to the table." "Is that not a good thing, Grand Wizard?" One of the Generals addressed the room. "Indeed, it is; however, the nonsense being purported by the takers of this potion is, well, to put it mildly, quite insane."

"Let me quote some of what has been said." 'Evolutionary *Dreams that purport to tell us of the Earth's origins, the abandonment of Religious doctrine, demilitarisation across Europe and the world, Conservation plans for the protection of natural species, a charter for the development of non-toxic chemicals to protect the food chain, the adoption of a woman's right to vote...*One of the Generals had made a sound, choking on his wine, *and rights within the household, the integration of a common currency for Europe and economic alliance within neighbouring states, especially Russia and the Eastern provinces.'* Members around the table had gasped in astonishment.

"And I quote, 'Europe as a whole continent would seek to benefit from the abandonment of borders and therefore rivalries and secure the next generation for the advancement

of food production, through planned technology working within the natural environment to secure resources for future societal growth. Continental Europe will always be at the mercy of incompatible political systems, which will seek to dominate the other through the acquisition of more territory by the use of force.'

"Poppycock!" General Barnpaler, sporting several striking scars on his face, scoffed and sat back in his seat and started to load his pipe with tobacco. The Grand Wizard sat back and sighed. "Gentlemen, some of these dreams, if realised, seek to undermine the very fabric of our god fearing nations, not to mention our right to arms and the wealth created for the top ten per cent of the voting majority." A communal *hear! Hear!* Erupted, the seated men billowed pipes and cigarettes and reflected their scowls within the wine glasses arrayed on the table top. *"A right to wage war is a god-given right!" One of the seated Generals shouted to the agreeing chorus. "Abandon God? Oh my, they are more foolish than I ever imagined!"* Cardinal Rufus had chortled, smiling at his dinner companions.

"Giannis, what do you say? The only one of us who has taken the Elixir." "The potion is strong, dreams I have, but money is a greater motivator," he had replied. *The men at the table laughed as one.*

He had to quell the Elixir; every fibre of his being had wanted to flay them all alive in that room, an instinct buried in the weaponry of the natural world. The fluid had coursed through him in that secret room, and he wondered if others had the same energy, drive and stamina it brought. Geo-political bantering and blustering fat men, it all paled into a tiny vacuum compared to what he knew. There was anxiety, but not anxiety about the open world where people looked in mirrors and put on uniforms and sequestered at bars and found lovers. It was a deep-seated anxiety about life and the Earth, and the compelling chemical dreams were now deeply ingrained within him.

He had been given the job by Intelligence to disappear Fieldlight, now an embarrassment to the high command. *I have to hand it to you, Mr Fieldlight; it was a good plan, German sniper rifle, concealed position. Only they got me to follow you a long time ago. I am glad I attempted to murder a war casualty and failed.*

The old Giannis was gone —the Giannis who hunted men because they were criminals or deserters. Now the new Giannis was dead, technically as well. Fieldlight, he suspected, was special like him. *So, we will see, I attempted to fulfil my mission, and what happens after, well, we will see.*

He had information about the Professor, the Cardinal, and the effect on women the Elixir was having. He had seen the mesmerising effects that the females had had on a group of men on leave from the front. Then he himself had been controlled, in a nice way, but controlled none the less. She had suggested he remove himself from the bar and he was gripped with an unquestioning force, leaving his half drunk beer and desired Bavarian sausage on the counter, and walking away from the Inn.

Afterwards he was shocked and couldn't understand why he was standing on a country road in the middle of nowhere. He realised Fieldlight was special at the depot, and then he noticed something he instinctively detected. The man cast an invisible light. *I am glad he got away. Did I subconsciously act foolishly, walking upright near the German line? Did I let him go the first time for a good reason?*

The shock of blackness enveloped him, and he was cast in a holding state of terminal chemistry. His mind set very slowly, and he was put in a state of tiny hibernation, a junction where chemistry and Physics met. He could feel his heart had stopped, and his wilting mind was only a small part of thought, a train that had entered a dark tunnel. He couldn't see or feel much. He had a dream in which he entered a small, brightly lit cave, where a stone altar protruded from the middle of the stone floor. Upon it stood a ticking, echoing clock made of glass, with cogs visible within.

He was an Instar like the others and had a second life, a second moult. He had taken the Elixir and knew that it contained a second chance if needed, how he knew he wasn't sure; an ingrained chemical signal, perhaps. He had been careless, exposing himself upright, and paid the price. His brains would regenerate, his torn skin would flex and heal over, and his broken skull would rapidly repair itself.

Several blastemas would form, with the cell masses mimicking the embryonic development of his origin in the womb. Retinoic acid markers would signal the devastated wound sites, and the strategy of healing wounds would begin forming his new brain, skull and optic nerve where his left eye had been shattered. He was in effect to be reborn whole, and the blackness of temporary coma enveloped him and set his mind into the most primitive state, the chemistry still active although his heart had stopped and his brain had shut down. The Instar Retinoic Acid oxygenated his brain and replaced the absent gas during the healing period, creating a super-oxygenated cocktail of chemical solutions and active nerve signals.

He had a dream in which he was an advanced machine, equipped with a switch that also served as a thinking mechanism. The machine was always on at an electrical power inlet, but it would shut down periodically to receive new information. Retinoic acid was like a small battery inside the machine that kept his life-clock working while he was shut down and healing. The rapid keratinocyte migration at his wound sites would allow a special form of cell layer to transmit the necessary information and form a signal centre, a small hospital in effect, within his brain and broken head. *Keratinocyte migration*, how do I know that?

Many hours after the round had hit his head, he awoke and saw the moon rising in his prone position. His neck was swollen and sore, but his head had healed, and his blood pressure had returned to normal; the fluid replenished to restore the plumbing system. The arterial pressure was low, and he still felt dizzy, so he waited. He lay and stretched his leg out from under his weight, where he had fallen on it. He noticed he must have been breathing for some time and looked up to the star-laden sky, biding his time.

No one came. Scared that they might bury him, but one man was a manageable corpse on a plain that had held thousands. It was vital that he could walk before dawn, he surmised in case someone showed interest in him. A few hours before dawn, his legs worked. His head felt like a cast, and his sight was a little blurry, but the Instar had moulted, and he was almost whole.

His clothes were encrusted with dirt congealed with brains. Someone had taken his pistol. In the darkness, he couldn't find his tin and swore silently. Shuffling back towards the old Allied line, stooping in shell-craters to hide any line of horizon sight and walking down to the river that was below the level of the village, where he met the tree-line. As he walked silently on the leaf litter, he realised with the moult he had become something different, not quite a homo-sapien anymore but a hybrid.

32

Wilhelm Scumarterschwartzer watched as the dead wasps shifted on his laboratory bench. From seemingly shrivelled forms that were drying in death, the small limbs of the wasps flexed, then gained their solution, and the Insecta rose on all six limbs and quivered as the weight of its thorax was raised from the flat surface in life. Wide-eyed, he knew the wasps had been there for at least the last day, and he never removed them because he was experimenting with the possibility of using the dry carcasses for other experiments. The movement caught the side of his peripheral vision as he jotted in his laboratory notebook, and he watched the transformation.

The enormous weight of the knowledge struck him, and he immediately realised the implications of what he had seen. If the wasps had reawakened from seemingly being dead, did it mean they were immortal? Had they been in a state of hibernation? His notepad had crushed one wasp, and that wasp, too, had risen; its damaged legs and thorax had, as far as he could see, regenerated. "Regeneration! Great Father of Life!"

Oh my. Oh my. Does that mean I am immortal, too? Can I hibernate? Great unseen gods, does that mean soldiers could raise themselves from the dead and recontinue an attack! His mind was momentarily flummoxed, causing his glasses to fly to the laboratory floor. An empty beaker rolled off the table, swept by his hand, and bounced on the floor off his rubber mat, causing the stand to rattle to the ground.

He experimented at once, his new Australian Laboratory on a small property surrounded by the fabulous Koala bears in the trees and the honey-eater birds that swam through the canopy. Gelda had burst into his Laboratory on the first day: *Wilhelm! It's eating the leaves, come and see!*

The wasps were brought in a large, sealed, glass aquarium-like box. He was already aware of the consequences of introducing the European-type wasp to the environment, so he kept them sealed within his laboratory. This is something else I need to publish: the introduction of species to other isolated environments and the consequences for native flora and fauna. Let's hope their ridiculous idea of introducing that South American Toad to the cane farms will be reconsidered.

I have found through my own research that the Cane Beetle simply walks up the cane stem, leaving the Toad at the bottom. The Toads are not long jumpers like native frogs here; instead, they are hoppers and cannot climb. Also, the toads have a poison on their backs, glands, a deterrent to predators. Who knows what trouble it will cause? I managed to give Jacobsen, their Chief Scientist, the Elixir in the guise of an aphrodisiac; let's hope he has success in more ways than one. The card night has proven more useful than I imagined. Once the Elixir is absorbed, he, too, will have the ability at least to think the right way.

§

So, let me see. What do I know about this cycle? He studied the drawings displayed within the lab book. The wasps are moulting; they are Instars, meaning they are within a developmental stage. Yes, yes, arthropod-specific. However, in this extraordinary case, they can rebuild their anatomical structures through cell regeneration. Good grief. They are complete. The one who was crushed has recovered completely. The exoskeleton is cast off during the moulting stage. Cast off after severe injury and seemingly death. There is definitely a stage of hibernation, we shall call it that for now. This, I suspect, is when the cell regeneration takes place. My word, my word.

The laboratory was dimmed, and it was late. Outside, he could hear the disconcerting grunting of the Koalas in the trees. He stared at the Elixir in a flask beside him. Next to the beaker was another test tube supported in a wire holder. Would the Instar come back from being poisoned? Yes, he had reluctantly tested it on a sample of mice. The mouse lay comatose, and he sat waiting after administering the poison, feeling like a murderer. Then its small eyes flickered, revealing the heartbeat of its tiny organ, visible through the skin and fur. In half an hour, the mouse had risen to a crouching position. Was all death reversible? In humans?

33

Gunter Scumarterschwartzer had met the Australian Corporal shortly after the Australian Seventh Division had organised a truce to bury the dead. He and his Sergeant walked the dirt of no-man's land, fairly sure now they wouldn't get shot, as they had seen the Australian Officer and Corporal Carter approach from the trench line at the same time. Sergeant Muller held the white flag, and the canvas fluttered over his shoulder, revealing its ability to halt the shooting.

At the time, he could feel his Father's Elixir in his tunic top pocket, a glass on fabric. The small weight of the vial was enough to tell it was secure. His own stash of Elixir he kept in his silver flask in the dugout. Muller eyed him with concern. "What's the problem?" "Be quick, no sudden movements, remember their sniper will be watching us."' It's done, don't worry." "Ok, Captain," Muller smiled, knowing he had been promoted for the occasion.

The distant Australians came closer; he could see the Officer was a Captain and the other man a Corporal; Intelligence. He was relieved; the Corporal had agreed to see what he had, what the Germans had produced that was changing the face of the war from within.

A small step toward a possible Armistice, a halt to the conflict, and the end of the war. The men approached now metres away. Muller saluted the Captain, and they shook hands. He took the corporal's hand and they looked for death in each other's eyes and found it in abundance."Well, gentlemen, what do we have to show each other?" The Captain offered them a cigarette, which they refused, now understanding the effect on their respiratory system. Müller smiled at him in humorous contempt, took one from the Captain, said "thank you," and inspected the brand, excited about a new variety. "Would you like some Schnapps?"

The front was temporarily silent for the meeting, but dead bodies didn't know a truce, and the putrid smell wafted from the Western side of the Allied Trench Line. Dead debranched trees stood as ruined stalks in spaces in no man's land, complementing the gloomy leaden sky and reflections of green from tepid pools of horror that had collected in shell holes.

"Take it and you will see, " he said, looking at the Australian Corporal. "What is it?" The Captain inspected the small vial of liquid, holding it up to the grey sky. "An Elixir, a new way of thinking" "How so?" Carter looked at him with some scepticism. "It provides a key to a crucial door that humans have not yet unlocked," the Captain and the Corporal said, looking at them, assessing the two madmen who had wasted their time. "Why would you give us this?" "Because we have taken it. We are here for the same reason, aren't we? A truce to bury the dead is what our superiors think. But we are here primarily to try to stop a war and save lives."

Certain high-ranking generals on both sides would consider this *nonsense*. Your translation is *Poppycock*. But not the ones who have taken it, the same ones who set up this meeting and are watching us at this very moment." The Captain gazed towards the German line. Carter looked at the dirt at his feet.

He looked out beyond the German line and waved his hand at the destruction. "No one can win this war, hasn't almost ten years taught us that? No one wants an Armistice that favours one side, which would lead to disaster for that Nation. We are ready to take equal responsibility for the destruction if you are. We have discussed this in detail in our negotiations, yes?"

"There are certain key figures on both sides that are perpetuating this conflict with their Social Darwinist outlooks. The mistake in their ideas lies in confusing instinct with behaviour. Mainly, Politicians are dithering, safe Politicians. Even the most noble Generals know it is a classic stalemate. There will no longer be a Cavalry charge through a gap to route the enemy. The romantic view of war as a part of a cultural right of passage is faulty, don't you agree? As front-line soldiers? The Elixir alters behaviour and provides an

194

understanding of human instinct." "That's a big call for such a little vial of liquid, Captain," the Corporal replied.

Carter looked at his superior, and the Captain said nothing but confirmed his gaze, seemingly unsure of the situation. Carter seemed impressed by the German Captain's English. "One vial is enough for many people, we have not yet managed to account for its strength" "We are to spike the drink of a General?" "Take it yourself first, then it will seem an easy task"

"A war stopped by a small vial of liquid?" "Stranger things have happened, Captain." "Have they?, I'm not sure" "Besides, is this what we have become? The Captain splayed his arm in an arc to show off the hell of no man's land. "Do we not have other aims as a species?" The German Captain handed him the vial with an outstretched arm. He took the glass and gave it to his superior. The four stood facing one another. "Well, I suppose we'd better bury some bodies," his superior said. Muller stood smiling, and offered them both a drink of Schnapps from a silver flask.

34

Gerry Ateskew prepared the Insecticide ingredients. *Powder One in the green tin, mixed to a 25:1 ratio, then Powder 2 in the blue tin, mixed to a 5:1 ratio. Let me check that again—Powder One, green, Powder Two, blue. The instructions on the two cans were simple yet partly obscure, written in tiny text on a white background, with the only distinction being the text, which was a slightly beige colour. How many times have I done this, and I still have to check it? Yes, Gerry, you still have to check it. Remember the third time you mixed it, and you got part one at a 5:1 ratio? Which resulted in a sticky consistency of useless Insecticide? And a day of shovelling concrete?* Carefully portioning the powders, he prepared the mix, the toxic fumes choking his senses and rising into the warehouse ceiling space.

§

Above, attached to the highest beam was a wasp nest. The meticulously prepared hundred octagon entrance hive was constructed from saliva and cellulite. An inverted cone shape descending from the steel to which it had been hung. The nest was built in the same colour as the steel; the Queen altered the saliva of the workers for camouflage.

The wasps flew out of the warehouse when the fumes of the insecticide mix alerted them to danger. Although terminal if it made contact with them, its dual purpose slowly synthesised over time, and the cocktail became a catalyst. The entire hive flew out and maintained a holding pattern above the factory, learning that the fumes dissipated within a certain amount of time. The small pupa inside the nest were still sealed and safe from the mix.

Over time, the wasps learned that once the fumes were mixed, their toxicity stopped, and they descended back to care for their young. The queen monitored the nest's surroundings and, in time, flew down to the pond-like pool and biped there. With fast precision, she aimed for the back of the limb joint, where the skin was softer and her barb could inject the most significant amount of acid.

The biped flailed about in frantic pain, sending the heavy object crashing, stumbled and fell within the pool. Queen wasp flew back up to the nest; the warning strike was enough as the biped had not directly threatened the young. The biped struggled in the mix, arms akimbo and mouth open, then lay still on the surface of the toxic pond, floating as so many of Insecta do with the effect of contact with liquid. Another biped entered the room later but did not enter the strike zone and retreated.

Many nests had been constructed over a long period, and the wasps had learned to adapt to the factory. Then, a small protein had been created within the insect's system and bound to the genetic RNA strand. A super-protein originated from an ancient pool formed in response to counteract toxicity, where a species had begun its life, a super-heated pool of reactive chemistry. The cellular organism then died suddenly as the Earth came too close to the sun, in a chance encounter at the dawn of time. The pool was heated, but it partially evaporated, and the temperature was too high for too long.

The protein stayed within the species in situ, inert. Passing from chain to chain of Insecta after the rise from swimming arachnids to flying adaptation, from fins to wings. Part one and Part two completed the chain of chemical change as the protein reawakened within the Queen and synthesised into the small sac of nerve toxin that fed the wasp's barb.

The path to natural selection was initiated, and the defence mechanism evolved into a commensal one; one species ensured safety from the threat, while the other facilitated the synthesis of the protein into the mammalian neurochemical pathway, thereby establishing an evolutionary knowledge

197

within a dexterous and apex-thinking brain. The Stone Age man was cast off, and the ape became aware of the universe.

Gerry Ateskew swam to the edge of the toxic pool and noticed he was ok. Shocked, he grabbed the side of the vat and hauled himself to the small square mixing deck, rolled like a wet piece of eroded river wood and lay still. The fumes had dissipated as the mix was set together. The humming of the mixing motor was all that he could discern apart from the naked bulb that hung from the beam above. Passing out several times, the bulb remained, casting him as part of the wooden vat in shadow and bleak light.

He awoke new and had dried. The crusted powder chalked his clothes, but as far as he could discern, it did not harm; his skin was untainted. He still lay in dread at what he had done, creating poison. One crooked arm raised and looked at the room, and searched for the tins that were laid on the shelf like disastrous bombs ready to be loaded into a terrible cannon. Part One and Part Two, on different shelves, he cast an eye across the metal containers. Standing. Not much time. The clock on the stained wall showed three-thirty, only two hours before the morning shift.

The entire plan within his mind had occurred to him in a rapid collation of specific philosophy and instinctual dreams; a cohesive, powerful resin. The hundred tins of Part One were tainted by an oxidising agent, which prevented mistakes from using too much water. Part One was rendered inert and hardened like concrete on the tins as he opened each one, then placed them back on the shelf. Working quickly, he poured several tins of Part Two into the vat, and the mix stalled, becoming glued up and bubbling in a ruined mass. He glanced at the clock. *Four-forty, I am done.*

His mind was clear and different, he realised as he walked from the factory across the wasteland. *I fell into the vat, why didn't I drown? An insect bit me, a bee, a wasp or something, that really hurt. What has happened here? My mind is clear,*

clear for the first time. The distant factories he surveyed as a future real estate agent and leader of men. Calm and calculated, the city lights shone in the distance.

Because he was the only one who knew the formula of the Insecticide, the factory halted production; the vat was also ruined, the mix now a semi-solid mire of concrete-like goo. The early shift workers milled around the factory floor, realising the Insecticide production line was no more. Inheriting the factory from his father, he closed the doors via an agent and distributed funds for the workers' redundancy, much to his accountant's dismay.

Teddy Barnett had stared at him as he visited his weather-board shack, shocked as he handed him his redundancy money and a gift for Mary. Barnett looked at the parcel and down to the ground and back at him and remained silent and nodded his thanks. He had momentarily gone inside and came back out with two cold beers and they had sat on the verandah silent for a time and watched as a rooster strutted in the garden. Barnett had turned to look at him and he had turned at the same time to say *"cheers"* and the small moment melted the awkwardness as they both smiled. "I still reckon the compressor was scarier than getting shot at" The rooster's eye was on them and then they started to laugh.

He took Pike-Pickard aside and thanked him for the work he had done; gave him his money, and left him to explain the closing of the Factory to the workers. Pike-Pickard said nothing but looked at him as if he had discovered his life. He shook Pike-Pickard's hand and apologised for his behaviour, wishing him luck at the front. He bought a suit, new shoes, and pinned a carnation to his lapel, then spent his time in the library.

In the coming months, he collected the cash he had saved and rented the factory to a wool wholesaler. Placed half his savings on the stock market after spending time researching the trends in manufacturing and where the gains were to be made from raw material production, combined with well-managed companies. In two months, his sole stock in the company had tripled, import tariffs had been abolished, and the prices he had predicted for its key manufacturing additive, a powdered additive for beauty cream, had been reduced.

The nature of the injury to his leg made him ineligible for service, so he bought a cane to advertise the fact, keeping meddling citizens at bay. His continued clarity of mind led to changes in his diet and habits. Discarded his cigarettes after reading a small article in the newspaper at the bottom of the second last page, where a tobacco advertisement was presented showing a well-dressed man smoking; behind him, an attractive woman was smiling.

Research may indicate smoking is related to lung cancer. A German scientist working in Dresden has discovered that inhalation of tobacco vapour into the human lung may cause deleterious effects. Bread and dripping were also discarded in favour of fresh berries and oats every morning. Exercising took him on long walks, and he also used the new Gymnasium to lift dumbbells and a medicine ball.

A man with spectacles and a white beard was pulling books from the shelf across from his reading cubicle, he noticed. The Library was closing in half an hour, and the man was hurrying to get what he needed, dropping a book and ignoring it as he concentrated on his search. The Library was fortunate to have an aisle in the research section where specific scientific articles could be accessed through the journals.

As the clock showed ten to five, he started to pack his work: several business articles and a study on the economics of the stock market. The street was dim, with a gathering storm billowing upwards to the South-West, an anvil in the afternoon light. The man he had seen was stopped by a light pole not far from the Library entrance, taping a poster around it. He waited, then stopped and looked at the notice.

Wilhelm Scumarterchwartzer presents The Elixir of Vigour, a potent potion of renewal and health. Demonstration of this remarkable Elixir's effects on mice will be demonstrated at the coming Carnival of Light, Circus by the River, 12th Feb, 1925, 8:00 pm. Big Top opened for nine shows, starting at 7:30 (On stage before the Trapeze act by Mr and Mrs Flycatcher).

The man noticed him and turned. "Hello, Sir, good day to you," German accent. "Good day. I see you have an Elixir on offer. Indeed, please come and see the effects of this potion. I guarantee no quackery, only knowledge" The German man looked at him with a precise stare, and he smiled, nodding.

35

A new age is dawning, subjects and priests of the order. He had a distinct memory of the latest sermon. *Our flock will be mighty and all empowered now, the age of godless, barren thought is now over, we have adapted and now are as one. It is a strong message from the Father, I know, but it is his way, our way, the Order's way.* "The Orders way," chanted the gathered. *"Get me out of here"* he had said to himself.

"Yes, Rufus, what do you have for me?" The Grand Wizard placed the enormous ledger on the oak table and sat back, rubbing his eyes. He heard another sound and guessed someone else was in the room, probably the Wizards shadow, his protection. The Wizard was getting younger; it seemed his new position was agreeing with him. A man of seventy now looked thirty.

The furrowed lines of Order service were barely visible now. The lines that in the past he had gazed at while in conversation with the Wizard were now smoothed out somewhat. The wizard's thin face resembled a shrewd donkey's, his blue eyes were succinct, his grey hair had turned brown, and he no longer wore spectacles. Excess fat from too many pies had diminished, and despite spending most of his time in a sedentary state, he looked healthy and fit. *How on earth has he achieved that? He hasn't even taken the Elixir.*

He could not spike the Grand Wizards' drink; he never drank with others in the same room. Denton Clever his attendant, was always lurking behind a curtain, it was simply too risky. He had to find a way to get the Wizard to ingest the Elixir but it was this task that was proving to be more difficult than he imagined. The kitchen was closely guarded.

They had wanted him to kill the man physically but he convinced them he was far more helpful as an agent for the Olduvai. *God forbid, Rufus the assassin. The pen is mightier than the sword.* He was now the Grand Wizard's staff head, Executive Officer, and assistant Grand Wizard. From his lofted position, he had access to the armed Priesthood, the Military wing of the Order.

He cleared his throat before talking. "It has been discovered, my Wizard, the Elixir, the transformative potion" There was a clanging sound outside and muffled chatter. The Grand Wizard placed both hands on top of his head in contemplation. "Well, yes, it was only a matter of time. How?" The Wizard turned and blew out breath, looking at him. "The origin is currently unknown, but it has been distributed. We suspect that an independent source, such as a Scientist or an organisation, has discovered it."

"The Olduvai, of course, are involved in its distribution." "So, the rest of the population is now in contact; we knew it would consume the population. And the Queens?" "None known, but undoubtedly active without knowing their potential, yet" The Grand Wizard grabbed a pencil and expertly twiddled the stick between his wiry fingers. He could hear the Order awakening through the stone echoes of the Cathedral; breakfast assembling in the hall.

"The front, what is happening?" "Destined to end in an agreeable and equal Armistice, my Eminence" "Mmm, pity it has given us some time to make the transition and remain shielded" "However, Grand Wizard, there is something else" "Oh?" "The new Instars are different. "Different? How?" The Wizard placed his pencil on the oak with precise lowering, as if it would disturb his hearing, and aligned it with the table's edge without a sound.

"There seems to be some gender differences. The Queens seem to be a different thing, a consequence of ingesting the Elixir." The Grand Wizard pursed his lips and frowned. "Which equates to what?" "We are trying to find out. We suspect this is female Instar-specific, something new." "Good hallowed fuckery, Rufus! Find out! We need to know what we are dealing with here. Fuck and fuckery titty fuck! The last thing we need are special females running around causing mayhem!" The Wizard stood in flustered annoyance and turned with hands on hips and strode to the centre of the Library in thought.

"The Orders line supersedes all else, Rufus! We need to prosper, not have another Holy War! Wars among states, fine, let them at it, it serves us well, keeps us in the dark and our flock closer beside us, but a direct threat? The slightest sniff Rufus, the slightest sniff, that's all it takes, ignore it, and we are in a hell of non-creation! It must be infiltrated, Rufus." "Yes, my Emminace"

"Don't Eminence me, Rufus, get on with it!" He bowed, looking down at the floor, and began to feel uncomfortable and sweaty. A line of light had penetrated the Library with the dawn. It was illuminating to see the portrait of the Wizard's predecessor, the Order's Cuthbert Tonkin, his grizzled, oil-colour canvas face seemingly mocking him from the flat wall. "Go! Go! Keep me informed, God damn it," The Wizard pointed to the door.

He fled the room and walked down the hall and passed the mess-hall entrance, no longer hungry. Denton Cleaver darted through a curtain and startled him, smiling craftily. "Your Emminance," he said with a smile. "Denton, what a lovely surprise," he uttered mimicking Denton's false regard. *Robed fool, he's always behind something.* The robe disappeared through another curtained gap.

His Word to Mudbank was essential. The armed Priests would want to search for them and eliminate anyone who had taken the Elixir. His orders would send them on a trek to nowhere, for now. Thanatos, the Greek, Mudbank had said, was after Fieldlight. He therefore had told Tempelton to help the press man, his brother, and protect Fieldlight but not kill Thanatos unless strictly necessary. Fieldlight had survived an impossible

204

attack, the Australian Fifteenth division. His German contact on the line had told him that the man rose after being gunned down, gunned down again, and then he rose again. *Had he taken the Elixir?* Harry Carter had pleaded with him to get the Sergeant off the line, once and for all for more reasons than one. *Harry, I do this for you my friend, but just you wait until I get my hands on you for spiking my port.* He smiled as he grabbed the telegraph from the Australian sniper.

Looks like hostilities have generally ceased on the line. Thanatos approached Fieldlight just outside Flurry in no-man's land. Looked like he was going to deal with Frank. There was a German in a shell-hole; they were together. I was about to take him out, and then another sniper shot him, ironically, probably from the German line to protect their man. Red and yellow artillery marker flags were spotted just before the shot.

I did not recover his body; there was no corpse when I managed to get to the site. Perhaps the sniper wounded him only. A small tin recovered, assumed to be Thanatos's, containing three photographs. One of you, Frank Fieldlight, a German Civilian, Professor Wilhelm Scumarterschwartzer. Continuing to shadow Fieldlight, what are your orders?

Quickly, he entered the radio room, noticing the drop in temperature of the stone room. The Telegraph machine sat near the picture of the Fifth Grand Wizard, a thin-faced monster in the dim light. Checking the Telegraph map, he knew Tempelton was near the Flurry bridge machine. *He will check the closest, then move on to the next if no message. Let's see, send one to Flurry and one to the depot.* Sitting, he crafted the cypher. He sneezed, wiped his nose, then crafted the telegraph.

Find Lucifer; he may be ascending. Shake the hand of the devil and report. Phoenix to be delivered to the shoulder of the river, and the scroll delivered. The sheep are scattering. Seek passage and avoid isolation. Fresh parchment lies in the wind.

205

For Private Tommy Church - Aus 7th Division AIF

In plain English, he checked the message to Tempelton's code name:

Meet Thanatos, suspect not dead; he may still be with us. Seek information. Get Fieldlight to Mudbank and share intelligence. Demobilise as ordered when the order comes to avoid disciplinary action. Will telegraph you.

Thinking about how much time he had before detection, he sent the telegraph, turning to check the room was still empty. Thoughts that he may be on a secret hit-list were always at the back of his mind. He glanced again at Archibald Boyd Franklin Harker, the oil painting of the Fifth Grand Wizard staring at him, him the traitor, the agent.

Staring at the former Grand Wizard, he pondered in thought, pursing his lips in thought. His predecessor, *Vice-Wizard Tuttleman,* had met his end in a Zeppelin accident. He had watched the Zeppelin dirigible as it was launched over the Orders Grand Picnic day field, rise to full height, then plunge to Earth in a spectacular impact, throwing out the twisting, dead occupants he remembered. What appeared to be two wine glasses flew in the air and landed, he discovered later, unbroken on the grass. A satisfactory outcome, one that removed him from office and ruined the day, was perfect. Unfortunate that the Grand Wizard was delayed; otherwise, he would have been in it as well. A terrible accident, I wonder. Was the Wizard Delayed?

The Olduvai were the missing link and remained hidden. Within their ranks were people who sought to bring the world into a different place, he and the Instars had tasted the true nature of life. Those who had taken the Elixir would, in time, realise their past, some would correct their worldly ways—people like Erich Ludendorff and Paul von Hindenburg.

206

Are we all altered Homo sapiens? Have we cross-pollinated with another species, the Insecta, and genetically mutated with them? Most thinking had changed by those that had consumed the Elixir. He was a shining example, his faith discarded. *Harry Carter saw to that.*

But, the archaic ways of thinking remain, people like the Wizard, the order. People who want war and death, social class and serfdom, societies for the privileged, power, and control.

36

Candice Thompson first noticed something different when she had to go to the front bar of the *Australian Hotel* on the town's main street. A man's bastion, she was greeted with all sorts of stares, especially since it was five fifty and the drinkers were sculling as many beers as possible before the pub closed at six, the *Six O'clock Swill*. The barman had the box. *How were my tins delivered here? He knew it was the beauty powder of all things!*

Entering, the men's gazes turned in disapproval generally as she made her way to the bar, the barman smiling, enjoying the spectacle. Nervously, she looked around when reaching the bar, the silver foot pole glistening, and the tiled bar green and smooth. Two young men undressed her in the corner. Several older farmers drank nearby, looking at the barman and understanding.

"Miss Thompson," "Mr Fieldlight," "I have your box here" The man's tone softened. She watched as he lifted the cardboard box and placed it on the bar. Several of the patrons were murmuring their disapproval at her presence in the men's public bar. The barman stared at the suspects, and the bar conversation continued as usual. Just audible, someone muttered *"Broad in the bar,"* another *"Great arse"* she discerned from the drunken banter. Above, cigarette haze hung like a winter troposphere near the ceiling. The barman rose to full height and eyed the suspects with a definitive *"shutup"* smile on his face.

"Thank you, Mr Fieldlight." She glanced around the bar and caught the eye of one of the men who sank back into his beer. "I don't know how they got this address, anyway." She looked at the barman; the man had a scar the entire length of his face that dissected his face from the top-right of his forehead to the lower left of his chin. The man looked familiar, but she couldn't place him. She realised she was sweating from the heat outside in contrast to the cool bar.

"Don't worry about the patrons, you are not drinking here, just picking up. He smiled. "Glad to help. Look, I wouldn't mind trying your powder, helps the skin you say?" "Yes, it has been good for scars and wounds, helps soften a little. Here no charge, try it Mr Fieldlight" She tried to ascertain his interest and felt nervous , inspecting the box. "Please, call me Frank"

She opened the box and checked that her tins were there, handed him one and smiled. As the lids closed, the bar had become silent, she noticed. The barman wiped the bar with a cloth and looked up to scan around, knowing also that something had changed.

The men were still drinking, but the conversation had stopped."Well, Frank, thanks again. I will be off." Frank extended his hand and smiled, which she took. As she left, the men in the crowded room parted to let her pass. One of the men moved a barstool, another slid a table. A man waited at the door and held it open. She smiled back at Frank as she left, thinking maybe it was him who changed the mood and then realised it was she who had changed somehow—a feeling of having power in that room, the opposite of how she felt when she arrived.

§

Frank continued to wipe the bar, the sound of cloth on wood suited the patron's murmur which had died down as Candice left and the solid awkward door closed on the dim public drinking hole. Her scent still permeated the room; a sweet musky lament. He glanced at the tin of powder, the label on the lid showed a drawing of an attractive woman. He lifted the tin to read the small print. *Distributed by Scumarterschwartzer and Ateskew Manufacturing - "For the new Australian man and Woman."*

Her electric presence permeated the room in a hanging stillness. The delivery he had diverted so he could see for himself; the Queen. In his now recurring dreams she appeared, wings and all. It settled within him and tempered his fatigue.

During the journey home on the Canadian transport freighter from Dover, the Captain placed a large mirror on deck so the men could see what they had become. Bullet holes where it seemed unlikely, scars of terminal history; he was still alive. Within his whiter scar-line he saw beauty and softness also; the Queen had somehow made it a miracle clay or a soft spatter of rain to sooth its passage.

He smiled and thought about Muller, the Germans, and how ironically they had wounded him then saved him. After Thanatos had disappeared they returned to the mass grave site and stood again and then sat, him and Muller, in solace, thinking about the men below.

As the last hour before closing time wore on, the pitch of the men's discussion became rowdier, then died off as one by one the staggering, laughing and wandering drunks left the door swinging more frequently from harsh pavement light and cavern night. Squinting at the last exit of the wobbling patron, the bar went momentarily dark again settling his eyes to the grain of the bar wood.

The last swing of the door revealed Donny Farrow, one arm and and a pinned shirt sleeve gazing through the dissipating bar haze. Outside, a man shouted and the clock on the Council tower rang - its echo crossing the street."Hector!" Donny turned around and looked outside, holding the door open. His cattle dog wobbled through the door and made a bee-line to him. Their eyes met."Crikey Frank, do you own this place?," Donny uttered, smiling, then watching Hector lie down on the cool pub floor.

Epilogue

Greg Fieldlight looked across at the large refrigerator with five compartments. The imposing, terrible steel monster had only finality, even in its design; a mirror of its dead occupants. Several other fridges carried the dead arrayed across the floor, slowing the decay. The Captain responsible saw him come into the room, and his face dropped further. "You're kidding, they're not going to report this, are they, literally?"

"Relax, I got permission to have a poke around. Besides, it would never get past censorship due to embarrassment alone. It's bad enough they lost their sons once, not to have to go through the fact that there was a body to bury, and now there isn't even that consolation. Not that they will ever know"

The Captain looked at the floor, visibly, genuinely upset. "Greg Fieldlight, Stringy Bark Times, official war Correspondent" He offered his hand outstretched. The Captain shook his hand. "Captain Miller, Morgue Section," Miller announced his position deadpan and grimly, he suspected for effect. "So how many bodies have we lost?" "I'm not sure at the moment, it depends on you," he said, looking at the Captain and waiting for the punch line. "Oh?" "If we can talk off the record, forever, I'll tell you, no one else knows yet. I am already waiting for a likely transfer to the front as punishment"

"Ok, off the record, you have my word" "Your Frank Fieldlights brother, aren't you?" "I am" They both looked at each other in recognition. "He's more famous than me" "Ha!" The Captain smiled. "He's gone back home?" "Having a beer as we speak," the Captain nodded longingly. "Good for him," he said genuinely.

"Twenty-two have gone missing." "Wow, I was told four." "Four lately, yes." The Captain walked over to a filing cabinet, leafed through a drawer, found a blue piece of paper, and handed it to him. "There, these guys from the Seventh Division were the latest." He glanced at the form, a record of the killed in action, their Morgue identification numbers clearly spelled out after their names.

Corporal Vince Reginald Horace Barton, (VC) - 5646211
Corporal Teddy Gerry Harris - 7865454
Colonel Johnathon Pike-Pickard - 8987868
Private Samuel Ronald Cowan - 3655329

"How?" He smiled, not understanding how bodies could go missing. "They were placed in the fridge on Monday, and on Tuesday, they were gone. I saw the Corporal arrange for their transfer the next day. Before you ask, the men working here have been cleared by the Military Police."

"What about medical staff, stealing cadavers for something, like that guy in the 1800s, who used to murder people and sell them to a doctor for a fee?" "That's not my department, and besides, if they did, they are bloody idiots" "Why?" "Because there are about forty corpses a day waiting outside at any one time, they could have easily taken one of them without breaking in here. I also know none of my men would be involved in that sort of thing ...if they had the time."

The Captain paused, then looked at him. "No one else comes here, for obvious reasons; there is enough death in their lives.," he said softly as not to disturb the dead. "So a Frankenstein scenario then," he smiled grimly. The Captain looked at him with a rye look. They both looked at the fridge, and there was a pause as they both pondered the dead.